"The loaf I take home is going to be my breakfast for the next week." Chloe's mouth watered.

"I hope you're planning on eating more than that," Edna teased. "The way you go, you'll probably burn that off by ten in the morning."

"I doubt that." Chloe had come to terms with the fact that she wasn't model-thin, but had no illusions about easily burning off a piece of toast.

"I told Chloe the same thing," Jamison said. "She's like the Energizer Bunny. She never stops."

Edna grinned. "Did she listen?"

"I doubt it."

Since her hands were full of dough, Chloe playfully nudged Jamison with her elbow. "First of all, I don't run around that much. I'm also right here, guys. I can speak for myself."

"I haven't forgotten," Jamison said.

As she met his gaze, a bit of warmth filled her insides. Jamison's brown eyes were sparkling and his rugged good looks were impossible to ignore...

Dear Reader,

Years ago, my husband and I would "adopt" a senior for the holidays. Our county had an amazing organization that cared for homebound senior citizens all year round. At Christmas, I loved receiving the wish lists, then running around to purchase everything requested. No one's names were ever shared. The organization asked that everything be wrapped and returned to their offices just before Christmas Day. I loved pulling into the parking lot with wrapped gifts for our mystery recipient. I always felt like an excited kid, and my heart would feel full.

I must admit that the drive home always felt bittersweet. I never needed to be thanked, but I did wish I could have been a fly on the wall when the gifts were delivered and eventually opened.

All those sweet memories came to pass when I was working on this book. I love writing Christmas novels and particularly enjoyed writing a Christmas romance filled with people trying to make the holidays a little brighter for someone in need.

Here's wishing you a happy holiday—and if you get a chance to do something nice for a stranger, I hope you will.

Blessings,

Shelley Shepard Gray

CHRISTMAS PROMISES

SHELLEY SHEPARD GRAY

HEARTWARMING

If you purchased this book without a cover you should be aware that this book is stolen property. It was reported as "unsold and destroyed" to the publisher, and neither the author nor the publisher has received any payment for this "stripped book."

Recycling programs for this product may not exist in your area.

ISBN-13: 978-1-335-46018-9

Christmas Promises

Copyright © 2025 by Shelley Sabga

All rights reserved. No part of this book may be used or reproduced in any manner whatsoever without written permission.

Without limiting the author's and publisher's exclusive rights, any unauthorized use of this publication to train generative artificial intelligence (AI) technologies is expressly prohibited.

This is a work of fiction. Names, characters, places and incidents are either the product of the author's imagination or are used fictitiously. Any resemblance to actual persons, living or dead, businesses, companies, events or locales is entirely coincidental.

For questions and comments about the quality of this book, please contact us at CustomerService@Harlequin.com.

TM and ® are trademarks of Harlequin Enterprises ULC.

 Harlequin Enterprises ULC
22 Adelaide St. West, 41st Floor
Toronto, Ontario M5H 4E3, Canada
www.Harlequin.com

Printed in U.S.A.

New York Times and *USA TODAY* bestselling author **Shelley Shepard Gray** has published over a hundred novels for a variety of publishers. She currently writes Amish and inspirational romances for Revell, Kensington and Harlequin. With over two million books in print, and translated into more than a dozen languages, her novels have been HOLT Medallion winners and Inspirational Readers' Choice and Carol Award finalists.

Shelley has been featured in the *The Philadelphia Inquirer*, *The Washington Post*, *TIME*, *Woman's World*, *First for Women* and *USA TODAY*.

She currently lives in northern Ohio, walks her dogs, bakes too much and writes full time.

Books by Shelley Shepard Gray

Harlequin Heartwarming

The Sargeant's Christmas Gift

A Matchmaker Knows Best Romance

Their Surprise Reunion

Inspirational Cold Case Collection

Widow's Secrets
Amish Jane Doe
Amish Fugitive

Visit the Author Profile page
at Harlequin.com for more titles.

Acknowledgments

I'm so very grateful to Johanna Raisanen,
Kathleen Scheibling and the whole team of folks at
Harlequin Heartwarming who do so much to make my
novels shine. Ladies, thanks for all your hard work
and care. Y'all inspire me to keep learning
and improving my craft.

CHAPTER ONE

November
Medina, Ohio

THE ROOM SMELLED like warm bread, vanilla and cinnamon. It was a tantalizing combination. Almost addicting. All Chloe Winner knew for sure was that it smelled delicious, and she didn't want to leave. "Your decision to make loaves of cinnamon bread once a month was inspired," she told Edna Wilson, the owner and director of Loaves of Love.

She chuckled. "I'm not sure if it was inspired, but all our clients have said they are enjoying the new recipe tremendously," Edna said in her usual modest way. "Not only is it fun to bake something that feels festive, but it's also good to change things up, I think."

The clients who Edna was referring to were folks in need of a helping hand. People from all walks of life who were experiencing food scarcity came to Loaves of Love to visit the food pantry. It was well stocked by both private and corporate donations. But something that Loaves of Love did that a lot of other food pantries didn't was offer a chance for the recipients and volunteers to help make bread for the community. Everyone enjoyed working together in workstations. It was uncommon not to hear happy chatter when entering the room.

When Chloe had started volunteering a couple of times a month, she'd worked with more than one man or woman who had stopped by for a helping hand but then ended up staying for an hour or two to help make loaves of bread. And, she believed, to nourish their souls.

She was pretty sure that had happened. But a lot of friendships had been made, too.

The camaraderie in the vast workroom was contagious. It was the norm for everyone to join other volunteers at their stations. Edna said it was a great way to learn from each other. Everyone worked in groups of four measuring ingredients, mixing, kneading bread and chatting. Making friends. She, for one, could attest to that. She'd met Jamison Smith the first time she'd volunteered there. They'd hit it off so well, now she often tried to coordinate her volunteer times with his.

Today, he'd been working by her side, and had been very amused by Chloe's excitement about the new bread. He'd been teasing her nonstop.

"I have a feeling the loaf I take home is going to be my breakfast for the next week." Her mouth watered as she imagined eating a thick slice of cinnamon bread toast every morning with her coffee.

"I hope you're planning on eating more than that, Chloe," Edna teased. "The way you go, you'll probably burn that off by ten in the morning."

"It would be nice if I did." Chloe knew she was rather full-figured. She'd long since come to terms with the fact that she wasn't model-thin, but had no illusions about easily burning off a piece of toast.

"I told Chloe the same thing," Jamison said. "She's like the Energizer Bunny. She never stops."

Edna grinned. "Did she listen?"

"I doubt it."

Since her gloved hands were full of dough, Chloe playfully nudged Jamison with her elbow. "First of all, I don't run around all that much. I'm an accountant, remember? And, besides, I'm also right here, guys. I can speak for myself."

"I haven't forgotten," Jamison said.

Meeting his gaze, a bit of warmth filled her insides. Jamison's brown eyes were sparkling and, yet again, his rugged California-boy good looks were impossible to ignore. Chloe was slowly beginning to learn that her "volunteer" friend—as she often referred to him—had a dry sense of humor and liked to tease.

Any retort Chloe would've made was cut short by Valerie, the volunteer receptionist. "Sorry to interrupt, Edna, but you're needed out front."

"Oh, dear." Turning to the two of them, Edna said, "Would one of you mind finishing up my loaf? It just needs to be rolled out sprinkled with the cinnamon mixture, then rolled back up and placed in the pan."

"I'm just about there, too," Chloe said quickly. "It's no problem to finish your loaf of bread as well."

"Thanks. Good to see you both," Edna said with a kind look before following Valerie to the entrance.

Chloe watched Edna peel off her gloves and apron as she walked, all while she said hello to several people who called out her name. "Edna's incredible, don't you think?" she asked Jamison.

He nodded. "Without a doubt. But you're not so bad yourself."

"Me?"

"Yeah, you. Every time we talk, I find out that you're even more accomplished than I thought."

"Come on."

"Be modest, if you want, but you've accomplished a ton and you're only thirty."

Jamison's words were sweet, but they were a little too generous. Chloe wasn't trying to do anything special, she was just trying to set herself up for success. Same as anyone else. "I'm not any more accomplished than any other woman my age."

"Mmm, sorry but I think you might be wrong." Picking up the rolling pin from the top of his workspace, Jamison began to roll out his dough. "Let's see. You own your own business, you volunteer in your free time, and are now looking after Madison."

"I like to be busy. And Madison is no trouble."

"Still, not everyone would take in a relative so she wouldn't have to move when her dad got transferred."

"A lot of people would do the same if the girl was Madison. She's not only responsible, but she's also been good company. Plus, she's my niece. Of course I wanted to take her in."

"Madison is also a senior in high school. I haven't met a high school senior yet who wasn't ready to push some boundaries and be more independent."

"Not Madison. She and I had a good talk before she moved in. She was onboard with my contract idea."

"I bet."

Jamison was teasing. Ever since he'd discovered that Chloe had put together a contract, he'd joshed her about it. She supposed she might have deserved the ribbing, too. She was nothing if not organized.

"Hey, writing out a contract before Madison moved in was a good idea," she retorted. "Now neither of us is going to get caught off guard. I know her schedule and she knows my boundaries. This school year is going to fly by without a blip in the radar."

"I hope you're right."

"I know I am," she said as she started to roll out the dough, too. "Besides, Adam's met her."

Something flashed in Jamison's eyes before he

looked down at his hands. "Oh, yeah. You two went out again last weekend, right?"

"Uh-huh. Adam met Madison the last time he picked me up for a date. He thought she was great. Just like I do."

"Oh. Well, that's good."

Confused by Jamison's new tone, Chloe glanced his way again. "I thought so, too. He seems like a good judge of character. Don't you think?"

"Since he's one of my best friends, I'd say so."

She still couldn't believe that Adam Dwyer, the lawyer she'd met at a local chamber of commerce meeting, was both Jamison's neighbor and one of his oldest friends. Talk about a small world.

But maybe she shouldn't have been all that surprised. Even though the guys were very different, they both were good men. Solid.

Thinking about how Jamison worked for the parks department and looked kind of like a Ken doll—the complete opposite of Adam's rather geeky, balding appearance—Chloe smiled. She could only imagine what the two of them must have been like when they were in junior high and high school together.

"Enough about me," she said as she walked around the other side of the station and rolled out Edna's dough. "What's new with you?"

"Me? Nothing."

"Come on. Did you go out on any dates last weekend?"

"Nope."

"Well, what's going on at work? Anything new in the park system?"

"Sorry, but there's nothing to speak of. I led two hikes on Saturday and will be doing my regular thing in Berea this week."

"Which is what?"

"Trail maintenance. Assessing parks. Helping out with the volunteers." He shrugged. "This is a busy time of year because of the holidays. Something different is going on every day. I enjoy it."

"Oh. Well, that's good." Chloe felt her comment was a little bit lacking but she didn't really know what else to say. Jamison Smith was a couple of years younger than her, but seemed to be light-years away in goals and motivation. She appreciated how content he seemed to be, but it still caught her off guard. She supposed it was because she always felt restless. Like she was missing out on something important.

He grinned at her. "It's very good."

Eager to get their conversation back on track, she cleared her throat. "So, what do you think? Do all three pans look like they're ready to get covered and rise again?"

"I'd say they're in good shape."

"Yeah. I think so, too." They shared a smile as they started to clean up all three stations.

She was so glad she started volunteering at Loaves of Love. Not only was she helping the community, but she could now make a great loaf of bread. Plus, she'd met so many nice people. Like Edna and Jamison. Looking at the three loaves in pans resting side by side, Chloe felt a little burst of satisfaction. Just like these loaves, everything in her life was going to turn out great. She just needed to keep working on herself and be patient. And, if she followed the directions carefully, everything in her future was going to be spectacular.

CHAPTER TWO

JAMISON SMITH FIGURED that he might be the only person in the small town of Medina, Ohio, who was glad that the temperatures had finally dropped and it was spitting snow. Not only did it finally feel like December, but he needed the distraction. The freezing rain stinging his nose and cheeks was just painful enough to make his eyes water. Sure, it didn't feel good, but it gave him something else to think about besides Chloe Winner as he walked home.

And...that was his real problem.

No matter how well they got along or laughed together, or seemed to be perfect for each other... she'd placed him firmly in the friend zone.

And yeah, though it was where his head knew he needed to stay, the rest of him didn't think it was a great place to be.

Actually, he hated it.

His subconscious kept imagining what it would be like if Chloe was his. He'd encourage her to stop working until late into the evening. He'd make sure she took care of herself as much as she tried to take care of others. He'd look out for her. Let her know that it was okay to ask for help. Yeah, he'd pretty much bend over backward to make sure she was happy, and he'd do that every day, too. It wouldn't be a chore.

But being with her wasn't meant to be, so he needed to learn to deal with it. Chloe not only didn't think about him in the romantic sense, she was dating his best friend Adam.

Adam really liked her, too.

Worse, when they were together, Jamison could see that they were a good match. Adam could make her happy.

Which sucked.

It would be one thing if Adam was a stranger, or if he was a jerk. But he was neither of those. Instead, Adam had been his best friend since junior high. Back when he'd been in sixth grade and Adam had been in seventh, Adam had saved his neck more than once.

Back then, he'd been having a tough time. His father had died from cancer and his mother had been struggling hard. In addition, he had his younger brother and sister to look after. Bud and Halley were twins, seven years younger, and desperately in need of a parent. Jamison had to fill in the gaps at home.

Even getting to school had been hard. Being the introverted guy who'd just lost his father had made everything worse.

He probably would have floundered bad if Adam hadn't been there.

The guy might have only been a year older than Jamison, but he'd been way ahead of him in the cool factor. In a lot of things. While Jamison's body had seemed happy to remain five foot five forever, Adam had grown four inches and gained thirty pounds the summer before his sixth-grade year. His growth spurt, combined with his confident demeanor and quick wit, had made him "the" guy in their junior high school.

Adam had somehow managed to get even more popular in seventh grade and by the time he was in eighth grade, pretty much every guy wanted to be like him and every girl wanted him to smile her way.

But even though he'd been all that and Jamison had been the runt on the football team, Adam's friendship had never faded. He'd stood up for him when most of the guys in the school had started to treat Jamison as an afterthought.

Just when he'd been ready to quit the football team and beg his mom to let him be homeschooled, Adam had gotten his dad to take both of them to the park a couple of nights a week to practice.

And though it took his body a full year to get with the program and start filling out, when he'd entered eighth grade, he was no longer the guy to be made fun of. He was big enough and good enough to play in almost every game. That acceptance had changed his life.

No, Adam had.

Even though Adam had repeatedly said that he hadn't done anything, Jamison knew the truth. And the truth was that he owed him. When they were both in high school, they'd remained good friends. They'd stayed good friends even when Adam had gone to college and law school, and Jamison had gone right to work for the parks department.

Looking back, he was still amazed about his buddy's loyalty. Jamison was a pretty good student and a pretty good athlete, but it was a far cry from Adam's high class ranking and stellar performance on both the debate and baseball fields.

While Jamison had gone to school and then went home to either work or help take care of his younger brother and sister, Adam had taken advanced courses, hung out with half the kids in the high school and dreamed about getting into a good college.

While Jamison had worked forty hours a week in the summers for the Medina Parks Department, Adam's family went on trips to Europe.

And when Jamison had needed a helping hand, Adam's parents had invited him over to their house for supper or just to hang out. In short, thanks to Adam, the Dwyers had been his second family. Their friendship had been so strong that when two houses in the historic downtown of Medina had gone on sale at the same time last year, they'd both decided to bite the bullet and become homeowners.

Even though his mother and Adam's parents had hinted that living so close to a good friend was a recipe for disaster.

So far, it hadn't been.

Sometimes, they barely saw each other. Jamison was good with that, too. After all, they had completely different jobs and obligations. Usually, the only time they ever did hang out together anymore was on Sunday afternoons to watch football on TV.

All that was why Jamison needed to stop thinking about Chloe. Even though Adam hadn't hinted that he was serious about her and Chloe hadn't shared any details about their dates, Jamison wasn't going to do anything that might make things awkward.

Sure, it pinched a bit, but whatever. Chloe was gorgeous, successful and such a good person that she took in her older sister's kid so Madison wouldn't have to change high schools for her senior year. Chloe deserved a guy who could afford to wine and dine her. A guy who was smart, educated and had a great family who would love her, too.

They belonged together.

And, if they didn't? Well, Chloe sure deserved someone better than him.

"Jamison?"

Turning, he saw Chloe's niece walking toward him. The girl had on a white puffy coat, jeans, boots and a purse big enough to carry about a week's worth of groceries. "Hey, Madison. What are you doing outside in this weather?"

She groaned. "I forgot my key. Were you at Loaves of Love, by any chance?"

"I sure was. I saw Chloe there."

"Okay, good. She didn't answer her phone when I called."

"I don't know why." Suddenly remembering an offhand comment she'd made, he said, "I think she mentioned stopping by her office before she went home."

"I was afraid of that."

"Why?"

"She puts her phone on mute if she talks to clients. And sometimes she forgets to take it off mute. That means it's really hard to get ahold of her."

"Ah."

"Yeah." Looking resigned but determined, she stuffed her hands in her pockets. "Well, thanks for the info. I'll walk over to her office."

Chloe's office was about four blocks in the opposite direction. It was really cold out and the girl looked exhausted. "Hey, wait a minute. My house is right around the corner. Why don't you come on in and wait for Chloe there?"

"Really? Are you sure you don't mind?"

"I don't mind. I'll put on the fireplace. You can sit there and watch TV or do homework." Catching sight of the amusement shining in her eyes, he added, "Or...do whatever you girls do while you're waiting."

She grinned. "I've got homework. Thanks. I mean, if it's not too much trouble."

Remembering he was holding a loaf of cinnamon bread in the paper bag in his hands, he said, "It's not. Plus, we made cinnamon bread at the food pantry today. I'll cut you a slice."

Her blue eyes lit up. "Oh, man. That bread is so good."

"Right? So, you ready to get warm?"

"More than ready. Thanks." As they started walking, she said, "I'll keep calling and texting Chloe. Hopefully I won't be in your living room too long."

"It's not a problem." When Madison still looked worried, he said, "You're not much younger than my brother and sister. I promise, I'm used to kids hanging out with me."

"How old are they?"

"They just turned twenty-one."

"They? They're twins?"

"Yep. And, just so you don't have to try to guess, I'm twenty-eight."

"Wow. Your parents sure took a break between kids."

He laughed. "Yeah. My mom used to say that Bud and Halley were her big surprise."

"I bet she had her hands full."

"Yeah. She sure did when they were small." He

felt his expression tighten. His father would've gotten a kick out of seeing the twins grow up. He'd be really proud of them.

"I have a younger sister, but we're just two years apart. I bet they were annoying."

"Sometimes, but most of the time they were fine. Which is good, since half the time I feel like their dad."

"Wow."

Hating that he'd shared too much, he cleared his throat. "The only reason I brought all that up is because I wanted you to know that I'm used to Halley and Bud over a lot. You being there isn't going to phase me."

Madison studied his face and then smiled.

It seemed more genuine. Relaxed. He was glad about that. "Do they live nearby?"

"They do when they're home. Bud goes to Bowling Green and Halley goes to the University of Kentucky."

"That's down in Lexington."

"Yeah. She wanted to go someplace far away and they got scholarships and part-time jobs so my mom said for them to go for it."

"Did you go there, too?"

He shook his head as he unlocked the front door and turned on the lights. "I didn't go to college. It wasn't for me."

"Wow. And your parents let you do that?"

"Yep." Jamison was pretty sure his smile was

as tight as his jaw felt. He'd never blamed anyone but his own mediocre grades for the fact that he'd never earned enough of a scholarship to even go somewhere local. But the truth was that sometimes he did want to yell out the truth. That his little brother and sister needed him because their mom had been either working or crying and no one else was around to pick up the slack.

Just as quickly, he felt a wave of shame wash over him. There was nothing wrong with his chosen path. He'd sure been successful. Probably made more money than a lot of people imagined.

Realizing that Madison was gazing at him with a worried expression, he pressed the button on the side of the fireplace. Immediately the pilot caught and the gas lit. Right next to the fireplace was this year's Charlie Brown tree. On it was a single strand of lights and about a dozen ornaments—all Snoopys, thanks to Bud and Halley. Clicking a button, he turned on the lights, too.

"Jamison, your tree."

He smirked. "Yeah, I know. But that's what you get when you work in the woods most of the year. I can't bear to cut down a healthy tree. This one wasn't going to make it to spring."

"I like it."

Smiling his thanks, he said, "The remote is on top of the coffee table. Do you want a glass of water or something?"

"Thanks, but I'm okay." Shrugging off her coat,

she pulled out her phone. "I'm going to hang out and try Chloe every couple of minutes."

"Sounds good. I need to, ah, get a couple of things done. Yell if you need something."

"Will do."

She was staring at her screen, though. Just like Halley did half the time she was over.

Walking into the kitchen, he opened a cabinet, pulled out a glass and filled it with the pitcher of filtered water he kept in the fridge.

After drinking half of it, he'd finally stopped thinking about things he couldn't control. Then, because he didn't feel right just leaving the girl alone while he went to his bedroom to change clothes, he started doing his least favorite kitchen chore: unloading the dishwasher.

He wasn't sure why he found such a simple thing so irritating. If anything, he should be giving thanks that he had a dishwasher in the first place. Growing up, his mother's dishwasher had never worked all that well. It needed to be replaced years before it had been. Because of that, he and the twins had washed most of the dishes by hand.

Thinking back to those years, he shook his head in wonder. Some nights there had been so many dishes in that kitchen sink and Bud had always somehow managed to get out of helping. Halley used to get so mad.

"I got ahold of her!" Madison called out.

Pleased to have a reason to stop sorting silverware, Jamison walked back to the living room. "What did she say?"

"She said that she's stuck on a call for another hour but she'd forgotten to tell me about the hide-a-key that's in a fake rock by the grill." Standing up, Madison reached for her coat. "I'm going to go look for it."

It was already dark out. "I'll walk you down and help you get in."

"You don't have to do that. I'll be fine."

"I'm sure you will. But I'll help you anyway." If the girl couldn't get inside, he had a feeling that she was just going to stand around until Chloe got back instead of returning to his place. "Blame it on the twins. They taught me that if something can go wrong, then it will."

She grinned at him. "I can't wait to meet them."

"You're sure to like them both. Everyone does," he added as he shrugged on his own coat. After grabbing his house keys and his cell phone, he walked to the door. "Ready?"

"Yeah."

Minutes later, they were walking on the sidewalk toward Chloe's house. "Where do you think Adam is?" she asked.

"I couldn't say. Maybe working still? Or playing basketball. He's on an indoor league in the winter at the rec center."

"Are you in that league, too?"

"Nope. I was never all that into basketball. And

I get a lot of exercise in my job. The last thing I want to do after working all day is go sweat in a gym with a bunch of old guys."

"Yeah. I wouldn't want to do that, either."

Enjoying the girl's company, he smiled as they continued on the sidewalk. Madison talked a little bit about her parents' transfer and how much she didn't want to start thinking about home being in Arkansas.

Maybe Jamison should have tried to get her to temper her argument. After all, it wasn't her father's fault that he was trying to earn a good living. But Jamison didn't have the heart to side with her parents. He didn't know them…and he could definitely see Madison's side of the story. He liked Medina. Liked it a lot. He couldn't imagine living anywhere else.

Plus, it was the girl's senior year. He could remember feeling a combination of nervousness and nostalgia about those days.

He hadn't wanted to miss a thing during his last days in high school.

"This is Chloe's house," Madison said, pulling him back to the present.

"I've walked by this place so many times. It was on the market just last year."

"Yep. That's when she bought it." Already tromping through the yard to where a gate on the right side was located, she said, "We've got to go this way to get to the grill."

Looking around, he noticed that everything looked taken care of but not with any real enthusiasm. He supposed that wasn't a fair criticism, though he didn't blame her if that was the case. Chloe had a new business to get off the ground and a high school senior to watch over.

He would, however, offer to help her get some lights installed. The house was completely dark. At the very least she needed some kind of light that turned on with a motion detector. Even some Christmas lights strung around some windows would help.

"Careful on the other side," Madison called out. "There's kind of a slope and it's slick."

She hadn't lied. The spitting snow did make it feel a bit like a sheet of ice. "I should've gone first."

"Why? I'm fine."

Following her to the grill, he said, "Where again did she say the hide-a-key was?"

"It's under a fake rock."

For the first time, she looked worried. "They all look the same to me."

"Mind if I take a look?"

"Help yourself."

Jamison crouched down by the grill. Moved two rocks, and uncovered the fake one. "Here we go." He flipped it over and pulled out the small insert. "Hold out your hand." When she did, he turned over the rock and the key fell into her palm.

"We did it."

"Let's see if it works. What do you think? Does it only work on the front door?"

"I don't know. I didn't ask."

"Go try, then."

Maddison tried to fit the key in the back door lock. "It doesn't work."

"Let's go try the front door."

Back they went, then tracked their way to the front door. "Let's see if this works," she said.

And, sure enough, the key slid into the lock easily. When she turned it to the right, a click sounded. She reached for the handle and turned.

They were inside.

"No alarm to dismantle, right?" He didn't hear anything, but some systems were silent.

"Nope. Chloe said it's a safe neighborhood." Turning on the lights, she turned to him. "Well, I'm in."

"You sure are. You good?"

"Yeah."

Pleased to have her settled, he took a step back.

"All right, then. I'll see you later. Oh, let me give you my number in case you need something before Chloe gets back."

"You sure you won't mind if I text?"

Uh-oh. She wasn't near as relaxed as she was pretending to be. "Not at all. Madison, I'll mind if you don't reach out if something's wrong."

"Thanks."

"Get out your phone. Let's make sure you've got my name and number in there."

"Just in case."

"Just in case," he repeated.

After she added him to her contacts and then texted him so he could do the same, Jamison studied her expression again. "I know you're a senior and all, but are you sure you're okay? I can stay here for a little while. You won't even have to entertain me. I can sit on the couch while you do your thing."

"Thanks, but I'll be fine now."

"Okay, then." She looked a little better. A little more at ease. His job there was done. "Have a good night."

"You, too."

He turned back out to the weather, frowning when he saw that the snow was falling down harder.

"Hey. Jamison?"

He turned back around. "Yeah?"

Her cheeks pinkened. "Thanks for, you know, taking care of me."

"You're welcome. Lock the door when I leave."

Walking home, he stuffed his hands in his pockets and replayed the last two hours. He was really glad that he'd been there for Madison. He knew Chloe would appreciate it, too.

And…that was the problem. No, his problem. No matter how hard he tried, he could never look at

Chloe as just a friend. The truth was that he liked her. A lot.

He liked everything about her. He liked how she looked. He liked her sense of humor. He liked how much she thought about other people.

He thought her lips were perfect. He ached to kiss her. Just once.

Okay, that was a lie.

He ached for her in a way that was wrong, given that she was dating his best friend. He was trying to come to terms with it, though.

After all, he didn't just like her. He was halfway in love with her.

He just hoped no one ever found out.

CHAPTER THREE

MADISON KNEW THAT a lot of people would disagree, but things in her life were currently not that great. Her parents had left and she now had to finish her senior year at her aunt's house.

Sure, she understood why her mom wanted to be with Dad when he accepted the transfer. Her dad was a good guy, but he wasn't all that capable with real life. Her dad could talk sports with anyone, could mow the lawn and was pretty good at golf. Other than that, he had no clue how to do much except for sell insurance.

Okay, that wasn't fair. Her father had an important job and did real well selling life insurance. But he had no clue how to cook, do laundry or even what to do if the internet went out. Mom did all of that.

And, when Mom did her church retreats two times a year or went on an antique hunt with her lady friends? Madison did those things for her father.

She'd gotten pretty good at making him eggs

and bacon or baking chicken and potatoes. And so far, she hadn't turned any of his undershirts pink.

So, she was okay with her parents being together. She was grateful that they'd let her stay in Medina, too. A lot of parents wouldn't have done that.

But she did miss them. Chloe was great and all, but she wasn't her mom and this house wasn't her home. Not even close, since all Chloe had done for Christmas was stick a dinky tree in the living room. Madison's mom went all out.

Plus, the TV situation was pretty bad. It turned out Chloe didn't watch a lot of TV and barely subscribed to any streaming services. She also didn't buy many good snacks. And she went to bed early.

So, living there was all right, but not excellent. And school was fine. She'd always been good at school and cheerleading kept her busy.

But she was tired. Varsity had a lot of practices, a lot of games, and because she was in a leadership role, she was supposed to go to some of the freshmen and JV squads, too.

And then there was Cope. Cope Swartz. Cope, short for Copeland Swartz, who was both one of the smartest kids in the grade but also one of the coolest. He also smoked. And, she was pretty certain, drank occasionally.

She also had a giant-sized crush on him and didn't know what to do about it.

Actually, she did know she should do, and that was stay far, far away from him. Guys like Cope were trouble. He'd even acted like she was ridiculous because she cheered. If he showed up at her house, her mother would have asked him a dozen personal questions and her father would forget that he was clueless and try to get involved in her social life

It would be embarrassing and awkward.

But her parents weren't around. Instead, she was living with her mom's younger sister, who was really nice but had a life of her own. Beyond making sure she had food and was reasonably happy, Chloe didn't have a lot to say about Madison's daily life.

Not that Chloe was supposed to, she kept reminding herself. Before her parents had agreed to let Madison stay, they'd had more than one long conversation about how it was Madison's good reputation that allowed her to stay behind. She'd never been the type of girl who needed her mother to watch over her every move. She'd always just done what she was supposed to.

Until now, it seemed. Now she was starting to think that she needed to live a little bit more and stress a little bit less.

After all, that's what everyone else in the senior class was doing.

Until recently, her idea of "living" and "stressing less" involved eating ice cream and just trying to get an A or a B on a test. Not a 100 percent. Now, though, she wanted to stay out later and get to know other people who weren't cheerleaders, AP students or varsity players.

Oh, who was she kidding? She wanted to get to know Cope better. The next time he stood by her locker and teased her about the way she took notes on every lecture, she wanted to tease him, too.

And when he asked her to go to a party with him, she wanted to say yes.

But that would be an invitation to go down a path she was supposed to stay far, far away from.

"You made a promise," she whispered to herself. "You need to keep it." *Think about Chloe. She'd be so upset if you start doing stupid stuff.*

Feeling better, Madison gave herself a mental pat on the back. That's what she needed to do. Be good and steady for a while longer. At least she'd have the perfect excuse not to answer her phone when Cope called.

When her phone picked that minute to ring, she groaned. When she saw who it was, she repeated all the promises she'd just made up.

Listened to it ring a second time.

Then a third.

And then, as it rang a fourth time, she picked it up. She might know what was "right," but she was also only human. It was Cope Swartz!

"Hello?"

"Madison, hey."

"Oh, hi." She hoped she sounded surprised and not breathless.

"You sound surprised. Do you not have me added to your contacts?"

"I guess not." She was such a liar.

"Wow. All right. What's going on?"

"I just got back to my aunt's."

"Your aunt's?"

"Yeah. She's my mom's younger sister. Her name is Chloe.

"She's also my godmother."

Realizing she'd probably told him way more than she'd intended to, she added, "Anyway, my dad got transferred and I didn't want to move to Arkansas so Chloe took me in so I could finish the school year here."

"That's nice of her."

"Yeah. It is." She needed to keep focusing on that instead of her tiny room and the lack of chips and crackers in the kitchen.

"What's she like?"

She leaned back in her chair. "I don't know."

"Sure, you do."

"Okay. She's...intense."

He chuckled. "I didn't expect you to say that."

"What did you expect me to say?"

"I don't know. Something generic. She's nice. She's mean." His voice thickened with humor. "That sounds stupid."

And that right there was the problem with Cope. She didn't think he sounded stupid at all. She thought he sounded kind of dreamy. And honest. "What are you doing?"

"I just got home from work."

"Where do you work?"

"Can you keep a secret?"

"I think so." Right away, all kinds of nefarious secret jobs began filling her imagination. Was he dealing drugs?

"You *think* so?"

"Well, I don't know. I mean, what if one day someone asked if I knew where you worked, and it was a matter of life or death. I'd probably tell someone then."

"Huh?"

"You asked." She was being honest. And she was also being ridiculous.

"Madison, I swear you're the funniest girl I've ever met."

That didn't sound good. Had she just ruined everything between them in two minutes? "Funny, ha ha, or funny, strange?"

"What do you think?"

He sounded like he was trying not to laugh. But not in a mean way. "The latter one."

He chuckled. "There you go again."

"Now what did I say?"

"Who says stuff like 'latter'?"

She rolled her eyes. "Me and probably a lot of others." When he didn't say anything, she blurted. "Do you really think I'm strange?"

"No. But you do make me laugh."

"I resent that," she joked. "I bet there are a lot of people in our school who are stranger than me."

"True."

"So, what's your job?"

"I don't think I'm going to tell you now."

"Why not? Is it because you really work at some top secret job that I couldn't divulge if you were in danger?"

"No, but I'm kind of enjoying the idea that you think I might. I mean, no one's ever thought I was that smart."

Great. Her attempt at humor had crashed and burned. "Fine. Well, thanks for calling," she said sarcastically.

"Wait, you want to get off the phone now?"

"Kind of. I mean, so far all that's happened is that you've made fun of me. I don't know why you called."

"Maybe I called because even though I think you're funny, smart and kind of strange, I still can't stop thinking about you."

She was pretty sure her whole body turned bright red. "Oh."

"Yeah, oh." His voice deepened. "Madison, want to go out sometime?"

Yes! she wanted to scream. But right on its heels was her promise to her parents. "To do what?"

"I don't know. Go out to eat?"

"Like a real date? Not a party?" She felt like eating her last words, but she didn't take them back.

"Yeah. Like a real date. Like I pick you up and drive you around and we eat." She could practically see him rolling his eyes.

"I can't go on Friday. There's a football game." She cringed. She'd just blurted that out. Like she was desperate. Like she'd never been asked out before.

"I know you can't, cheerleader girl. Look, I better check my work schedule. When I know I have a night off, I'll see if you do, too. Okay?"

His voice had lowered. Not a lot, just enough to be that perfect combination of teasing and romantic.

Okay, Cope had probably never been either teasing or romantic. But boy did he sound tempting.

She knew she should say no. He really didn't have a good reputation. She was pretty sure that all the rumors about him weren't false. He really was trouble.

Plus, all of her friends would be shocked if they found out she was going out with him. Her friends would tell her to say no. Her mother would refuse to let her go out with someone with his reputation.

In addition, she was supposed to be biding her time in Medina until she got her college acceptance letters, picked a place and started planning her future.

But she was so tired of always doing the right

thing. And it wasn't like he was offering to take her to some wild party in the outskirts of town. He'd asked her out on a date. To dinner.

And she wanted to go so bad.

"Madison?"

She closed her eyes. Mentally jumped. "Okay."

"Cool. I'll text you tomorrow."

He hung up before she could say a thing in return. Which was kind of a rude thing to do.

So why was she already thinking about what she was going to wear on Saturday night?

She was in so much trouble.

CHAPTER FOUR

CHLOE FELT TERRIBLE about dropping the ball on her parenting duties. She really did. She'd promised Rhonda and Jerry that she'd look out for their girl. Instead, it looked as if Madison was the one looking out for her.

Glancing at the clock again, Chloe winced. She shouldn't have worked so late. Or, at the very least, she should've come home and worked from there.

She'd just taken on a new account, her biggest client yet. The only kicker was that they wanted her to work on their accounts at their offices part of the time. When she'd accepted the job, it had made sense. The two brothers had grown their business from the guest bedroom in one of their houses to a small office, to a remodeled building in the heart of downtown Medina. They had a lot of moving parts and a lot of questions. As their new accountant, she'd had questions, too. It would've been difficult to do a good job if she had to constantly play phone tag or trade emails and texts with them.

But the drawback was that she'd felt a little trapped there. She'd stayed too late, which meant that when she dropped by her own office, she discovered a pile of work to do there.

Instead of reminding herself that nothing was extremely urgent, she'd sat down, put her phone on mute, and lost track of time. She'd put their needs before her niece's.

Still berating herself for not answering Madison's call, and then not hurrying home when she'd discovered that the poor girl was at Jamison's and then that he was going to have to help her hunt for the hide-a-key, Chloe walked in the door with a box of cupcakes from the bakery next to her office. Chocolate cupcakes with red and green sprinkles didn't solve all problems, but Chloe hoped that it would soothe some hurt feelings.

Maybe that, and a pizza?

She'd walked into the house armed with apologies, only to find that Madison had not only turned on the fireplace, but had starting making pasta for dinner.

"Hey," Madison said. "I thought I'd cut up the grilled chicken we had left over from last night and put it and some peppers and broccoli in some ziti. Is that okay?"

"Of course. It's better than okay." Tossing her bag on the coffee table, she hurried over to give the girl a quick hug. "I'm so sorry, Madison. I feel terrible that you had such a bad afternoon."

"Why? You're not the one who forgot her key."

"I should've never put my phone on silent. And

I really should've come straight home to help you get inside."

"I'm not ten." Lifting her chin a bit, her voice cooled. "In a couple of months, I'll be on my own at school."

"I know, but I promised your parents I'd look after you." Rhonda was going to be so mad.

"You are looking after me. It's fine."

There was an edge to Madison's voice now. Chloe wondered if it was because she felt as though Chloe was treating her like a little kid, or if she was harboring some kind of resentment toward her parents for leaving—or for making her live with a relative instead of allowing her to live on her own.

Or maybe she was simply trying to cook?

Chloe tried to remember how she'd felt at eighteen, but she couldn't draw many comparisons. She'd been awkward and single-minded. She'd wanted to get into a good college, obtain a decent scholarship and ultimately a big job at an accounting firm. That was it.

And while she had done all those things, she couldn't exactly say that her laser-focused goals had been the right ones. Looking back, she wished someone had given her younger self some honest advice. Like that there was more to life than a good paycheck at a well-known accounting firm.

It was a useless wish. If she hadn't worked so hard to get in that firm, she never would've been able to leave, which meant she would be still working for another person instead of owning her own business.

Plus, even if she'd been given well-intentioned advice, she probably wouldn't have listened anyway. She, too, had thought she'd known best for herself.

Feeling like she was making things worse instead of better, Chloe finally let it drop. "Even though I'm not great at taking care of you, I did manage to pick up some cupcakes from the Blue Door Café." She smiled. "I even managed to snag two of the chocolate with peppermint frosting."

"No way." That seemed to have been the magic thing to say. Madison put down the wooden spoon she was holding and turned to reach for the distinctive blue bakery box. "I love this place."

"I do, too. I also picked up two chocolate peanut better fudge and two of the marble layered raspberry. Have you tried those? The frosting is dark chocolate."

"I haven't, but I will." Madison opened the box with a grin. "Look how cute those sprinkles are! They're in the shape of reindeer! You have just made my day."

"Now I know what to get you when you're stressed out about college aps," she teased. "Madison, I really am sorry that I wasn't there for you today."

"I was fine."

"I hate to think of you hunting around in the backyard for that key."

"Jamison found it really fast."

"I'm glad Jamison had time to do that."

"Yeah. He said that he didn't feel comfortable sending me home to a dark house. He really is a nice guy, Chloe."

"He sure is."

"He said you two haven't known each other very long?"

"He's right. We haven't. I met Adam and him about the same time. Adam, at a chamber of commerce party and Jamison through Loaves of Love. I couldn't believe it when I discovered that they not only knew each other but were next-door neighbors."

"I guess the three of you were destined to be friends."

"I guess so." Still surprised that the guys, so seemingly different were also best friends, she shrugged. "I'm just glad Jamison was there for you today." She owed him a phone call.

"Yeah." Madison turned back to the pasta.

"I'm going to change, then I'll help you get dinner on the table."

"Sure thing."

Walking down the hall to her room, Chloe allowed herself to take a moment to appreciate the plush quilted headboard in shades of ivory and white, the dresser and bedside tables that were painted a soft antique ivory, and her brand-new comforter. It was made of velvet, in a yummy shade of celery green, and had been an unexpected find in an outlet store a few months ago.

In short, the bedroom was a replica of her college dream bedroom. It was plush and feminine and pretty. Even the glass bedside lamp looked expensive and soothing. Every time she went to sleep, she was reminded about how all those years working in a big firm had paid off.

Telling herself that there was no need to continually regret something she couldn't change, she walked to her closet, put on her favorite leggings and old hoodie, and then returned to the kitchen to help Madison finish dinner.

Later, after they'd eaten, the dishes were done and Madison had retreated to her room for the night, Chloe parked herself in front of the fireplace, found an old version of *A Christmas Carol*, put it on mute, and gave Jamison a call.

"I can't think you enough for being there for Madison," she said after they exchanged pleasantries.

"You've already thanked me and so did Madison. Don't worry about it."

"You know I'm going to."

"It's done. I'm going to tell you the same thing I told your niece. I practically raised the twins. Helping her out was no big deal."

"You're sure?"

"Positive. Today was nothing compared to the time Bud locked his keys in his car at the mall at the movie theater. He called me at midnight. His date was there, shivering. I had to spend half the time sliding a coat hanger through the window to pop the lock and the other half trying to calm her down. And glare at my brother when he couldn't keep his hands off her."

Picturing the scene, she started laughing. "Okay, you win. That sounds awful."

"It was awkward as all get-out. We laugh about it now."

Feeling another wave of confusing warmth run through her, Chloe sucked in a breath. She wasn't supposed to feel this way about him. They were friends. "Well, uh, I better get off the phone."

"Oh. Sure."

"Sorry. I didn't mean to sound so abrupt. It's just that I remembered that I haven't called Adam yet. He's probably wondering what happened."

"Or he could call you," he said after a brief pause.

He did have a point. Maybe he was right, too. But, that didn't mean that she should be talking to Jamison instead. "I told Adam I'd call when I was done with dinner. I'm sure he doesn't want to bother me."

"Oh, yeah. Sure."

"He's really considerate about things like that."

"I didn't say Adam wasn't."

"I'll see you later. Are you volunteering at Loaves of Love this weekend?"

"I'm planning on being there sometime Saturday morning. You?"

"Yes. I'll look for you."

"Great. Night, Chloe."

"Night," she said softly before disconnecting. Eager to put the awkward conversation out of her mind, Chloe quickly dialed Adam's number.

When it rang four times before his recording announced for her to leave a message, she tried not to wonder what he was doing.

Just like she tried not to wonder why she wasn't all that upset about not hearing his voice.

Or that he never called her back the rest of the night.

CHAPTER FIVE

"JAMISON, YOU ARE just the man I wanted to see," Edna called out when he walked through the main door of Loaves of Love on Saturday morning. "I need your help."

Edna was standing in front of the reception area. As usual, she was wearing jeans with a faint crease in the legs, a chunky sweater and tennis shoes. A new diamond ring sparkled on her left hand, reminding him that she might be in her sixties, but she was also a newlywed. "What's going on?"

"Wayne accepted a donation of ground beef, but no one has divided it into portions or placed it in ziplock bags yet." She sighed. "There's a lot of it. Would you mind helping him weigh the meat and then bag and tag it?"

"Of course."

Looking a little hesitant, she added, "He might need some help bringing it all inside. He has frozen chicken, too."

"I can help with whatever he needs."

"Thank you. I was going to ask Sean Copeland to lend a hand, but he has another commitment with his family so he couldn't come in today. Do you know Sean?"

"The high school coach? Yep. He's a good guy." Winking at Edna, he added, "He's a newlywed, too, I think."

Twin patches of color appeared on her cheeks. "Yes, he is. He and Kayla are doing well…and she just had a baby! A little girl named Aubrie."

He grinned. "I heard that news as well." Actually, for weeks all conversation among the volunteers had seemed to center around either Edna and Wayne or Kayla and Sean. Everyone loved the idea that couples were finding happiness within the walls of the organization. "Is Wayne in the back?"

"Yep."

"I'll head there now."

"Thanks."

Just as he was about to head down the hall, he turned back. "Hey, Edna, if you see Chloe, tell her that I'm here, but in the back. Okay?"

"I sure will." Her voice warmed. "Do you need to see Chloe immediately, Jamison? If so, I can send her to the back the minute she arrives."

"Oh, no. It's nothing like that. I…well, when we were talking on the phone the other night, I mentioned that I'd see her here today."

"I see." A pleased smile formed on her lips. " I'll be happy to let her know where you are."

There was a glint in the lady's eyes that was vaguely disturbing. Sean had once mentioned that

Edna had given both him and Kayla advice when they experienced a bump in their relationship. Even though he and Chloe didn't have that type of relationship, he didn't want Edna to say something to make things awkward between the two of them.

Luckily, he was able to put all thoughts of Edna matchmaking out of his mind when he walked into the pantry's large space.

Metal shelves were neatly lined up and different types of foods were organized in rows. At the end of each row was a sign that announced the contents of each row.

The floor was linoleum, and the walls had recently been painted a buttery yellow. Hanging on the walls were photographs of farm animals in black wooden frames. Recently, Edna had purchased a half-dozen shopping buggies that had removable baskets on the top and the bottom. Altogether, the room looked like a cross between a library and a small country grocery store. It was certainly inviting.

"Jamison, am I glad to see you," Wayne boomed in a deep voice. "Some of these packages of meat are heavier than they look."

When he spied the two giant packages on the butcher block table, Jamison thought that they looked very heavy. It was going to be a good workout. "I'm happy to help. How about you let me do the lifting and you direct?"

"That works for me. My younger self would object but my current bones are thanking you."

He grinned. "I have a feeling that one day I'm going to blink and feel the same way."

"Bite your tongue. You've got years and years until you get to be my age."

Jamison didn't respond, but memories of his father dying too young always tainted any picture he had in his mind of being a contented old guy.

Pushing those thoughts away, he walked to the truck outside and pulled out the first carton. Just like Wayne had promised, the container was heavy. At least forty pounds.

The cardboard container didn't seem very secure, either. He groaned as he carefully picked up the first box and carried it in. The last thing he wanted was for the cardboard to rip and all the meat to fall on the floor.

"You okay, buddy?" Wayne called out.

"Yep. How do you want to handle this? Unpack and sort as we go? Or, would you rather unload the truck first?"

"Unload first. Edna might get another delivery before we're finished."

"That works for me."

He spent the next half hour working up a sweat in the cold air as he carried box after box of poultry, pork and hamburger and sorting it into family-size portions and then storing in the giant freezer in the storage area.

Just as he got everything unloaded, his cell phone rang. Seeing that it was Bud, he picked up. "Hi. Everything okay?"

"Yeah. I just had a couple of minutes before class to say hi."

Jamison could tell he was walking on campus. Faint laughter was in the background and Bud was slightly out of breath. "I'm glad you did. How are things?" His little brother rarely called for no reason other than to say hello. Through the years, he'd become the twins' first line of defense. They called him before Mom when they were in trouble, needed extra cash, or were worried about something.

"Um, okay. Hey, you sound like you're hiking. I thought you were off work today."

"I am off, but I'm over at Loaves of Love. They got a shipment of meat and needed some help unloading the truck."

"So of course you stepped in." There was humor in his brother's voice. Bud and Halley liked to tease him about never being able to refuse doing a favor for someone.

"I did. It's all good, though. We're almost done. So, what class are you headed to?"

"Physics."

His little brother was so smart. He was a hard worker, too. Jamison knew he was trying to graduate early, so he was taking a couple of classes on Saturdays. "Better you than me."

"Eh, it's fine. It's better than my morning class."

"Which was?"

"Communication. We have to debate and give speeches."

"Now, that I could do," he teased.

When Wayne looked at him curiously, Jamison held up a finger, signaling that he needed five more minutes. "Bud, I'm glad you called but this is a tough time for me to talk. How about I call you in a couple of hours? You going to be around after your class?"

"Yeah. I don't work at the restaurant until tonight."

"Okay. I'll try you in around—"

"Wait. I was hoping to ask you for something. I promise, it's quick."

Here it was. Reminding himself that Bud rarely called for money and that he did work every Saturday night at a high end restaurant, he asked, "How much do you need?"

"It's not money, J."

"What is it, then?"

"I was wondering...could I come stay with you next weekend?"

"Of course."

He breathed a sigh of relief. "Thanks. I appreciate it."

"You know you never have to worry about staying with me," he added, confused why Bud was acting like this was a big deal. "All you have to do is tell me when you're showing up."

"You know I wouldn't do that to you."

"Why don't you want to be at Mom's?"

"Because I'm going to be seeing my girlfriend's parents on Saturday. I'm not ready for Mom to meet Jenny yet."

"Am I going to get to meet Jenny?"

"Yeah. She wants to meet you. She met Halley a couple of weeks ago."

He was serious about this girl. If he was so serious, why didn't he want their mother to meet her, too? Warning bells rang in his head but Jamison knew how his brother would react to a bunch of questions fired on the fly. "It's your call," he said slowly. "But we should probably talk about that when you're here."

"I know. That's fine. I've got to go."

"Hold on. You coming Friday night or Saturday?"

"I'm not sure. I'm hoping for Friday afternoon, but if I get an extra shift at work, it might not be until sometime Saturday."

"No worries. Come when you can. If I'm not home, you can let yourself in. I'll text you the garage code in case you forget your key."

"I won't forget the key and I already know the code. But thanks."

"Of course. See you then."

"Yeah, see you."

When they disconnected, Jamison stuffed the phone back in his pocket. Bud and this Jenny were now going to be on his mind. Briefly he wondered if he should give Halley a call and get the lowdown on their brother's love life. She would know...but she would probably go against him. The twins were a united front.

Wayne interrupted his thoughts. "If I didn't know better, I would guess that you were talking to your son."

Turning to face Wayne, he said, "That was my younger brother, Bud. He's seven years younger than me."

"That's quite a gap."

"Yeah."

"Sounds like you two are close."

"We are." Feeling compelled to share more than he usually did, he added, "Our dad died young. I helped raise him and his twin sister, Halley. So, yeah. Sometimes it does feel like I'm talking to my son."

"I'm sorry for your loss. Boy, losing your dad when you were just a kid had to be difficult. How old were you?"

"Twelve."

"That was awfully young to lose a dad—and to be saddled with so much responsibility."

"It was a lot but my mom had her hands full." She'd also kind of shut down for a while. For years.

"Sounds like you had your hands full, too. I bet that was hard."

Jamison had never liked people making a big

deal about him caring for Bud and Halley. "It wasn't so bad."

"You loved them."

"Yeah." And he still did. No, he always would.

The lines around Wayne's mouth seemed to deepen as he crossed his arms over his chest. "It may sound corny, but I've found that love can make just about any job bearable. I mean, if you're doing it because your heart is involved."

Thinking back to when he'd first started doing more and more for Halley and Bud, Jamison shrugged. "I do love them, but I can't say that I thought about that so much when they were home. I just did what had to be done."

"Kind of like this chore in front of us now," Wayne said.

"I don't know. Maybe you're doing this out of love for Edna, but I'm guessing your motivation might be more old-school."

"You'd be right. This is not my favorite job here. You and me are sorting meat because it needs to be done."

"And because everyone who receives it is going to have a decent meal with it."

"Yes. Absolutely because of that."

They shared a smile as they got to work. As Jamison packaged products and dutifully labeled and dated the freezer bags for Edna, he pushed aside all his worries about Bud. If something was really wrong, Bud would've told him.

Maybe Bud was afraid their mother was going to say that he shouldn't be seeing any girl so seriously. Or warn him off from proposing or something.

Proposing? Where had that come from?

Bud was a long way from marriage…and then he remembered that a handful of friends from college married right out of college.

Maybe Bud wasn't too young to be in love after all.

And that…unfortunately, brought his mind ack to Chloe again. He was stepping to the side for Adam because Chloe seemed to like him the best and Adam had started dating her first. And, of course, they appeared to be a good match.

No, that wasn't right. They were a good match. Both Chloe and Adam had gone to college and were driven. They were both making a lot of money. Probably more than he ever would.

Plus, Adam had asked her out first. So, no way could Jamison interfere.

Missing out with Chloe pinched, but he could deal with it. He had no choice.

Because even though he was loyal to Adam, there was only one real reason he was determined to keep all his feelings for Chloe firmly under lock and key.

He wasn't stepping aside because it was something that had to be done. He was doing that because he loved her.

Man, even admitting it to himself was tough.

Way harder than looking after Halley and Bud had ever been.

There was no doubt about it—unrequited love sucked.

EDNA LOVED MANY things about being married to Wayne, but one of the things she loved the best was that he loved celebrating Christmas as much as she did.

Soon after they returned from their honeymoon in Hawaii, they'd bought a new sectional for the living room. It was plush, comfy, and electric. With just a push of a button, she could recline with her feet propped up perfectly. Wayne could do the same thing on his side. As the wind picked up outside, she stretched her toes a little bit closer to the roaring fire. And smiled at their stockings hanging on the mantel.

"What's put that smile on your face, Edna?" Wayne asked. "Is it because you're watching *The Bishop's Wife* for about the seventh time this month?"

"No, though who could blame me? Cary Grant makes the best angel." When he rolled his eyes, she chuckled. "Actually, I was thinking about how festive the living room looks. I love looking at all the decorations."

"Me, too, though we might have gone overboard with all the trees."

Turning down the volume, she said, "There's

nothing wrong with having four Christmas trees. It makes every room bright and cheery."

"You'll get no argument from me about that." Wayne crossed his ankles with a pleased smile. "Deciding to get this ocean-liner-sized couch was a good idea."

"It's called a sectional."

"I'll just call it comfortable." After taking a sip of his drink, he said, "Did I tell you that I had a good time working with Jamison today?"

"Sorting meat?"

"Yep. He's a hard worker, of course. But catching up with him made the time go by faster."

It was almost impossible for her to not think about how eager Jamison had been to see Chloe. "What did he have to say? Anything interesting?"

"His brother called."

"I think his name is Bud?"

Wayne smiled at her. "It is. I tell you what, Jamison talks to that boy like he's his father. And a good one, too." Staring at the television screen, he added, "That man is going to make some woman a great husband."

She'd thought the same thing for some time. "I agree," she replied. Maybe a little too brightly.

"Uh-oh. You aren't thinking of matchmaking again, are you?"

"Of course not, honey." But that wasn't really the truth. Watching the movie again, she felt her insides melt as she watched Cary give David Niven a good talking to. It was her favorite scene. Well, that and when Cary and Loretta Young were ice skating.

Cary wasn't just an angel sent down from Heaven. He was a matchmaking one. Which meant matchmaking wasn't always a bad thing. Not really.

"You know, Wayne, the truth is that some couples just need a little help. A little push in the right direction."

"We didn't."

"That's true." Smiling, she added, "But we were the exception. I mean, look at Kayla and Sean. They're really happy." They'd also benefitted from a little bit of meddling.

"I can't deny that. But you can't expect to get such good results with Jamison and...whoever you have in mind."

Chloe Winner. That was who she had in mind. And if Wayne wasn't so bullheaded, he'd open his eyes and realize that Chloe and Jamison were meant to be together.

But maybe it would be best to not get Wayne involved. He could ruin everything. "Oh, turn it up, honey. This is the best part."

"You say that about every scene."

"That's because every scene is wonderful."

"I think you have a secret crush on Cary Grant, Edna," he grumbled as he dutifully turned up the volume. "Tomorrow night, we're watching *Christmas Vacation*."

"Whatever you want to watch tomorrow night is fine with me, Wayne," she said in a sweet voice.

When he laughed, she couldn't help but chuckle a little bit, too. They both knew that by the time tomorrow night rolled around, they'd be watching another old black and white movie. He might control the remote during basketball season, but she always got her way when it came to Christmas movies.

CHAPTER SIX

"You're starting to be hard to get a hold of, Chloe," Adam said as he helped her out of her car at noon on a couple of days later. "Thank goodness you were free for lunch today. Otherwise, I don't know when we'd see each other again. It could be another week."

Slightly stung by his greeting, Chloe held out her cheek when he leaned down to kiss it. "I haven't been that bad."

After closing her door, he paid the parking meter using the app on his phone. The action was smooth and seamless. If she hadn't struggled with getting the stupid thing to sync with her phone the other day, Chloe wouldn't have even been aware of his actions.

But she had and she was. Somehow Adam made everything he did seem effortless. He also took care to do little things like that so she wouldn't have to even think about them.

It was part of his personality, she supposed. Adam Dwyer was successful in life. Now, though, she was beginning to wonder if his consideration toward her was one of the reasons she'd started dating him several months ago. For most of her life, she'd only been able to count on herself to get things done. It was nice to be cared for. Was it bad that she allowed him to do so?

After a pause, Adam's voice gentled. "Hey, I'm not complaining," he said as he reached for her hand.

Like always, her hand felt comfortable in his. Adam's palm was just calloused enough to show that he didn't mind getting his hands dirty. In addition, he never held her hand too tightly or too long. Just enough to show her he cared. Or to help her over a step or move through a crowd. It made her feel secure.

But even though she enjoyed being by his side, it didn't mean she'd loved being greeted by a complaint. "You're complaining a little bit," she teased.

"Yeah, I guess I am." He met her gaze before looking away again. "But I understand where you're coming from. You've got a new business to run. And a girl to keep track of. Then, of course, there's all your Loaves of Love stuff."

She couldn't help but notice that he didn't sound all that enthused about either Madison or her volunteer job. And, since he hadn't actually said her name, did that mean he'd already forgotten it?

Did that even matter? She wasn't sure.

Honestly, Chloe was starting to think that maybe she was the one with the problems. She might be acting too sensitive. She was pretty sure that she had already forgotten some of the names of the guys on his basketball team and he mentioned them all the time.

"You've been busy, too, Adam," she said at last. "If you're not working on a court case, you're playing basketball." Or watching football. Or getting together with his college buddies for happy hour someplace.

"I guess that's true." Looking down at their linked hands, he squeezed hers gently. "This is why we're so well suited. We not only have a lot of interests and hobbies, but we're also building our careers. We're two extremely motivated young professionals who support each other's lives."

She thought that kind of sounded like a caption on a magazine photo. Or, maybe it was true and the description fit him well.

She wasn't sure about herself, though. One of the reasons she'd decided to open her own business was to have more time instead of constantly working overtime in order to obtain a partnership. She wanted to have more time for people she cared about. She'd wanted to have a boyfriend.

"I do think we're well suited," she said at last.

"Of course we are." Looking down at her with a fond expression, Adam added, "One day, years from now, we're going to be glad we did all this. We're going to be lounging next to our pool or sitting on leather recliners in our very own media room decorated with Browns and Cavs memorabilia."

"Adam, really?"

"Come on. You'll be a sports fan soon. Anyway, my point is that one day we're going to look back on this time in our lives and be glad we went full throttle. We're going to look at each other and think that we couldn't be happier."

She giggled until she realized he was being serious.

And, it seemed, he was serious about her. Guys didn't say words like "years from now" without realizing how it would sound.

So, Adam really did intend to have a great life. With her. And…well, she might be on board with her own backyard pool, but sitting on a recliner in front of a giant television had never been on her list of wants. "I might take a pass on the leather recliner," she teased. And the Browns stuff on the walls.

"That's all right. You can hang out in the pool with all the kids." He grinned.

There it was again. The subtle (okay, maybe not so subtle) reminder that he was not only in this relationship for the long haul, but he had a particular idea of what it would be like.

Chloe knew she should feel happy and excited about that. She'd been alone for far too much of her life. Being with a guy like Adam, who was secure and solid, would mean that she'd never have to worry about paying bills or having food on the table.

She should probably be feeling a sense of peace, too. She'd dated more than one guy who never wanted to think about anything beyond the upcoming weekend. Adam, on the other hand, went out of his way to make sure she knew she was important to him.

Shouldn't she think that was wonderful? Shouldn't she want that in her future husband?

"Chloe?"

Snapping out of her daze, she dropped his hand. "I'm sorry. I meant to say yes." He frowned. "I mean, right."

A line formed between his brows. "I'm holding the door open for you, sweetheart. Are you ready to go inside?"

It was thirty degrees out and the poor hostess had been getting blasted with cold air while she'd been lost in thought. "Oh! Sorry." She hurried through and mentally splashed cold water on her cheeks. She needed to get her act together.

"I think we're going to have to meet for lunch more often," he teased as he guided her to the hostess table with his hand lightly grazing the small of her back. "You've been working so hard, you're hardly able to relax." Smiling at the attractive redhead, he said, "Dwyer. Table for two."

"Yes, Mr. Dwyer. We have your table ready. Right this way."

As they walked to a table in front of the fireplace, she sighed in appreciation. The restaurant had covered the mantel with fresh greenery and gold and silver ornaments. "This is wonderful."

"I knew you'd like to sit in front of the fire."

Like always, Adam helped her with her chair before he took his own chair.

Which was so very Adam. He had impeccable manners and always made her feel like she was worth all the trouble he went to, even if it was just taking her out to lunch on a Tuesday. Noticing he was reading the menu with interest, she studied him yet again. He had dark hair that was receding quickly, matching dark brown eyes that were always alert. Adam was slim and just a few inches under six feet tall. He didn't tower over her, and his muscles were carefully toned and hidden under tailored slacks and starched cotton shirts.

Whenever they went for a bike ride or a walk on the weekends, his shorts or sweats always were branded some kind of expensive outdoor clothing label, and his T-shirts were always loose, comfortable and looked brand-new.

All in all, Adam was attractive, but his good looks had more to do with his personality traits than God-given handsomeness.

With a start, she realized it was his personality and drive that she liked. She wasn't exactly attracted to his physique. She should probably figure that out. A wife should probably think her husband was desirable.

Shouldn't she?

"Do you already know what you're getting?"

"Not yet. I was just thinking that you were right. I think I do need to take a few more breaks throughout the week. This restaurant is gorgeous. It's awfully fancy for a quick lunch, though. I would've been happy to go anywhere."

"You're special to me, Chloe. I don't want to take you just anywhere. Ever."

She tucked her head. His words were lovely, but they felt too much. Too much for a couple who had only gone on about a dozen dates over the last four or five months. She wasn't dating anyone but him, but they'd never talked about being exclusive.

But maybe it was understood?

Seeking to lighten the mood, she said, "If you take me here again, I'm going to think this is the only place we should go."

"See, just listen to me and I'll steer you in the right direction."

He was grinning as he said that. It was obvious he was teasing.

But she didn't exactly appreciate the joke. So, even though it would maybe be easier if she giggled and moved the conversation forward, she couldn't do it. "I kind of stopped allowing people to steer me in any direction back in high school."

"Whoa." He held up his hands. "You took that completely wrong."

"I'm sorry if I did." When Adam continued to look at her like he'd been blindsided, she inwardly sighed. "Let's just drop it, okay?"

"Yeah, sure, though I'm not exactly sure what we have to drop. I still am not quite sure what I said that got you so riled up."

"I'm not riled." Yes, her voice was still tense. So Adam probably had a very good reason to be taken off guard by her reaction. "Let's talk about you for a change. How's that case you were working on?"

"Which one?"

"The one about the family contesting the will?"

He lifted one shoulder. "It's going. You know I can't discuss the details with you. Attorney-client privilege, you know."

"I wasn't looking for details." She was just trying to make conversation.

"Let's not discuss my cases. That way I won't be tempted to tell you something I shouldn't. I'm sure you understand."

"Of course I do," she said quickly. And she did understand. But the look he'd given her stung. All she'd wanted to do was talk about something else. Not dodge another conversational land mine. "I think I might get the beef short ribs. What about you?"

"I'm trying to eat healthier. Probably the fish."

"The salmon does sound pretty good."

"I thought so. You might want to get it, too. Calories add up, right? Especially since we're having this bread and butter, and it's Christmastime."

As if on cue, their server returned to their side. "You two made your choices yet?"

"I believe so," Adam said. "Chloe, are you ready? As much as I'd like to linger, I can't stay that long. I've got to get back to work, you know."

The pretty server shared a commiserating smile with him before turning to her. "Miss?"

"I'll have the salmon."

"Of course. Grilled or pan fried?"

"Grilled. With mixed vegetables."

"It comes with a choice of potato, rice or additional vegetables. What is your preference?"

Though the extra veggies would be best, she wanted something more filling. "The loaded baked potato. Please."

"Good choice. And you, sir?"

"The tilapia, vegetables and a salad instead of the potato."

"Coming right up."

When she left, Chloe took a big sip of water and looked out the window. If Adam was going to give her advice about the appropriate side dish, she was going to say something she'd regret.

"Hey," he said in a low tone. "Chloe?"

Turning to face him, she kept her expression carefully blank. "Yes?"

"I'm sorry."

"About what?"

"I shouldn't have said a word about the short ribs. Or the fact that we've been eating bread, too."

"You know I volunteer at Loaves of Love."

"I know. What about it?"

"Well, since you live next to Jamison, you probably realize that we can take home a loaf of bread when we volunteer."

"He mentioned that." He tilted his head to one side. "What about it?"

Instead of feeling self-conscious about her curves, she said, "What it means is that I like bread. A lot. Obviously, I'm not going to pass it up here."

Adam looked slightly shocked. "I didn't think you ate a whole loaf every week."

"I don't eat a whole loaf. Madison is living with me. She has some, too. Don't worry about me putting on too much weight."

"I'm not. It didn't cross my mind."

"Sorry, but it kind of sounded that way."

He frowned. "Chloe, I'm not sure what's going on. Everything I say seems to be the wrong thing."

"I feel like you've been giving me advice that I didn't ask for since we sat down. First that I need to work less and then that I shouldn't want to eat beef, and now that I need to be careful about how much bread I eat."

His eyes widened. "You know I think you're gorgeous and successful. I don't want to change you. I'm just making conversation." He leaned forward.

"Chloe, didn't you hear me when I talked about my dream for the future? You're in it."

She gave herself a mental kick in the shins. "I'm sorry for jumping all over you. I guess I'm tired."

Sweet compassion entered his eyes. "How about the next time we share dinner, you come over to my place. I'll cook."

"I didn't know you liked to cook."

"I don't know if I do or not, but I'm hoping that's the case. I just signed up for some cooking classes."

"Really?"

"I just bought the most gorgeous hickory wood dining room table from down in Amish country. It cost an arm and a leg, but it's smooth as butter. It can even sit twelve."

"Twelve?"

He grinned. "I hear you. You're right. It's massive. But I didn't want to buy something just to have to replace it fifteen or twenty years from now."

"That's thinking ahead."

"It is, but I figured if anyone would understand where I'm coming from it would be you. I mean, you're the queen of long-range planning, right?"

She knew Adam was giving her a compliment, but it felt a little hollow. Not his words as much as the way they made her feel. She supposed it had to do with the fact that she wasn't feeling too sure that her long-range planning had served her all that well. "I used to be."

"But not anymore?"

"I'm not sure," she said honestly.

Just as she'd taken a deep breath in order to share how confused she'd been feeling, Adam spoke again. "Here's the deal. Even though I want the table to eventually host dinner parties for my wife and I and then one day Sunday dinners with our children, I also want to use it now."

"You're right. It's not like you must put in all of the table's leaves."

"Exactly. That's why I signed up for cooking classes. I figure if I spent so much money on that thing I better learn how to make something more than grilled chicken."

His explanation, though a little frightening—when it came to hosting dinner parties—did make a lot of sense. Smiling at him, she said, "Whenever you're ready to demonstrate your new skills, I'll be ready to come over to dinner." Just to show him she had no hard feelings about their earlier conversation, she added, "I'll bring the bread. And dessert."

He chuckled. "That's my girl."

She smiled but everything inside of her started twisting again. Shouldn't she feel more at peace with him? Shouldn't she be beyond questioning his comments?

Something wasn't quite right between them. Not for the long haul. Not for falling in love.

At least, she'd never imagined that falling in love would feel like this. She'd thought it would be more consuming. Like, she'd feel a physical reaction that she couldn't control. Like her heart would beat faster or her palms would sweat. Or something…

Like butterflies.

Yep, she could really go for some butterflies.

She'd thought that was where they'd been headed, though. It was disappointing. Especially because Adam seemed like everything she'd ever wanted. Everything she should want.

He was everything she'd ever expected to want.

Which meant, she supposed, that she needed to give some thought to everything that might be unexpected.

It sounded both exhilarating but scary, too. Kind of like jumping off the high diving board in the pool.

She just hoped she wouldn't land so hard that she wouldn't be able to catch her breath. If that happened, she would never recover.

CHAPTER SEVEN

"Hey, Madison, do you have plans on Saturday night?" Chloe asked from the doorway of her bedroom.

Looking up from her laptop, where she was completing yet another college application, Madison felt a twinge of worry. Her aunt rarely asked about her weekend plans. At first it had seemed odd since her mom had used to want to know everything Madison was doing.

But then, after getting to know her better, she'd realized that Chloe didn't want to interfere with Madison's many activities. All she'd ever wanted to know was when Madison was leaving and returning home. It had been obvious that she'd been bending over backward to be accommodating to Madison's social life and school schedule.

Not that Madison was going out all the time anyway. Though she enjoyed spending time with her friends, she was kind of over the high school social scene. She no longer had any desire to go to any of the big parties after football games. She'd done plenty of that her sophomore and junior years.

Now all she wanted to do was finally figure out where she was going to go to college in August. Well, that, and stress about her parents making her spend the summer in Arkansas.

What was funny was that lately, she had been home on the weekend. Of course, the one time Chloe seemed interested in doing something with her, she had plans.

Not quite concrete plans, but plans all the same.

"I might," she said slowly. "Why?"

"Oh, no reason. I...well, I had just thought it might be fun if we did a girls' night." Her expression lighting up, she said, "I thought we could go into Cleveland. Maybe go to Playhouse Square. Everything downtown will be covered with lights. It will be gorgeous."

"Like, go see a play?" Everyone knew that downtown Cleveland had a big arts district and that a lot of the national tours started there. Playhouse Square was an area of old, gorgeous theaters. There was even a giant chandelier hanging in the middle of one of the streets. She'd only been there once before, and never at night.

Looking amused, Chloe nodded. "Yes, exactly like go see a play. Have you ever been to see a play there?"

"My parents took me to see *The Lion King* when I was little."

"That's a good one. I saw it, too. There are quite a few plays on right now that sound good to me."

Looking a little hesitant, she continued. "If you'd like, we could pick one, then drive down early, go out to eat and then go to the show."

"That sounds amazing."

"I know I'd love it." Looking more excited, Chloe added, "We'll make a night of it. Want me to give you the link of the plays?"

"Um, not yet. I mean, that's sounds really fun, and I do want to go, but I need to check with the guy I've been talking to. We were going to try to go out last weekend but he had to work. He said he'd make sure he was free this week, but I'm not sure. If he's still planning on it, maybe we could go on Sunday? Or next weekend?"

"We're supposed to get a big snowstorm midweek. It might not happen, but if it does, I don't want to worry about driving around at night. I'd be up for a Sunday matinee this weekend, though. We could go to church, then head downtown for brunch and then a play. What do you think?"

Relieved that her aunt wasn't upset, she smiled. "I think that sounds awesome. Thank you."

"Of course." Looking pleased, she said, "Okay, let me look at choices and tickets and then you can pick which play you want to see."

"That's so nice, but honestly, I'd be fine with any of them. It's not like I've been to Playhouse Square lately. Whatever you want to see is great."

"I want you to be happy."

Chloe was so nice. Madison wondered when

she'd last really thanked her for taking her in. "I'll be happy no matter what. That's sweet of you to ask me. I'm looking forward to it."

Walking closer, Chloe sat down on the cozy chair in the corner of Madison's room. "When you first moved in, I didn't want to suffocate you with rules and plans. But I think I might have gone too far in the other direction. I don't want you to ever feel as if I'm ignoring you."

"I haven't felt that way at all. You've been great, Chloe. Thank you for letting me live with you this year."

"Oh, no. Don't start that again. I'm just glad that it worked out. So, I know you've got a football game to cheer for on Friday night. Want to tell me about this possible date on Saturday?"

No, she didn't. Not because she thought it wasn't Chloe's business, but because she wasn't sure how she felt about Cope. She liked him, but she was a little worried about why she liked a guy who was so different than anyone she'd ever been interested in.

Hedging a bit, she said, "There's not a lot to tell yet. I've started talking to this guy named Cope and he calls me a lot."

Looking concerned, she said, "Where did you meet him?"

"At school. He's not a stranger, I've known him for a while. Well, I've known of him. We've had a couple of classes together when we were sophomores."

"And you two recently clicked?"

"Yes." Moving her computer off her lap, she shifted, folding her legs close to her chest. "I know that probably sounds weird."

"Not really. By the time I got to my senior year in high school, I was ready to have some more friends. I was tired of hanging out with the same people and listening to the same stories."

That sounded very familiar. "I think that's what I've been doing."

Chloe chuckled. "I'm pretty sure you're not the only one. I think every senior gets ready to move on before May arrives. It's good to shake things up a bit."

"I guess that's what happened to me." She shrugged. "One day, Cope and I were the only two people walking in the hall. Since neither of us were in a hurry to return to class, we started talking. Then we started talking some more. Now we've become pretty close and the other night he asked me out on a 'real' date. He wants to pick me up and take me out to dinner and everything."

"Wow. I didn't even think teenagers did 'real' dates anymore."

Pleased that her aunt looked impressed, Madison grinned. "Same. The last guy I dated seriously, all we ever did was hang out at games or at other people's houses. This is different."

"How come you aren't sure about Saturday night,

then?" She frowned. "Is it just his schedule...or do you not like him?"

"I'm pretty sure I do." She paused, then blurted, "It's more like he's really different than other boys I usually hang out with."

Chloe frowned. "Different, how?"

"He's not part of a great crowd," she said. "Some people even say he has a bad reputation."

Chloe's expression was worried now. "What does he do? Is he drinking?"

It was tempting to lie and make Cope sound like he'd never done a thing he shouldn't, but that wasn't him, and she didn't want to lie about him, either.

Weighing her words, she replied, "I think he drinks some, but a lot of kids in high school do." Shifting her legs again, Madison added, "Don't get freaked out. I'm not interested in drinking or smoking or drugs. That's not my thing."

"Drinking, smoking and drugs," she repeated. Looking stricken, she stood up. "Wait. Is he doing all three?"

"No." Just probably two out of three. She was pretty sure she'd smelled cigarette smoke on him once. "I know he doesn't do drugs." There was no way she'd hang out with him if he did.

"What does your mom say? Does she know this Cope guy?"

"She hasn't said anything. Because I, uh, haven't told her about him."

Chloe sat back down. "Why not?"

"Because she'll start digging and make up her mind about him which wouldn't be fair."

"Are you sure?"

"I'm not sneaking around, Chloe. If my parents ask who I'm going out with on Saturday night, I'll tell them the truth. But I'm also not going to voluntarily get my mom involved in my life when I'm an adult and about to graduate high school." Besides, she'd left. Sure, Dad's needs and her sister, Eileen, were important, too. But didn't she count?

Chloe looked worried, but whatever she spied in Madison's face must have told her something, because she said, "How come you aren't sure you're still going to go out with him on Saturday night?"

"He hasn't mentioned it since we rescheduled. I'm starting to think he forgot."

Chloe smiled. "He didn't forget."

"How can you be so sure?"

"Because that's how confident guys are. Since you said yes when he asked, in his mind it's all set."

Madison didn't want to be mean, but she was pretty sure that Chloe wasn't an expert on dating. Adam was kind of a dud. Plus, everything she knew about Chloe signaled that she'd had no time for boys in high school, college or when she was at the big accounting firm.

All that meant that chances were better than good that her aunt probably had no clue about how guys like Cope did things. About how a lot of guys did things. Slowly, she said, "That's how you run,

Aunt Chloe. You are super organized and honest and dependable. I don't think Cope is like that."

Concern clouded her aunt's eyes. "If you think he's the type of guy to lie to you, then you shouldn't give him the time of day."

"I don't think he's a liar. It's more like he's just really, uh…cool." Which sounded like she was in fifth grade. She shook her head. "In a good way."

"Are you sure?"

"Well, no. We don't know each other that well. But he's not a bad person. I know that."

After a long pause, Chloe nodded her head. "Okay, then."

"Okay, then…?"

"Okay, then give him the benefit of the doubt. Now, it's not even six o'clock. How about we head to the mall, get some fast food and I'll get you something to wear for your date?"

"That isn't necessary."

"That's why it's called *fun*. We're going to do something that we want to do. Not something that we have to do. Plus, all the stores will be decorated for Christmas. Now, do you want to go?"

Anything was better than sitting around waiting for Cope to text or call. "Sure."

"Great." Smiling big, she said, "Go get ready. We'll leave in ten minutes, if that's okay with you?"

"Yep. I'll be ready."

"I know you will, honey," her aunt said softly. "Cope might not be super dependable, but you are."

Two hours later, they were driving home again, and she had a new pair of jeans and a sweater in the trunk of Chloe's car. To her surprise, Chloe had bought some things for herself, too. She'd bought a pair of jeans, two sweaters, a flowy dress and some suede scrunchy boots.

They'd also eaten a ton of pizza at the food court before Chloe took her to the cookie factory, where they picked out a dozen warm cookies.

"Those cookies smell so good," Chloe said. "You've got to stop me before I eat five of them tonight."

"You should eat five, if you want five." When she spied her aunt grimace, she said, "Okay, I'll stop you after you eat four."

"I'll do the same for you."

"Thanks." Glancing at her in the dim light of the vehicle, Madison said, "This was fun. I liked walking around the mall with you. Thanks for the clothes, too."

"Anytime."

"And thanks for inviting me to a play on Sunday."

"Like I said, I want to go with you, honey."

Madison felt herself soften at the endearment. "I, uh, just want to tell you not to worry that I'm going to start taking advantage of you."

"What are you talking about?"

"My parents made me promise that I wasn't going to ask you for things."

"You haven't." Frowning, she added, "You never ask for anything."

"You know what they meant. It's enough that you've taken me in."

"Just so we understand each other, and I'm going to be completely honest… Madison, I love you. You're family. I've been glad to be able to give you a place to live this school year. But more importantly, I like having you here," she said as she gently brushed a strand of hair off her cheek. "You're easy to get along with and good company."

"Thanks."

"There's one more thing, and this might make me sound mean, but I kind of didn't think it was fair that your parents just up and left. Even though they wanted to get your sister Eileen settled in her new school, I thought your dad and mom should've tried harder to stay until you graduated in May. The inconvenience for them would've been far less of an impact of you having to move, or live with a relative your senior year."

It was like someone finally understood her feelings. Feeling a little choked up, she said, "Thanks for saying that."

"Oh, honey. You've been keeping a lot of stuff inside, huh?"

She shrugged. "Kind of." She didn't want to say anything more, because she was afraid that once she started, she wouldn't stop whining.

"Just for the record, I wasn't just spouting off

words, Madison. I meant them," she said as she pulled in. "I care about you."

"Same."

Just as they were walking in the house, Madison heard her phone ring. Pulling it out of her purse, she was totally ready to fill her mother in on their shopping trip when she realized that it wasn't her mother at all.

Cope was calling.

"Hey," she said.

"Hey. What's going on?"

"I just got back from the mall." She smiled at Chloe as she headed toward her room.

"Madison?" Chloe called out.

"Hold on, Cope." Covering her phone, she said, "Yeah?"

"Is it him?" she whispered.

"Yeah." She couldn't help but grin when Chloe gave her a goofy thumbs-up.

"Sorry. I had to tell my aunt something. Anyway, that's where I was."

"I'm surprised you went out there by yourself at night."

"I didn't go by myself. My aunt and I went together. We ate pizza at the food court and then looked at all the shops."

"No way, really?"

He sounded like he was trying not to laugh at her lame night, which didn't make her happy. "Yeah, Cope. That's what I really did."

"Whoa. Sorry if I said the wrong thing. It's just that I didn't think anyone still did that."

Realizing that she sounded rude, Chloe chuckled under her breath. "I didn't think so, either," she allowed. "But, you know what? I'm glad we went. It was fun and the pizza was even pretty good."

"I guess that means I don't have to do too much to impress you on Saturday night, then, huh?"

"So, we're still on?"

"Yeah. I was able to get off work. Is it still okay with you?"

"It is. Though, I'm expecting something just as good as mall pizza," she joked. "Sbarro pizza is a pretty high bar, you know."

"Sky-high."

"It's not like I say yes to dates with just any guy, you know?" she continued to joke.

"I'm glad you don't. I think that means that I might have a chance with you."

He sounded serious, which was crazy because it wasn't like they knew too much about each other. "Cope, that's really sweet."

"Hey, I know you were joking around. I probably shouldn't have said that just now. Sorry if it was too much."

"It wasn't," she said softly. "So, enough about me. What have you been doing tonight?"

"Compared to your night at the mall, mine was pretty lame. I worked and then went home and ate leftovers."

Once again, she was struck by how much she'd misjudged his life. He hadn't been out partying. "I'm sorry you had to work."

"It was fine. I like the overtime."

"Do you like working at the hardware store?"

"It's all right. My boss is cool, so I'm good with it."

"How long have you been there?"

"Almost four years."

"What? You started there when you were fourteen?"

Sounding like he was trying not to laugh, he said, "I was thirteen, actually."

"You started working at thirteen?" Yeah, she was making a big deal about that, but it kind of was a big deal. It seemed awfully young to have a "real" job.

"Some kids babysit, I worked at the hardware store."

"I didn't think that was legal."

He laughed. "To hire a thirteen-year-old? It wasn't. The manager paid me under the table for a year."

"What did your parents say?"

"What do you think? They were good with it."

"Yeah. I guess that's obvious. But I feel bad for you."

"Don't."

"Wow." She wanted to ask him why. Wanted to ask a lot of things about his job, but it was obvious that he didn't want to share the details with her.

She wondered how many secrets he had.

"I still want to take you out on Saturday night. Is that okay with you?"

"Yes."

"I'll pick you up at six thirty."

"I'll be ready."

"Do you have a curfew? I didn't even ask."

"Yeah. I need to be in by midnight. Is that okay?" she asked hesitantly. A lot of kids she knew could stay out as long as they wanted.

"It's fine. See you then."

"Yeah. See you then. Get some rest."

"You, too. Later."

"Later." She disconnected, tossed her phone on the bed, and then thought some more about Cope. A tingling sense of anticipation hit her hard.

She wondered how she'd feel tomorrow and then finally on Saturday. Would the tingles continue? Or, would she realize that Cope was nothing like she thought he was? There was a chance that would happen.

Then, there she'd be again. Applying to colleges, checking her email and waiting to finally move on.

CHAPTER EIGHT

CHLOE HAD ARRIVED at Loaves of Love too late on Saturday morning to bake bread, but she'd come in plenty of time to monitor the last set of loaves in the oven and clean the kitchen. This was the third time she'd taken over the last shift, and there was a part of her that enjoyed it the most.

It was quiet, the kitchen was filled with neatly wrapped loaves, and it smelled heavenly. It was one of the few times in her week when she allowed herself to simply sit. She didn't make to-do lists and she didn't play on her phone. She simply wiped counters, mopped the floor and allowed herself to relax.

After reassuring Edna that she wouldn't leave the building before double- and triple-checking that everything was turned off and locked up, Chloe happily hopped up on a stool, sipped the large cup of coffee she'd brought with her from home and waited for the last two volunteers to hand her their loaves of bread.

"Here you go," a lady in her thirties said as she placed two loaf pans in front of Chloe. "My mom and I were starting to think our loaves were never going to rise."

"I've thought the same thing myself. I know the saying about a watched pot never boiling is popular, but I think all of us would say the same thing happens with a loaf of bread dough."

She chuckled. "Exactly."

Since the woman seemed anxious to chat, Chloe added, "Is this your first time volunteering here?"

The woman nodded. "My name's Nan." Lowering her voice, she added, "I actually came in to help my mom pick up some food. She's on a tight budget and I...well, I can't always take care of her and my son and husband, you know?"

"I understand. Everyone needs a helping hand now and then. That's why Edna started this place."

"Mom and I had a good time making bread." Looking wistful, Nan added, "It was the first time in ages that we weren't worrying about something. Plus, the couple across from us were a lot of fun."

"I hope you'll come back and bake bread with us again, even if you don't need a helping hand. It's kind of neat that a group of strangers can bond together over yeast and flour, isn't it?"

Nan's tentative smile brightened. "It really is. Mom kept saying that working in this kitchen is a lot more fun than doing the same thing at home."

"I've said that, too."

"Nan, you ready?"

Glancing in her mother's direction, Nan said,

"Looks like Mom is ready to go. After we clean up our spaces, we're going to head out."

"Sounds good. Have a good rest of your day."

Just as Nan was about to reach for her purse, she turned back to Chloe. "Are you here all by yourself now?"

"I think so. There might be a volunteer still in the food pantry."

"This is a big building. Would you like us to stay?"

"Thanks, but I'll be fine. I lock the doors."

"So you'll be safe."

"Yep. Plus, I kind of like being here alone. There's something so peaceful about watching bread bake in the peace and quiet." Gesturing toward the tall metal cart, she said, "I get to organize the fruits of today's labor."

Looking at the dozens of loaves, the lady whistled low. "No wonder it smells so good in here. Everyone made a lot of bread today."

"It's incredible, right? Don't forget to take two loaves when you leave."

"We won't. See you later."

"Yep. See you."

She couldn't help but smile as she watched Nan walk to a little cubby near the door and pull out two paper sacks stuffed with groceries. She didn't always know who was a recipient and who was a volunteer and she was glad about that. She knew food insecurity could happen to anyone at any time. But Chloe would be lying if she said that seeing the obvious joy the donations gave to a recipient didn't make her day.

After Nan and her mother walked out of the workroom, and then out the front entrance, silence descended.

She checked the timers near the ovens. One batch would be done baking in seven minutes, the other twelve. Then all she had to do was bake the five loaves on the counter, which would take thirty minutes. All in all, she should be able to leave within two hours.

That meant she had lots of time for quiet bliss. No work to do on her laptop. No phone calls to return. No bathroom to clean or kitchen floor to wash. And finally, no Madison to chat with.

She loved her job and she loved her niece. But she also needed some downtime.

And…some time with Adam, too.

Smiling at the thought of surprising him with dinner, she began to mentally take stock of the freezer. She was pretty sure she had a lot of frozen chicken. Maybe Adam would want pasta? They could open a bottle of wine, eat on the couch, watch some series everyone was talking about. It would be nice. Hopping off her stool, she started walking up and down the vacant workspaces, double-checking that every spot was neatly wiped down and all the containers were put away.

Just as she was putting an industrial-sized container of salt away, the first oven dinged.

Quickly, she hurried to the back, put on kitchen mitts and pulled out ten loaves of bread. After placing the pans on a set of racks, she put in those last five loaves and set the timer again.

In five minutes, she would start taking out all the loaves from their pans. After they cooled, she'd slip them into plastic sleeves. Right about then, it would be time to empty the second oven and turn it off.

"You've got this," Chloe told herself.

She did, too. In some ways, she enjoyed this part of the bread baking process even more than making the actual bread. Her mind thrived on order and organization. She loved putting everything in its proper place. She also felt like she was not only helping the food bank's recipients but also Edna when she stayed late. She now knew that until recently, Edna was the only person to ever work the closing shift at Loaves of Love.

Just when she was about to start taking out the cooled loaves from their pans, there was a banging on the front door.

Her first instinct was to ignore it—after all, they were supposed to be closed. But maybe it was Nan? She could have forgotten her phone or something.

"Hello?" a voice called out. "Can anyone let me in?"

She knew that voice! Hurrying toward the front, she clicked open the door. "Jamison, what are you doing here?"

"I could ask the same of you," he said, as he walked inside with a cold burst of air.

"I'm closing the kitchen for Edna tonight and locking up. What about you?"

"The same." He looked sheepish. "Except I'm late. I meant to get here a half hour ago. I was stuck at work."

"On a Saturday?"

"Yep. I had a scheduled tour along the Rocky River."

"That sounds...fun."

He laughed. "It was. The group's energy was infectious. It made the time go by fast, though it was cold."

Taking a better look at him, she noticed that his cheeks were slightly windburned. He was also wearing thick twill pants, a Carhartt coat, brown work boots, and a gray-and-green flannel with a sparkling white undershirt peeking out of the collar. "You look nice," she said before she could stop herself.

"Thanks, but you probably don't want to stand too close to me. When I wasn't walking along the river, I led the women's hiking club today. We went seven miles."

"You lead women's hiking clubs?" She probably sounded incredulous. But it was probably better than sounding jealous.

Which she was, though she had no right to be. She

and Jamison were just friends. Just good friends. She was dating someone else seriously.

Well, kind of seriously.

But even so, she kind of felt possessive of him. Hmm. Or maybe it was more like a protective feeling? Like he was so nice that he probably had no idea that women watched him all the time. She could just see all those female wannabe hikers gazing at Jamison like he was their own personal guide and Sherpa.

"You're frowning. What did I say that irritated you?"

"Nothing." When one of his eyebrows rose, she exhaled. "Fine. I was thinking about all those women who probably signed up just to get to be around you."

He started laughing.

It was a big, loud sound. Loose. Like he wasn't guarding himself around her. That made her feel good.

But made her feel a little awkward, too. Because she knew she shouldn't be feeling so easy with him.

When his hand pulled at hers, it took her off guard. Especially when his gentle tug brought her closer. Close enough to hug. Almost close enough to kiss. Her attention shifted to his lips.

Imagined what it would feel like to kiss him. Probably pretty darn good.

There she went again, thinking things she shouldn't. She had to get some control of herself, which meant that she had to push him away. Whenever he was around, she could hardly think straight. "Jamison, stop."

He did immediately. Scanning her face, his expression softened. "Sorry for laughing, but I couldn't help myself. Chloe Winner, you crack me up."

"I'm not sure what I said that was so funny."

"Ah, women signing up to go hiking in the bitter cold because they want to be near me. That's what was funny."

Did he never look in the mirror? "It's not that funny. I could be right." She honestly wouldn't have been shocked to discover that he had a fan club.

"If you saw these women, you would know that I was the last thing on their minds."

"Why is that?" Suddenly not liking that he acted like they weren't good enough, she said, "What was wrong with them? Were they too old? Too young?"

"Nothing is wrong with them. It's more like they're way too motivated to do anything more than glance my way. They're part of a 'women who hike' group. The group gives out badges and medals and stuff for miles hiked per month. Trust me, all those gals wanted was for me to guide them around a seven-mile hike and then sign their forms."

"Oh."

"Yeah, oh." Still holding her hand, he ran a finger along her knuckles before releasing it. "Thanks for the smile, though."

"Anytime."

"Now, what can I do to help you clean up? What still needs to be done?"

"Oh my goodness. I need to check on that bread!" Turning around, she hurried back into the kitchen and rushed to the ovens. Sure enough, the second oven's timer had gone off. Muttering to herself, she grabbed two kitchen mitts and pulled open the door.

"Hey, I'll do this. You check the other oven."

Realizing that his long arms had a much easier time than hers did reaching all the loaf pans, she did as he asked. "The other batch is fine. They still need a few more minutes."

"Okay."

As Jamison continued to pull out the loaf pans, she went back to bagging the bread she'd taken out of the oven thirty minutes ago.

From then on, they worked in companionable silence. Jamison helped her take out the last batch of bread, sweep, then wash bread pans, then bag the last batch of cooled bread. Finally, he mopped while she wiped the last of the counters.

When she turned off the last lights and walked out the front door with a loaf of bread in one hand and her purse in the other, two more hours had gone by.

"I'm starving," Jamison said. "Do you want to grab something to eat?"

She was hungry, too. Too hungry to whip up some fantasy pasta dish to impress Adam. Mentally promising herself to cook for Adam very soon, she replied, "Let me check on Madison. She has a date tonight, but she might need me for something." Quickly pressing her number, she was glad that the girl answered immediately.

"Hey, Chloe."

"Hey. I just finished at Loaves of Love. Jamison stopped by to help me take care of the last set of bread in the ovens and clean up. We're thinking of grabbing something to eat."

"Okay. Have fun."

Feeling guilty, "Hold on. Would you like to join us? You're welcome to."

"No thanks. I'm going out to dinner, remember?"

"I remembered. But, um, do you need anything?"

"I'm good. I'm about to take a shower."

"Okay. So, I'll see you when you get home?"

"I guess so."

"Home at midnight?" That was her curfew.

"Yes, ma'am," she teased. "Just like the contract said."

She felt a little foolish now. Madison was such a good girl. She probably could stay out all night and never get into trouble. "Okay, I'll see you then."

"You don't need to stay up for me."

"If I'm asleep, put your shoes out by my bedroom door. Then, if I wake up in the middle of the night worried, I'll know you got home okay."

"Really?"

"Sorry, but yes. I take my job as your guardian seriously."

"Fine. I'll do that."

"Thanks. Now go have a good time. You can tell me all about it on our drive downtown tomorrow."

"I can't wait to see *A Christmas Carol*."

"I'm excited, too! Plus, we're going to a famous bistro in one of the big hotels nearby for brunch."

Pleased to hear genuine enthusiasm in Madison's voice, Chloe exhaled. "It's going to be fabulous. Bye."

"Bye, honey."

"What did she say?" Jamison asked after she slipped her phone back in her coat pocket.

"That she's fine. I'm free to grab something to eat."

"Good." Walking toward his vehicle, he opened the door. "Hop in. After we eat, I'll take you back here for your car."

"Sounds good." She accepted his hand as he helped her climb into the truck. Minutes later, when he was driving her to a new Mexican restaurant, she completely relaxed. Being with him was so easy.

She hoped Chloe had just as good a time on her date tonight.

Though, Chloe reminded herself, she wasn't on a date. She was just grabbing something to eat with a friend. Adam's best friend.

CHAPTER NINE

JAMISON DIDN'T BELIEVE in fate. He believed in coincidence, and he was pretty sure that everything happened for a reason. Most of the time.

But the day's events were making him change his mind. He was sure that a higher power had turned his well-intentioned quick stop at Loaves of Love into one of the best afternoons of his week. Not only that, but his time with Chloe wasn't over yet. They now had a dinner date planned.

So, perhaps he was a believer in something greater than himself after all. Whether it was fate, divine providence or that the universe had aligned all the stars in his favor, he didn't care. All Jamison did know was that he was going to go with it.

Even though Adam really liked this woman and there was a very good chance that Jamison was going to regret his decision, he wasn't going to pass up this opportunity. A tornado was going to have to suddenly tear through the downtown streets for him to not take advantage of the situation.

As Jamison drove the short distance to his favorite restaurant with Chloe in his passenger seat, he found himself continually glancing at her. She had a smile on her face. No, she was beaming.

And chatty.

She loved seeing all the greenery, wreaths and Christmas lights in the town square. And the wooden cutouts of reindeer in the front yard of a home. And the way someone had covered their mailbox in wrapping paper and a jaunty red bow.

It had been hard not to smirk when she'd talked about that. Did anyone but Chloe Winner actually use the word *jaunty* in conversation? He doubted it.

Her colorful commentary, combined with the fact that she'd taken over his stereo and put on her Chloe's Christmas Playlist, made him feel like he'd just stepped into a Christmas movie.

The way she was smiling hinted that he'd been doing everything right. If listening to Bing Crosby and Nat King Cole meant that Chloe would keep smiling, he'd do it every day.

When she finally stopped to take a breath, Jamison glanced her way. "You really like Christmas, don't you?"

She nodded. "Of course I do. But, who doesn't?"

"No, I mean, you are looking at the decorations and lights like you're a kid and it's the first time at the county fair." He frowned. "Or maybe Harry Potter World, or something."

She laughed. "Yeah, I guess I am a little too into everything. You're right. In spite of the fact that I should've decorated my own house more, I do like the way so many people go all out."

"You like the music, too," he teased.

"Yep. I could listen to Bing Crosby all night. But, it's more than that. I like how everyone tries so hard to do their part for the season. Everything makes the whole town feel a little magical. Special." She shrugged. "And yes, I know I'm probably too old to be excited about some Christmas lights."

"I don't think you're too old. It's cute." When she smiled, he added, "I bet your house now looks like a Hallmark movie came to life in your living room."

"Honestly, I just got my tree up. It's just a little three feet one, too. I wish I had a decent-sized one."

"Sorry, but that's not much of an excuse," he teased. "There's a tree lot right downtown. Or you could go another route and run to the supercenter and buy one."

"I know. But it's always seemed like too much trouble. Plus, I don't know if you noticed, but I'm not that big. I'd have a hard time pulling a tree down from the top of my car. Or even unloading a big Christmas tree box."

"There's no one in your family you could ask?" Or Adam? Why the heck hadn't Adam been running around town, buying trees and greenery? How come he hadn't put lights on the trees in her front yard?

"Not really. I mean, my parents passed away."

He was about to ask about cousins or uncles or even Madison's extended family, then decided that it didn't matter if they had been willing to help her out or not. "Give me a day and I'll help you with the tree. Or tomorrow. I can get your tree tomorrow."

"That's so nice of you, but I already have plans to take Madison downtown to see a play."

"Maybe another day, then?"

Her eyebrows rose, like he'd just offered something over-the-top. "Maybe. I'd hate to ask you to do that, though."

"You didn't ask. I offered."

"That's sweet of you." But then her smile quickly faded as she gasped. "I should probably ask Adam, though."

Bitter disappointment coursed through him. He struggled to keep his expression neutral. "Oh. Yeah. You probably should."

"Do you think he'd mind? Do you think he'd help if I made him dinner or something?"

He hated how tentative she sounded. Hated that she actually thought Adam would only put up her tree if a meal was involved.

"I don't think he'd mind at all." He made a mental note to tell him to step up and help his girl out. If Adam was as serious about Chloe as he said he was, then he needed to get with the program. Trees, lights and Bing Crosby were in his future and he needed to make sure she was happy.

"Okay. Maybe I'll ask him next time we talk."

Next time we talk. It sounded hesitant.

Which, unfortunately, gave him hope.

Sure, Jamison kind of felt like a heel, but a part of him was celebrating big-time. If Adam wasn't texting her often or calling her every night at the very least, then maybe they weren't as serious as he thought.

Pulling into the parking lot, he cleared his throat. "I didn't even ask. Do you like Mexican food?"

"Do I like tacos, fajitas, and rice and beans? Absolutely."

Relief poured through him as her voice brightened again. "Dumb question, huh?"

"Only slightly. I'm excited to finally eat here. I bet I'm one of the very few people who hasn't stopped by."

"If you like Mexican, I'm surprised you haven't given it a try."

"There was an hour line the two times I tried to get in. I can't believe there aren't more cars here right now."

Grinning in appreciation, he turned off the ignition. "Me, neither, but I'm glad about it. Hold tight, and I'll come around and help you down."

He exited his side and circled around the vehicle before she'd had a chance to protest that she was fine. He'd done that on purpose. The truth was that, yeah, Chloe wasn't very tall and getting in and out of his truck meant the assist of the running board. But really, he just wanted an excuse to touch her again.

No, he wasn't proud of that fact, but it wasn't going to stop him.

"Here. Let me help you," he murmured as he reached for her arm. When she leaned close and he caught the scent of her shampoo, he pretended that was a normal thing for him to notice.

Yep, that was him. The kind of guy who smelled women's hair. No, Chloe's hair.

As a flicker of guilt slid into his head in the form of Adam, Jamison reminded himself that all they were doing was grabbing a quick bite to eat. Two people who would've otherwise been eating home alone. Nothing wrong with that.

And as for him smelling her...well, that was just a natural reaction. She smelled good and he noticed. Nothing creepy about that.

Okay, maybe it was a little creepy.

For a moment, Jamison considered texting Adam to see if he wanted to join them, but he disregarded the idea just as quickly. It wouldn't be right to ask him without asking Chloe first, and then if they had to talk about it, and then wait for a response... well, they would've probably already finished their meal if they'd done all that.

"What do you usually get?" she asked as they walked inside the small restaurant that incongruously was located in a historic Victorian home.

"I usually stick to a combination plate. What about you?"

"Tacos." She smiled, gazing at the surrounding walls. Taco, Tacos had adopted an eclectic Day of the Dead theme. There were brightly colored drawings of skeletons and birds on almost every flat surface. Mariachi music poured from speakers. The scarred, uneven wood floor gave it a homey feeling.

And now there were white lights lining the walls and someone had decorated a cactus with red ribbons.

But his favorite part of the place—besides the food—was Ricky and Manuel. The two brothers owned the place and insisted on manning the hostess table. Which meant they greeted everyone with the same amount of infectious enthusiasm.

"James!" Manuel called out. "Long time, no see."

"That's not true. I was in here last month with some guys from work."

"That's still too long." When he eyed Chloe, Manuel's expression warmed. "Who do we have here?"

"Hi, I'm Chloe."

"I'm Manuel. It's good you're taking care of James tonight. We'd been telling him that he needs a woman."

Feeling his skin heat, he tried to send a meaningful cease-and-desist glare Manuel's way, but the man only had eyes for the petite blonde by his side.

Who looked very amused. "This is news to me," Chloe said. "Does Jamison need taking care of?"

"To be sure. He's always in a hurry. Or alone too much. But now, things have changed!" He clapped. "It's a Christmas miracle!"

"We're just friends, Manny," Jamison said quickly.

Manuel's eyebrows pulled together. "Just friends? You sure?"

"Very sure." Kind of.

He was sure unless Adam didn't get his act together around her.

"We're friends, but good ones, right, Jamison?" Chloe said. Before he could answer, she added, "He and I met a couple of months ago and hit it off."

"Hmm," Manuel said. "Sounds like it was meant to be."

Since that was uncomfortably close to what he'd been thinking, Jamison said, "We met while volunteering over at Loaves of Love."

"We sure did," Chloe said. "Have you been there, Manuel?"

He frowned, obviously trying to place it. "Isn't that the food bank?"

"Yes, but you can volunteer to bake bread there, too," she said.

Ricky sauntered over in time to hear the last of that comment. "I know all about Loaves and Love. Sometimes, when we have extra, I send Edna some lettuce and tomatoes. But I've never made bread there."

"You should give it a try. Kneading dough is stress relieving."

"I'm sure it is, if you've been sitting in an office all day. If you were me, you would not want to bake bread after cooking here all day."

He looked so appalled, Jamison chuckled. "Point taken. Ricky, this is Chloe.

"And we need a table, please," Jamison added as smoothly as he was able. When there was a line of people, the brothers were efficient. When there was no one else and it was an off-time, like it was now, they had a habit of chatting about everything under the sun.

"Of course. This way."

Chloe smiled at him as they followed Ricky into the room to the left, what must have been the original owner's library. Bookshelves lined one wall. Instead of tearing them down, Ricky and Manuel had painted them black, then had hired an artist to paint a picture on every third or fourth shelf.

In no time at all, they'd ordered sodas, had a basket of warm chips and bowls of salsa in front of them, and Chloe was leaning back in her chair with a smile on her face.

"I already can't wait to come back and I haven't even looked at the menu yet."

"I think the food is just as good. I hope you feel the same way."

"Me, too."

She was all smiles, making him realize that she

was at her best around other people. "Sometimes I can't believe that you are an accountant."

"Why do you say that?"

"I mean, I'm sure you're good at your job, but it seems like such a solitary profession and you always light up around other people."

"I'm around other people at work. I just happen to be up close and personal with a bunch of numbers, too."

"I hear you."

"Back when I was working at a big firm, I did feel like I was isolated sometimes," she confided. "Now that I have my own little business in downtown Medina, things have been different. The clients I've taken on live and work here, too. They're depending on me to help them for years. They want my guidance when they relocate, expand their business, even try a new venture. It fills a need I hadn't realized I had."

"I can see that being important to you."

"Really? Most people only think of me as being extremely driven."

"Like, to a fault?"

"I guess." She averted her eyes as she picked up another chip.

"Chloe, there's nothing wrong with being driven or wanting to be successful. Not for a man and not for a woman."

"I didn't say there was. It's just…well, I guess it's like the Christmas decoration thing. I don't always pursue other parts of my life as intensely as I have work. But I'm trying to get better."

"You don't have a thing to get better," he whispered.

Her eyes widened. And he felt his neck heat. He shouldn't have said that. Shouldn't have even thought it. "Sorry, I meant to say that everyone is working on something. You aren't the only one trying to get better."

"Oh. Of course."

She smiled at him, but there was something different in her gaze now.

He'd give a lot if someone could tell him what that gaze meant.

CHAPTER TEN

Chloe felt uncharacteristically shy when Jamison drove her back to her car after dinner. It was hard to shake the feeling, though. In the span of just a few hours, so much had changed between them.

Or, perhaps, it was merely her perception of how things were.

As awkward and strange as she felt, she understood the reason. It had been the first time she and Jamison had been out alone. Every other time they'd seen each other, they'd been in the company of a bunch of volunteers at Loaves of Love. Or she'd seen both him and Adam at one of their houses.

Or they'd been walking back and forth from the parking lot. Each one of those situations had a different feel to it. They were either preoccupied with other things, or in a hurry to get someplace else, or so surrounded by people that their conversations had been chatty and lighthearted.

But tonight, even though they'd been in the very casual and kitschy Taco, Tacos, she'd been aware of every little thing Jamison did. She'd noticed how his brown eyes took in all the people sitting around them—and how they focused on her whenever she spoke. How carefully he ate his meal. Each bite had been cut into a neat bite before it was consumed.

How he sometimes rolled his shoulders back, as if one of them pained him. How he took the time to ask her specific questions about her job and her interests.

It was going to be very hard to only think of him as her "volunteer buddy" or "Adam's best friend." She was also starting to realize that it was no longer possible to ignore how attractive he was.

Or how, when he'd helped her climb into his truck, his gaze had lingered on her lips. And that she hadn't hated the idea of kissing him.

That wasn't good. Irritated with herself, she tried to tell herself that the reason she was suddenly so enraptured with Jamison was that he seemed to notice every little thing about her. No one had ever done that.

She supposed that wasn't true. Her parents had noticed a lot of things about her likes and her interests, but they'd usually been preoccupied with making sure the bills were paid and there was food on the table. Later, after her parents' sudden passing, she'd decided it was easier to only count on herself.

But as far as Jamison noticing how much she liked Christmas decorations and holiday festivities. How his careful coaxing had even encouraged her to admit her secret desire to blow a ton of money at a fancy Christmas boutique and buy an armful of gorgeous ornaments and pricey lawn ornaments…and a tree?

Well, no one had ever really cared. Just like it never seemed to matter to Adam that she liked steaks and burgers and didn't always want to choose fish or a salad when she went out to eat.

Hmm. Perhaps she was simply blowing everything out of proportion? Maybe Jamison was just being nice. After all, he was her friend.

Yeah. He was just like one of her girlfriends, she supposed. Except for…

"Hey, Chloe…you okay?" Jamison asked as he turned left at a light.

"Yeah, why?"

"No reason, except that you've gotten pretty quiet all of the sudden."

Blinking, she focused on the street signs. They were almost back to her car and she'd barely said five words. "Sorry about that." Smiling, she added, "I'm fine. I must be in an enchilada-induced coma."

He grinned. "I feel the same way, except mine is from tacos and tamales. I always eat too much there. It's so good."

"At least you'll have the opportunity to work it off when you go back to work on Monday. You'll be working on trails next week, right?"

"Yep. At least for half the time. The other half will be in the office in meetings. Plus, I'll probably go on a run tomorrow."

"Maybe I'll work out during my lunch on Monday, too." Of course, her lunch workouts usually involved a leisurely stroll. Or, if she was feeling frisky, she might go to the gym for twenty minutes and walk on the treadmill. Neither activity would probably negate all the calories she'd consumed tonight.

"If you end up working out, let me know."

"Why?" Spying his grin, she got suspicious.

"Because I'm going to want a record of that."

She couldn't help but start laughing. "I know. I should be better." Looking down at her thighs, which were not very toned at all, she said, "Every New Year I tell myself that I've got to get a handle on my body."

"Hey, you know I'm just teasing you, right? And I wasn't thinking about your curves. I was just joshing you about going to the gym."

He said "curves." What did that mean? "Don't worry. I wasn't offended."

"For the record, I think you look great." He grimaced. "And now I think I've just made things worse. I probably shouldn't have said that."

"I heard a compliment, J. Not anything weird."

"Yeah?"

He looked so worried, she nodded. "Yeah. I promise. I'm thirty years old. I'll take compliments wherever I can get them."

Parking his truck next to her car, he unhooked his seat belt, then folded his arms over his chest.

"Thirty isn't old, and I'm sure you get your share of compliments all the time."

"Not really." And yes…she should have kept her mouth shut.

"What? Adam isn't telling you how gorgeous you are with those blue eyes, blond hair?"

She laughed. Hoping that it came off as amused instead of suddenly depressed. "You know Adam."

He stared at her for a long moment. "I thought I did, but maybe not." Looking away, he added, "Of course, I've never been the type to notice how he is with girlfriends."

This whole conversation was quickly going downhill fast. Not only was she continually imagining just how different Jamison might act if he was her boyfriend, but she was starting to dwell on all the ways Adam was coming up short in the romance department.

"You know, I should probably get going. Madison is out on a date, but I want to be home in case she needs something."

"Right." He opened his door. "I'll come around."

He was out of the truck before she had the opportunity to point out that she might be short, but she could climb in and out of a truck without assistance.

But then there he was, opening her door, helping her unbuckle the seat belt she'd forgotten to unclip. And when he bypassed her hand and wrapped his hands around her waist and pulled her down, Chloe could almost pretend that it didn't matter.

But it did.

Because she'd placed her own hands on his shoulders, leaning close. Close enough for parts of her to brush against him. And then she'd slid down to the ground, brushing against him again.

He didn't let go of her immediately. Instead, he closed his eyes. Breathed deep.

And then he bent down and kissed her cheek.

"Night, Chloe," he said before walking away.

"Yeah. Night."

Only the clicking of his driver's door shutting brought her out of her fog.

Quickly, she got into her own vehicle, started the engine and then fastened her seat belt.

Pasted on a smile and shifted the car into Drive.

And headed home.

Only after she'd entered the garage had she realized that she'd forgotten to turn on the heater. One chaste peck on her cheek had heated her up.

This wasn't good!

"You, Chloe Winner, are a hot mess."

It was true and she had no idea what to do about that.

CHAPTER ELEVEN

MADISON HAD IMAGINED all kinds of scenarios for her date with Cope. Most of them had either included him being late or not showing up at all.

She'd also prepared herself for him to either take her to some fast-food restaurant or a pizza place and then ask her to split the tab. She'd already made peace with that. They were in high school. He'd worked overtime last night, and wasn't shy about letting her know that he worked a lot. Obviously, he needed money. Maybe he even had to help pay for some bills at home. One of the juniors on the varsity cheerleader squad had confided that she babysat as much as possible to help her mom with their rent.

Besides, she'd said yes to dinner with Cope because he'd asked and she was eager to try to figure out why she liked him so much. It didn't matter to her where they went. Maybe, by the end of the night, she'd know the answer to that.

Right on the heels of all her unicorn dreams were her worst imaginings. Those included Cope showing up buzzed, with a friend, or being so rude and irritating that she had to pull out her phone and call for an Uber.

All that added to doubts about her outfit—a black short skirt, black tights and a thin, loose-fitting blue sweater. Maybe she should've just worn jeans and tennis shoes? Leggings? Did she look like she was trying too hard?

When Cope knocked on the door at exactly six thirty, it threw her a little off-kilter. And when she noticed that he was in dark jeans, boots and a Henley, her heart melted a little bit. He hadn't forgotten, he wasn't acting like he didn't care, and he had somehow managed to look even better than she'd ever thought he could in the first place.

"Hey," he said when she opened the door.

"Is this okay?" she blurted.

His head tilted slightly to one side. "What are you talking about?"

"My outfit. Is it too dressy?"

"I don't know."

"I didn't know where we were going. I could change."

"Don't. You're okay." He grinned.

So far, she was making a fool of herself. "Are you laughing at me?"

"Madison, did you hear me laughing?"

"No. But maybe you were laughing inside."

"I don't even know what that means." Before she could make a bigger fool of herself, he looked around. "So, this is where you live?"

"Yeah. This is Chloe's place." She tried to see it through his eyes. It was small but pretty and still was didn't even have a Christmas tree in it.

"It's nice."

"I like it, too. It's a bungalow and was built right before WWII broke out." She bit her lip. Man, she sure wished she could stop talking.

"I've driven by all these houses tons of times, but I've never been inside one."

There was something in his tone that sounded off. "Really? Where do you live?"

"Not here," he said cryptically. "You ready?"

"Yeah." She grabbed her coat and her purse, then followed him out the door. "I've got to set the alarm and lock the door," she said as she punched in the code and then locked the dead bolt with her key. Turning to smile at him, she said, "I'm ready now."

"Don't you want to put on your coat?"

"Oh. Yeah."

"Here." Next thing she knew, he'd taken her coat and was holding it so she could slide her arms inside. Their close proximity allowed her to get another chance to smell his cologne.

Then she noticed his car.

It was an old Toyota 4Runner. Black with gray interior. "Do you drive this to school?" she asked. Chloe was sure she would've noticed it in the parking lot.

"No."

"How come?" It was really cool.

Looking uncomfortable, he shrugged. "I don't know. It's my dad's. He doesn't like either of us to drive it much," he said after they both got in and he turned on the ignition.

"What do you usually drive to school?"

"An old Civic." He shrugged. "Sometimes I just walk."

"I haven't noticed that, either." She felt her cheeks get hot. What was she doing, quizzing him about his vehicles? "I'm sorry. I just realized that I sound like a stalker."

"You didn't. But I don't care what you ask me. Ask me whatever you want."

"I won't. I guess you can tell I'm a little jealous, huh? When my parents moved, they took the car I shared with my little sister. So now I don't have a car. I'm always trying to catch a ride."

Cope's expression softened. "That sucks. I'm sorry."

"Me, too, but it's okay." Since she'd just been complaining about it, she felt kind of stupid. Obviously, she wasn't okay about it. "I mean, yeah, the selfish part of me wishes that I still had it, but I got to stay here instead of leaving."

"I get that."

She shrugged. "I'm pretty busy, so it's not like I got all that much time to go places anyway."

"You ready to eat?"

"Yes. I'm starved."

He chuckled. "Good."

As he pulled away from the curb, she was able to get a better look at him. She noticed he was wearing a white undershirt under his Henley. It wasn't skintight, but it sure wasn't loose. It showed off his broad shoulders and his biceps. He might not be a jock living in the weight room but it was obvious that he worked out somewhere.

She just realized that she was able to check him out so easily because he didn't have a coat on. Curious, she glanced over her shoulder. There wasn't a coat in sight.

The 4Runner was standard. His right hand rested on the gearshift, switching gears as they drove out of the downtown area and toward the outskirts of Medina. "What are you looking for?"

"Your coat."

"Why?"

"Because it's December and really cold out." The temperature was probably in the midtwenties. By any stretch of the imagination, it was cold.

He smirked. "Don't need to worry about me. I've got one in the back."

"Are you sure? I looked in the back seat."

"It's in the far back, Maddie." In a touch softer voice, he murmured. "It's cute you care, but don't worry about me."

She wasn't all that thrilled to be called cute, but she pushed the comment aside to concentrate on the more important thing. "Why do you have it way back there?"

As he slowed toward a red light, he shot her a curious look. "Why do you care?"

His voice was a little harsh. Maybe a little bit sarcastic, too. He thought she was being weird. And maybe she was. She was a senior in high school. She was eighteen, an adult. Most importantly, she was on a date with a guy she'd had a crush on for months. A guy at least three dozen girls she knew would give a lot to have his attention. She should focus on being attractive. Maybe even a little sexy.

Shouldn't she be thinking about all those other things instead of his warmth?

Yes. Yes, she should. It embarrassed her.

"I don't know," she said quickly. "I... I guess I didn't want you to be cold." She clenched her right hand. "You know, now that I hear the words out loud, I realize how stupid it sounds. Sorry."

"Hey. No." He took a breath. "I'm the one who's sorry. I shouldn't have sounded like that."

"Why did you, then?"

He was staring at the road. There wasn't a lot of traffic. The sky was clear, though. A lot of stars were out. So was the moon. Between those things and the colorful Christmas lights that seemed to dot every other business on the street, she got a pretty good look at his expression. It looked tight. Maybe strained?

Something was definitely on his mind that he didn't want to talk about. And here she'd gone, pushing again. Her mouth was turning dry. "Hey, it's none of my business. You don't have to answer."

"Yeah, I do." He glanced at her. "And I will, once we get inside."

She realized that while she'd been watching him intently, Cope had pulled into a parking lot of a little restaurant she'd never noticed before. The sign above the door said Sergio's. As he parked, she noticed that there were about a dozen cars in the parking lot.

"Have you been here before?" he asked.

"No. What kind of food is it?"

"Slavic."

"What kind of food is that?"

He smiled. "Think sausage, potatoes, cabbage and beets."

"Oh."

His smirk grew into a full-fledged grin. "There are other things to eat, too. It's all good, I promise."

"I'm looking forward to it," she said as she opened her door. Of course, she would've said that no matter where he took her, but she was telling the truth. This restaurant seemed to be a little like Cope. Different. A little off the beaten path.

New.

He had already come around by the time she'd gotten out and grabbed her purse. "I'll help you down."

She didn't need his help. But did the fact that one of his hands was holding hers and the other was around her waist make her feel like maybe she hadn't just ruined everything with her nosy questions? Yes. Yes, it did.

After he closed her door and locked it, he held out his hand for her to take. Slipping her hand in his, she decided that holding hands with him didn't feel awkward at all.

Especially since his palm was warm and dry and he was holding her hand in a relaxed grip. Some guys clasped her hand too tightly.

Inside the restaurant, music was playing, the walls were filled with old-world-looking decorations and framed flags. And, there was an unusual smell in the air. Something spicy and different. Like paprika.

"Cope!" a man called out as he stepped forward, clasping him in one of those old-man hugs. Slaps on the back and gruff. "I told Anna to keep on the lookout for you. Everyone has been wanting your table."

"I thought you wrote me on the books."

"I did, but you know how people are. It's cold and the table is in front of the fireplace. It's a good spot." Turning to Madison, the man said, "Welcome."

"Thank you," she said.

"Uncle Sergio, this is Madison."

"So I see. It's good to meet you, Madison. I hope this boy is treating you nice."

"I just picked her up. Don't embarrass her, Uncle."

"Never." Grabbing two menus wrapped in plastic covers, he said, "Let's get you out of the doorway. It's cold outside."

When Cope gestured for her to precede him, she followed his uncle into a small room with six or seven tables. Each one was covered in crisp white tablecloths and had red cloth napkins on top of each plate.

When he came to a stop in front of a big stone fireplace with a crackling fire inside, she couldn't believe it. Here they were, two high school kids, and they had the best table in the house. Sergio waited while she slid off her coat, then took it while she sat down.

"I'll hang this on a hook by the door."

"Thank you."

"Here are your menus. I'll send someone over to tell you all about the specials, but my advice is to get the celery soup." He winked at her, then clasped Cope on the shoulder before walking away.

Madison noticed more than one couple about her parents' age eyeing them with interest. Another lady was frowning. She decided that lady was jealous that they'd gotten such a prime spot. When she directed her attention toward Cope, she realized he was watching her.

"You all right?" he asked.

"Yes. Of course. Sorry, I'm…well, I'm just trying to wrap my head around tonight."

"Why?"

"Well, obviously, we don't know each other that well. I kept thinking about how you said you made good money working overtime last night. I don't know why, but I figured we'd go eat pizza, or something."

He looked offended. "I'm not going to take you out for pizza."

"Cope, it wasn't like I knew your uncle had a restaurant."

"Yeah, I guess that's fair."

"Why didn't you tell me this was where we were going?"

"I wanted to surprise you."

"Well, it worked. I'm surprised."

He didn't look all that happy about her reaction, though. Madison bit her bottom lip. It was probably because she'd been doing such a bad job as a date. So far, all she'd done was complain about her lack of vehicle and question him about his vehicles and the fact that he wasn't wearing a coat. "I'm sorry," she whispered.

"About what?"

"You went to a lot of trouble and I've been kind of acting like a brat."

"Not to me." Glancing over her shoulder, his expression turned stoic. "What would you like to drink?"

She looked up to see their server. She was blonde, was wearing a dress that looked like a cross between an Amish-looking dress and a dirndl from the Alps. She was also smiling at Cope.

"I heard you were coming in tonight, Cope. How are you?"

"I'm good, Anna. This is Madison. Mad, what would you like to drink?"

"Water?"

"We'll have two waters."

Anna propped a hand on her hip. "That's it?"

"That's it for now. Thanks."

She turned away with a flash of skirts.

Madison raised her eyebrows. "I guess you two know each other?"

"Yeah."

"And...are you going to expand on that?"

"There's nothing much to say. I'd rather talk about something else."

"Okay. How about you tell me something about yourself?"

The guarded look returned to his eyes. "Like what?"

"Like what you said we'd talk about when we got here."

"All right."

When he didn't say anything for a couple of seconds, she said, "Cope, I really am trying to get to know you, but I feel like you're hiding something from me."

"I guess I am."

"What?" A dozen awful ideas popped into her

head, starting and ending with the fact that he really wasn't into her.

Looking pained, he took a breath. "See—"

"Here's your water," Anna interrupted. "Do you want to hear about the specials?"

"Yeah," Cope said.

"Our soup tonight is cream of celery and our special is pork Milanese. Oh. And the cabbage rolls are really popular tonight. If you want some, let me know, 'cause they're about to be sold out. Are you ready to order?"

"We're gonna need a couple of minutes."

When Anna flounced off yet again, Madison couldn't help but giggle. "She's full of attitude, isn't she?"

"Unfortunately." He sighed. "I've known her most of my life. She was like this when she was seven years old, too."

"Is she your cousin?"

"Kind of. We should look at the menus."

Everything sounded good, but unfamiliar. It also wasn't cheap. "What are you getting?"

"The pork Milanese. And the soup. What about you?"

"I guess the same."

Cope waved Anna over, they gave her their orders and menus, and after she left, they were finally alone.

Then she sat back and folded her arms over her chest. Sure, she wasn't giving him a lot of choice, but she was done waiting. She wanted to get the bad news—whatever it was—over. Then she could deal with the fallout.

"Fine. Here's the deal. I don't have a great life at home. My mom died of cancer about four years ago and my father never recovered. To make things even more awkward between us, I am working at the hardware store, and I do like it, but it's not like it's a great job or anything. The fact is that the only reason I could take you here is because my uncle is letting us eat for free."

"Oh."

"Yeah, oh." Looking even more torn up, he said, "I'm pretty sure that I'm the exact opposite of every other guy you've gone out with."

"I guess you are." But that was a good thing, she thought. She liked that he was honest and wasn't going on and on about himself like so many other guys in their senior class.

"That's all you're going to say?"

"About that? Yeah."

Cope turned his head. Stared at the fireplace beside them. "So, that's how mixed-up I am. The only way I could take you out to eat was at my uncle's restaurant. You, on the other hand, are trying to choose what fancy college you want to apply to."

"That's not the only thing I do."

"I know. You run around in those little skirts at halftime and take a bunch of AP classes."

"I wouldn't call my cheerleader uniform a little skirt."

"You would if you were a guy."

"Cope!"

"Sorry." He chuckled before looking serious again. "You might have been worried about what to wear, but I've been worried that the minute you got to know me better you'd be trying to get a ride home."

"I'm not stuck-up."

"I didn't say you were."

"And I don't care about the money thing."

"You will. You told me your parents moved because your father got this big promotion and your mother is trying to sell you on the new house because it has a pool."

She'd been sounding like a spoiled brat. "You didn't have to take me out to a fancy restaurant, Cope. We could've had sandwiches at my house or something."

"Yeah, I did. I wanted to pick you up in a car, take you somewhere decent and pretend that this was a real date."

"It is."

"I don't know. I kind of think it was a real date but now it's... I don't know what it is."

There was so much self-doubt and hesitancy in his voice she wanted to reached for his hands and hold on to them tight. Since that would be weird, Madison did the only thing she could. She looked at him in the eyes and said, "This is a real date, Cope."

Before too long, Anna brought their soup and hot bread. Eventually, their empty bowls were replaced with the breaded pork dish. Madison was glad she'd never been shy about eating a lot, because everything was so good.

While they ate, they talked about a bunch of other stuff. Movies. Teachers. A couple of people in their class who neither of them particularly liked. Cope started smiling more easily and once he even looked at her like she was something special.

Madison was already dreading the end of their night.

After Anna had taken their plates and his uncle Sergio had stopped by to say that apple strudel with ice cream was on the way, Madison got up her nerve. "Hey, Cope, if I asked you something, would you promise to think about it before answering?"

"Maybe."

"If we go out again, would you let me pay next time?"

"You want to go out with me again, Madison?"

"Yes." She swallowed. "I mean, if you do."

"I do want to take you out, but there's no way you're paying."

"I wouldn't care."

"I would."

"Cope…there's nothing wrong with you using your money to pay for other things."

"I don't want your pity, Maddie."

Maddie. Goose bumps formed on her arms. Reminding her that whatever she was feeling about him wasn't superficial. It was something deep and emotional. It might not make sense on paper but it couldn't be denied. "That's what I want," she murmured.

His hazel eyes darkened with anger. "You want my pity?"

"No. I want you to call me Maddie. I want you to look at me like I'm not an afterthought. Like you're looking at me now."

A new emotion flared in his eyes. "You better be careful."

"Why?"

"I'm about to kiss you right here in my uncle's restaurant."

She giggled.

He didn't. "I'll call you Maddie as much as you want. I'll look at you like I think you're something special because I think you are. If that's what you want."

"That's what I want."

"I'm not going to be okay with you paying for my dinner."

"We'll figure something else out, then. Maybe something that isn't fancy like this. Maybe we could just hang out."

When he smiled at her, she knew that it hadn't

just been her imagination. There really was something good between them.

And there was no way she was going to go to college across the country. No way on earth.

CHAPTER TWELVE

NEITHER OF THEM had gotten a lot of sleep the night before. Madison, because she'd walked in the front door at exactly midnight, and Chloe because no matter what she'd said she'd do, she hadn't been able to go to sleep until she'd known that Madison was back safe and the front door was locked.

When her alarm had gone off at seven that morning, Chloe had seriously considered tossing her phone across the room.

Or, at the very least, decided not to attend church after all. Missing a Sunday service wasn't that big of a deal, was it?

But then, just as she'd decided to roll over and go back to sleep, Rhonda's voice rang in her ears—along with her own promise. She'd promised to do her best to parent Madison in her parents' absence. That included church.

So she'd roused a sleepy teenager and accompanied her to church. After, they'd gone back to her house, had more coffee and gotten dressed for their big day at Playhouse Square.

Of course the weather had to get involved. The

temperature had dropped and it was spitting snow, lengthening the drive by another twenty minutes.

When they'd arrived at the restaurant in the Renaissance Hotel for brunch, she'd already felt exhausted. Going back home and curling up on the couch to watch old Christmas movies sounded perfect. Wearing her favorite old sweats sounded even better. Instead, she put on a good face.

"I think you're going to love the menu here," she told Madison. "I've had both the pecan waffles and the spinach omelet before."

"It all looks really good." She smiled, but it didn't reach her eyes.

Hoping the girl was simply tired, Chloe pretended not to notice. She ordered eggs benedict with a fresh pastry on the side. Sure, the meal was about a thousand calories, but they were spending a special day together. As she hoped, by the time she'd taken her third bite, her mood had improved dramatically.

Until she noticed that Madison was only picking at her omelet. "Is something wrong with your breakfast, Madison?"

"Hmm? Oh, no." She picked up a piece of fruit. "I, uh, just had a lot to eat last night."

"You went out for Ukrainian?"

"It was something like that. 'Slavic,' Cope said. I had a pork dish and some kind of celery soup. Both were so good. I couldn't believe that Cope's uncle owned the restaurant."

"It's nice that he took you there so you could meet someone in his family."

Madison's expression brightened. "His Uncle Sergio was really nice. Cope seemed different around him."

"How so?"

She shrugged. "I don't know. Maybe more relaxed? Maybe happier?"

"Maybe it was because he was with you."

She rolled her eyes. "It wasn't that."

"But you had a good time?"

"Yeah," she said softly. "I learned a lot about him. He's different than I thought."

"It sounds like maybe you feel better about his reputation?"

"Yeah. There's all these rumors circling around him, but I realized that most of them were just gossip." She paused. "Or, maybe he's just different than most of my friends."

Thinking about how she'd been so motivated in high school, Chloe said, "I've always thought different was good. Everyone can't be like everyone else."

"Yeah." Her niece took another bite of her omelet. Then another one.

Pleased that Madison's mood was improving, Chloe relaxed and enjoyed another bite of her chocolate croissant.

"Hey, you haven't told me about your date."

"A date? I didn't go on one."

"Uh, yeah, you did. Didn't you go out to eat with Jamison?"

"Yes, but we just got a bite to eat after we volunteered." She nodded, reinforcing her statement. They'd simply been two friends sharing a meal. That was it.

"Was it just the two of you?"

"Yes."

"Then it was a date." Madison smiled like she was the expert on such things. "So, how was it?"

"It was fine. Jamison and I always have a good time together, but we were not out on a date." She was starting to feel like she was getting interrogated. And not in a good way, either.

"Where did you eat?"

Relief filled her as the topic moved forward. "Taco, Tacos. Have you been there?"

"Yep. My mom loves that place. Did you get tacos?"

"No. A combo platter. Jamison got tacos, though." Realizing that Madison was looking at her intently, obviously waiting for more information, Chloe shrugged. "It was really good."

"What else happened?"

"Nothing. We cleaned the kitchen at Loaves of Love, realized we were both hungry. Jamison drove me to eat Mexican food, and then he took me back to my car."

"You didn't tell me that he drove."

"It made sense to only take one vehicle."

"Mmm-hmm."

Chloe was losing patience. "Madison, stop looking for something that isn't there. While you were out with Cope, I grabbed something to eat with a friend. That's all it was, too. Just a meal together."

"Would you do it again?"

Taken off guard by the way Madison was watching her, Chloe reached for her coffee cup and held it between her hands. "I don't know. I imagine so." If she ever figured out things with Adam.

"Good."

"You are too funny, girl. Making mountains out of molehills."

"Maybe, but I still think that he's a better match for you."

"Than who?" Of course she was playing dumb. But would anyone blame her? The sad truth was that Madison had probably been on dates with more men than she had.

"Than Adam."

The girl had said his name like he was a roach that had gotten into the house. Lifting her chin, she said, "Adam is very nice and we have a lot in common."

"Sorry, but I didn't see that."

"Really?"

"Really. He didn't seem very genuine to me."

"Well, he is. He's perfectly nice." Since Madison continued to look unimpressed, she added, "He's also smart and we have some things in common."

"Like what?"

"Well, we both put ourselves through college. We are also career driven." But even she had to admit that didn't mean much.

"What else?"

"I don't know. Does it matter?"

"Uh-huh. Both of you going to college doesn't mean much." She waved a hand. "A lot of people go to college. And a lot of people don't and do just fine, right?"

"Well, yes. I didn't say that they didn't."

"Plus, pretty much everyone wants to make money in their job, right?"

"I suppose."

Madison leaned forward. "What does Jamison not have that you want?"

Nothing. She honestly couldn't think of a single thing about him that didn't interest her. But how could she say that out loud? She had a feeling that if she put her true feelings out into the atmosphere, something tragic was going to occur. Like Adam would hear about it.

Or Jamison would, and be shocked and appalled. He seemed perfectly happy for them to be buddies.

"Don't you know?" Madison pressed.

"I know. But I don't think this is a suitable conversation."

"Why not?"

"Because…" Because she wasn't ready for it. "Because I'm your aunt."

"Oh. Yeah. And I'm just a kid."

"Exactly."

Madison giggled. "Oh, Chloe."

"What now?"

"You've got yourself a love triangle."

"I... I do not."

"Okay, but you know what they say." Her eyes brightened with mirth. "If it walks like a duck..."

"I've always hated that saying."

"It's no wonder, 'cause it sure fits you."

The server's appearance felt like a lifeline. "Ladies, do you need anything else?"

"Just the check, please. We've got play tickets."

"Oh! How fun. What are you going to see?"

"*A Christmas Carol*," Madison said.

"Ohh. That's a good one. Have you seen it before? Some families go every year."

"We haven't, but maybe this is the start of a new tradition, right, Aunt Chloe?"

Looking at Madison in surprise, Chloe said, "Maybe so."

After she gave the server a credit card, she continued, "You're going to be going off to college next year, honey. As much as I'd love for this to be our new tradition, I can't imagine that you'll be around here next Christmas."

"How come?"

"Because you're going to be home with your family in Arkansas, right?"

"I guess...though anything is possible at Christmas, right?"

"Right." Chloe smiled, not wanting to ruin Madison's happy smile. But she honestly had no idea how anything different could ever happen."

CHAPTER THIRTEEN

A COUPLE OF days after his night at Taco, Tacos with Chloe, Jamison was at home, making coffee when Bud finally walked into his house. Even though he'd said he was going to get there last Friday or Saturday, he'd been texting Jamison regularly about the changes in his schedule.

Jamison took another sip of coffee as he watched his brother juggle two duffel bags of laundry, a loaded backpack, a cooler and a phone to his ear.

As usual, Bud had about a dozen things going at the same time. Bud could multitask like no other. "Hey, you made good time," he said. "I didn't expect you for another thirty minutes."

"One sec, J," Bud said. Returning to his phone call, he lowered his voice. "I know. Yes, I hear what you're saying. Hmm. Yeah, I'll call later." Looking at Jamison, he added, "I'll tell J. What? No, I don't mind. *Of course* I don't mind. Yeah. You, too. Bye." Tossing his phone on the table by the door, he said, "Sorry about that."

"No worries. Let me guess, you were talking to Halley?"

He grinned. "Yep. And, as usual, she had a lot to say."

Crossing the room, Jamison took in the lines of stress around Bud's eyes, the stretched-out pullover, the boots with missing laces on his feet and his smile. All in all, the kid looked good. "It's good to see you," he said, wrapping him in a hug.

Like always, Bud hugged him back. Leaned into him for good measure. And like always, Jamison felt a touch of parental pride. Though they all still had their mother, Halley and Bud had never been shy about saying that Jamison had been the person in their lives that they'd always depended on.

He didn't know if they'd ever think of him as just their brother. If they didn't, it wouldn't bother him. He didn't think he could ever look at his siblings and only think of them as his younger brother and sister. In a lot of ways, he felt like their dad.

"I'm glad you got here safe and sound. How were the roads?"

"Fine. No traffic to speak of. I usually stop for fast food but I figured you'd probably have something better." Toeing off his boots, he looked toward the kitchen. "Please tell me you have food."

"I have food." Slapping him on the back, he said, "Come on. I'll make you a sandwich. Turkey, ham or roast beef?"

"You have all three?"

"Yep."

"Okay. How about turkey and ham? But I'll make it."

"Of course you will." He attempted to make his voice a little gruff, just to show Bud that he wasn't going to baby him. But, that still didn't stop Jamison from getting out the deli meat, cheese, mayo, lettuce and chips. "You bring home some laundry?"

"Yep," Bud said as he got out a plate and knife, then hunted in a cabinet for bread. "And don't worry. I'll do that, too. It's cheaper here than at my apartment."

"I know." Jamison got himself a glass of water and then moved to one of the barstools while Bud made his sandwich.

"Oh, man. You've got good bread. Did you go to Loaves of Love today?"

"Nope. I had to work this morning, but only a half day. I had a couple of things to do before you got here." Such as go to the grocery store.

"I'm so glad I'm done with another semester. Only two more to go."

"How do you think you did?"

Bud shrugged as he grabbed a bag of chips. "Fine."

That was his brother. School had come easy for Bud. In some ways, life did, too. He'd never been the type of person to sweat the small stuff.

"When will you get your grades? Or find out about your next classes?"

"I got my grades and I figured out my classes a while ago. You don't have to worry about that."

"Oh. I guess you're right. I didn't know how you registered for your classes."

Bud shrugged. "Why would you?"

"Yeah. You're right." He'd never gone to college. "I wouldn't."

"Hey. I didn't mean it in a bad way," he said as he sat down, a bag of chips under one arm since his hands were full of his plate and a can of soda. "It's just, you've got your own life."

"I know what you meant."

Bud looked like he was going to say something but changed his mind. Instead, he took a second bite of his sandwich, pulled open the bag of chips and promptly popped two in his mouth. The kid was hungry.

Jamison sipped water, thinking that he probably looked the same way half the time when he came home after working outside all day.

Less than ten minutes later, Bud's plate was empty. "That was so good. Thanks."

"It was a sandwich."

"I know. But still."

"Hate to bring this up, but Mom would've made sure she had food for you, too."

Some of Bud's easy expression faded. "I know."

"Tell me why you don't want her to meet Jenny."

"I'm just not ready for that."

"What do you think Mom's going to do?" He was

pretty curious. Sure, there had been a time when their mother wasn't all that dependable, but she'd never been mean.

He averted his eyes. "I don't know."

"Look, I haven't said a word to her about you coming in. I didn't even mention your visit to Halley when she called yesterday, and I was tempted."

"Thanks."

"You're welcome. But I need to know what your secret is."

"All right, fine. I don't like Ronnie."

Well, that took him off guard. "Who's Ronnie?"

"He's Mom's boyfriend." Obviously catching his shocked expression, Bud frowned. "Hasn't Mom told you about him?"

"No. I haven't heard a word."

"Huh."

"Bud, what do you know that I don't? How come I haven't met this Ronnie guy?"

"I don't know…but it could be because it was pretty obvious that I wasn't a fan." He waved a hand. "And you know how it goes. Halley and I are always her tryouts. If something she does goes over well with us, then she tells you."

"That's not how it goes."

"It is."

"Bud—"

"Jamison, Mom does that with a lot of things. She doesn't like to look bad in front of you. So she tests out her news with either Halley or me first."

He leaned back in his chair. "When she goes on vacation. When she went on that cruise for single women. When she got that new job. When she painted the house white."

"I still can't believe she painted over all that brick."

"See? You have opinions and you aren't shy about sharing them. That gets on Mom's nerves."

Jamison figured that was fair. As much as he'd wanted to change and be less judgmental, he still gave her a hard time about things. Feeling guilty about that, he stuffed his hands in his pockets. "Tell me about Ronnie."

Bud rolled his eyes as he stood up and started to clean up his mess. "He's annoying."

"What does he do?"

"First, he touches Mom all the time."

Jamison felt a twinge of distaste but pushed it away. "Well, you know Mom. She's pretty."

"Yeah, she's pretty. And I even get that they're probably doing all kinds of stuff I don't want to know about. But it's like Ronnie can't leave her alone. He runs his fingers along her hand. Or her arm. Or plays with her hair. Once I saw him pat her rear end, too."

"What?"

"It's gross, J. And the worst part is Mom looks only kind of okay with it."

"What does that mean?"

"It means that I don't know if she's as into all that PDA as he is."

"Maybe she should tell him to leave her alone." He mentally rolled his eyes. So much for him deciding to keep his opinions to himself.

"It's beyond that. They're serious. Plus, Ronnie was trying to give me advice."

"What?" Yeah, he'd barked that question, but he couldn't help himself. The more he was learning about Ronnie, the less he wanted him in their mother's life. Or in the twins' lives.

"Yeah. He had the nerve to say something like he has grown kids of his own, too, so I should feel free to call him if I need something." He lowered his voice. "And then he gave me a lecture about how Mom's house wasn't just a place for me to do laundry."

"Where else are you supposed to do it?"

Bud grinned. "Here, obviously."

Jamison chuckled before his protective instincts took hold. "Has Halley met him?"

"Oh, yeah."

He couldn't believe that he'd been oblivious to everything that had been happening. "What happened? Did Ronnie order her around, too?"

"Yep."

And that was all it took for him to be completely against this Ronnie guy. "He has no right to order around Halley."

"I said the same thing to Mom before I left."

"What did you say?"

"That even though I was glad she wasn't sitting home alone, I thought that she could do a whole lot better than that guy."

"You did better than I would have."

"Come on, J. You know how hard it is to tell Mom something she doesn't want to hear. She either pretends she doesn't hear us or cries."

"I know." Though, the truth was he usually did speak his mind to her. He'd been an adult a long time now. And Mom sometimes forgot that neither Bud nor Halley were completely grown-up. They still needed her to be their mother. "I'll call Halley soon to see what she thinks."

"She's not going to tell you much. She doesn't want to get in the middle of an argument between you and Mom."

"Still, I'm going to call."

"I know. You're going to do what you want, no matter what."

Meeting his brother's gaze, Jamison reckoned he was probably right. Around the outside world he was as easygoing as he could be. With his brother and sister, though? He was some kind of papa bear, ready and willing to do whatever he needed in order to make sure they were safe and happy.

"So, are you going to tell me about Jenny?"

For the first time, Bud's guard went up. "What do you want to know?"

"Oh, I don't know. How you met her. How the

two of you got so serious so fast. When I'm going to get to meet her. Things like that."

His brother's expression eased. "I met Jenny when we were both waiting for the campus shuttle one night and she was on her own. Her girlfriend she'd gone to a party with had ditched her and she was really bummed. I ended up walking her to her dorm because it wasn't safe for her to be going alone. And then, I asked for her number. We went on from there."

"Just like that?"

"Yeah. Well, more or less." Bud grinned, then seemed to look at him a little bit closer. "Wait, you look confused. How come?"

"No reason."

"Are you sure?"

His brother's genuine concern prompted him to let down his guard more than he usually did. "I haven't been in love before."

"How come?"

"I don't know. Maybe I haven't met the right person yet. Or I've been too busy. Maybe I haven't had the opportunity."

"Sure you have."

"What is that supposed to mean?"

"I don't think you've put yourself out there, Jamison. Go out more with your friends."

"I do. Adam is next door."

"Yeah, but he's all corporate lawyer stuff now, isn't he?"

"He is, but he's still the same. Besides, he's dating Chloe pretty seriously."

"I thought Chloe was your friend at the bakery place you volunteer."

"She is." And...why had he decided to mention her?

"And aren't the two of you close?"

"We are, but that's it." Kind of. He'd never tell Bud, but there had been something intense going on between him and Chloe on Saturday night. More than once, he'd considered kissing her. He hadn't, of course, but something had told him that she wouldn't have minded. "She's dating Adam. And you know how that goes."

"Yeah."

He shook his head as he stood up. "Why don't you work on your laundry and call your girl and figure out what you're going to do. I'm going to call Halley."

"Good luck with that."

"Thanks, I'll probably need it," he joked. And after he got off the phone with Halley, maybe he'd even do a little bit of thinking about how he was going to put a little distance between Chloe and himself.

He needed to do that for both of their sakes.

Otherwise, he was going to lose both her friendship and Adam's, too. He didn't think he could bear that.

CHAPTER FOURTEEN

MADISON WAS STILL wearing a dreamy expression on Monday morning. Since it was final week, Madison had a light schedule. Most of her finals had already been completed through her advanced placement classes.

Chloe noticed it the day before, too. Maddie had seemed preoccupied when she first got up and had coffee, when they walked three blocks to the old stone church on the corner, and even when she was talking to a couple of her friends before they headed downtown.

Chloe had kept hoping that Madison would confide in her about her date with Cope, but, just like the day before, she didn't seem inclined to say much more than that she had a good time.

Even though Chloe knew it wasn't very fair to feel slighted, she kind of did. She'd thought they had a closer relationship and hadn't expected to be kept in the dark. She would have loved to hear all the details of the girl's new romance.

On another note, she was a little jealous, too. Although she was with Adam now and had occasionally gone out in high school and college, she could honestly say that she'd never worn a dreamy, infatuated expression any morning after a date, let alone two days after. So, she was curious about what had caused Madison to feel so smitten. Was this Cope guy all that special?

Was it how Madison always acted after a date? Was she simply a girl who loved being in love?

Or was Chloe once again overanalyzing the situation? Maybe all that was going on was that Madison was being a high school senior. Maybe she wasn't acting besotted at all. Maybe all that was happening was that she was tired and wanted a nap.

When they walked through her front door, Chloe breathed a sigh of relief. She was going to do some work for a little bit, then vacuum and dust. Then she was going to make some soup for supper. None of that was very appealing, but it was a lot better than trying not to stare at Madison and read her mind.

After Madison hung up her coat, she turned to Chloe. "What are you doing tonight?"

"A little bit of accounting and housework. What about you?"

"I'm going to call my parents and work on college applications."

"Again?" It was hard not to smile.

"Yeah. They're never ending."

"How many colleges are you applying to?" She'd thought Madison was a pretty good student with decent test scores. Plus, Jerry had a good job. A really good job. Chloe was pretty sure that Madison wasn't going to have to rely on obtaining a handful of financial scholarships like she'd had to do.

"Twelve so far."

"Twelve? Why so many?"

Madison sat down on the sofa. "Mom and Dad want me to apply to a few colleges in Arkansas, since that's where they are. So those two. Then I'm applying to five of my 'dream' schools. You know, Ivy League and big colleges out of state." She sighed. "Then, of course, are all the colleges in Ohio."

"If you got to choose, what would be your first pick?"

"It used to be Yale or Princeton or Vanderbilt, but now I'm thinking somewhere a lot closer. Like Case Western."

"Case is in Cleveland."

"I know. I've visited the campus."

"You really want to stay close to where you grew up?" She could've sworn that Rhonda had said that Madison was almost guaranteed to get into an Ivy League university.

"I didn't, but I might want to be close now."

"Why?"

For the first time, Madison appeared guarded. "I don't know."

Maybe the right thing to do would be to drop it, but since she'd also taken her college goals very seriously, Chloe felt obligated to impart a little bit of the wisdom she'd gleaned. "Before you waste a ton more hours filling out applications and spend more money sending in transcripts and test scores, you might want to make a list."

"What kind of list?"

"I made lists about my goals. I wanted to get into one of the top three accounting firms, so I tailored all my college choices toward that."

"That sounds intense." Madison wrinkled her nose.

Remembering all the nights she'd stressed about grades and finals, Chloe nodded. "It was. But in the end, I did meet my goal. I interned at a big firm the summer after my junior year and was one of a select few to get offered a job at the end of the session." Sure, she sounded a little braggy, but she figured it was worth it to prove her point.

But instead of looking relieved that she wasn't the only one to be stressing about her future or even impressed that Chloe had done so well on her own, Madison drummed her fingers on her thigh. "That's great that everything worked out for you. But, um, I'm thinking about things a little differently."

"You are? How so?"

"Even though I want to get a good job one day, I'm thinking about other things besides that."

"What other things?" Before she could answer, Chloe blurted, "Do you want to be near some of your friends?"

"Kind of." She pursed her lips, then added, "If I tell you something, will you promise not to tell my parents?"

"I do, unless you're about to tell me something that might harm you or someone else."

Madison started laughing. "Aunt Chloe, you are always so serious! Where do you get this stuff?"

Completely embarrassed, she was sure her face was turning five shades of red. "I don't know. I'm trying my best to be a good parental figure here."

"Sorry, but I have two parents. How about you just be Chloe?"

The girl was right. She needed to relax and stop being Madison's caretaker, college guru and substitute mother. She needed to just be Chloe. "I can do that. And, about the other...well, you know what I meant."

"I get it. If I tell you I have a secret drug habit, you're going to tell my parents."

"Yes, but I'm being serious. And secret drug habits are bad."

Madison's eyes lit up. "I'm thinking that maybe all drug habits are bad, too."

"Whatever." Boy, she was failing miserably. The truth was that she'd been thinking more along the lines of Madison feeling depressed or something, but it was probably not a great idea to share that. She didn't think depression was ever something to joke about.

Madison studied her face. Seemed to mentally

weigh the pros and cons of continuing, then came to a conclusion. "All right, fine. Here's my secret. I think I want to stay nearby because of Cope."

"The guy you went out with for the first time the other night?" She was feeling pretty good about not sounding completely shocked.

"Yeah." She looked sheepish. "I know, dumb, right?"

Her old self would have told Madison yes. For so long, she had told herself that only thinking about a big goal and financial independence was what was important.

Now she knew better.

Yes, having enough money to pay her bills was a wonderful thing, but it wasn't the key to happiness. She'd learned that lesson in spades. Now that she'd uprooted her whole life because everything she'd sacrificed so much for had made her miserable, she wasn't sure that she trusted her opinions. "It's not dumb."

Hope flared in the girl's eyes before she firmly squashed it down. "I bet you don't understand."

"You're right. I don't. You're acting like you and Cope are serious, but you've really only been on one date."

"Yeah, but I've known him for years, Chloe," she added quickly. "We didn't really talk until we were in the same English class. And then, I don't know, if we saw each other in the halls or after school or something, we'd talk. Then we started texting. And then calling. And FaceTiming."

"So this date has been a long time coming."

"It's more like the change in our relationship has."

"You know, I wasn't going to say anything, but you've seemed distracted a lot recently. Was your date that special?"

She didn't hesitate even for a second. "Yes."

"Why? What happened?" When Madison's eyes widened, Chloe said quickly, "I don't want to get into your personal business, but I'm curious. I've been on my share of dates but I'm positive I never walked around looking like I was floating on air the morning after."

"He made me feel special, Chloe." She lowered her voice. "Cope made me feel like he was as into the date as I was. Guys don't usually act like that. And all he did was kiss me good-night."

"I hope that's all he did."

"No, you don't understand. He didn't try for more. He acted like that was enough. Like me being me was enough." She drew a deep breath. "But he's not going to go to college. He's staying here."

"What is he going to do?"

"He's been working for a builder for years. They've been training him. He wants to build houses. He says he wants to work with his hands and make things that he can see. Plus, he really likes his bosses. Don't you think that's cool?"

"I guess so."

Madison nodded. "I do, too. I think it's really cool that he already knows what he wants to do with his life."

"What do you think your parents are going to say if you do decide to go local? And, no, I'm not going to tell them anything."

Her eyes lit up, like she was secretly amused. "Oh, they're going to hate it."

Chloe thought the same thing. Rhonda and Jerry had always had high hopes for Madison. Case Western was a great school and not easy to get into. It had a great reputation and if Madison chose to attend, she'd get a fine education there. That wasn't the issue. The issue was that her dreams had changed and they no longer aligned with her parents'.

"No matter what you do, I hope you're happy. That's the most important thing."

"I agree."

"I can't wait to meet Cope. I mean, whenever you're ready for me to meet him."

Madison grinned. "Since I think he's going to be coming over a lot, I'm sure you will meet him." After a slight pause, she added, "You know, when you're not working or volunteering. Or...going out with Adam."

"You made Adam sound like an afterthought."

"Do you really like him? I mean, like I like Cope?"

"I don't know."

"Really? You guys have gone on lots of dates. Like, for months."

Put that way, it did sound like things should have moved on by now. "We have gone on quite a few dates. They've been nice, too."

"Nice?"

"Nice is good. But see, because we're adults and not teenagers, there's a lot of things to consider."

Her brows lifted. "Like what?"

"Like even though we're compatible, I'm not a hundred percent positive that our visions for our futures coincide."

Madison giggled. "You're missing the point of love, Chloe."

"Oh, yeah? What's the point of love?" she joked.

"That you don't want to be with anyone else because he makes you so happy inside that you feel like you glow."

Boy, talk about poetic teenage girl language! "I don't think I'm supposed to glow anymore."

"Sorry, but I think you are. Maybe you should date someone else."

"It's not all that easy finding a good guy, Madison."

"Sure it is. I mean, first you met this Adam guy, and then you met hunky Jamison while volunteering."

"Hunky Jamison?"

"Well, yeah. I mean, he's old but he's really cute.

And he's so nice, too. He told me all about Bud and Halley. He really loves them."

It took her a minute to remember who they were. "His brother and sister?"

"Yeah. They're twins and he helped raise them because his dad died when they were really young."

"I... I didn't know that."

"Well, you should have heard him when Bud called. He was all like, 'Do you need me? Is everything okay?' Wouldn't that be something, to have a big brother like that?"

"It would." It would be even better if that was how a boyfriend was, though. Would Jamison be that way with her? Pick up the phone when she called, no matter what he was doing? Give her his complete attention. Or, more importantly, encourage her to give him her complete attention, too.

Visions of lounging on a couch, their legs tangled together, his arm curved around her back. Holding her close. The two of them watching a movie that neither of them cared about. She'd be so focused on the way he felt, the way he always smelled faintly of the outdoors and coffee—she would feel content and happy.

And he would feel the same.

Feeling uncomfortable with the direction her thoughts were heading, she stood up. "If I'm going to get any housework done, I better go change clothes."

"Yeah, me, too."

"It's supposed to snow tonight and tomorrow. I thought I'd make a big pot of soup. Okay with you?"

"Sure, Chloe. Anything is good."

"I'm glad we talked, honey. I like having you here."

"I like it, too."

Her smile was sweet. Genuine. A warmth with a new ease filtered through her. Life was imperfect but it was imperfect in the more perfect of ways. It probably didn't make a lick of sense to anyone but her—but to her, it felt crystal clear.

CHAPTER FIFTEEN

FILLING OUT COLLEGE apps took time but not all of her attention. As she cut and pasted essays, answered the usual questions, she thought about Chloe and how she looked mystified when Madison had told her about how she felt about Cope.

Her aunt hadn't looked any more at ease when they talked about Adam, either. Madison hadn't been surprised. Even though that guy seemed to check a lot of Chloe's boxes, they didn't seem like all that great of a pairing. Chloe needed someone fun.

Thinking of how Chloe had barely decorated her house for Christmas, Madison decided that her aunt needed a guy who would look out for her, too.

Not take care of her—Chloe could do that just fine. What she needed was someone who would bring her a cup of coffee in the morning or make dinner, or convince her to even sleep in on a Saturday and do nothing but read for a couple of hours in the afternoon. The woman really needed to learn how to relax. Madison was pretty sure that Adam wasn't the guy to do that for Chloe.

Or at least, not without her mentioning it first.

However, her eyes had sure lit up when Madison had brought up Jamison.

That meant something.

Or...maybe it meant something to her. She liked the fact that Jamison had a lot in common with Cope. Jamison had also bypassed college and liked to work outside. He also seemed to be one of the few people who could encourage Chloe to stop working all day and all night. Her aunt needed to get out of her accounting world as much as possible.

Chloe needed to drop Adam and start dating Jamison.

Unfortunately, she had no idea how to make that happen. She was only eighteen years old and living with Chloe for a limited amount of time. How could she get Chloe together with the right guy without making them miserable?

It seemed almost impossible.

When her cell rang, Madison reached for it, in relief. Chloe's love life was wearing her out! Sure, it was either going to be one of her girlfriends from cheerleading or maybe Cope. Instead it was her mom.

Feeling a mixture of happiness and unease, she picked it up. "Hey, Mom."

"Madison, I'm so glad you picked up. I was afraid you were at a game or en route to one."

"Nope." No matter how many times Madison

sent her mom the schedule, she never seemed to look at it. "You called at a perfect time."

"Well, if you aren't at a game, what are you up to?"

"Working on college applications."

"Still? Honey, I thought you were done with those."

"I decided to fill out a couple more."

"Why, Maddie?" Her voice turned even more worried. "Honey, I promise, Vanderbilt or Yale are going to want to snap you up. And if they don't, I'm pretty sure you've got a good chance at Stanford. Then, there's always Cornell."

"I know."

"Then…what's going on? You said you applied to the University of Arkansas, too, just in case you want to live close to home. I can't think of a single scenario that you haven't covered."

Since there was one more scenario…the one where she went to Case and stayed close to Cope, Madison bit her lip. "I guess I can't help myself," she joked. Sure, she could probably tell her mother all about her thought process but there was no reason to get her spun up. Not yet. "What's going on with you?"

"Furniture shopping."

"You're still decorating the house?" Her mom and dad had gotten rid of a lot of the furniture from the house she'd grown up in, saying it had been built for teenagers, dogs and busy schedules.

Now that they were essentially empty nesters and living in a warmer climate, her mother wanted a fresh look.

Or, maybe she just wanted a whole house of new furniture.

"I have a feeling I'm going to be working on this house for the next two years, Maddie. It's all taking far longer than anticipated. Everything seems to be backordered and will take months to come in. I'll be lucky if your game room is completed by May."

"What game room is that?" And May? No way was she going to be moving to Arkansas in five months.

"It's a surprise for you, honey. There's a space in the upstairs for you to hang out with your friends. Plus, there's a little television nook. You're going to love it."

Friends? What friends did her mother think were coming over in Arkansas? And for what? She would likely be moving on campus at the beginning of August. "You didn't need to do that, Mom."

"Eileen said the same thing, but she doesn't understand that you need a place to feel comfortable."

"I'm going to be in college."

"Yes, but maybe not until mid or late August. Honestly, university probably won't even start until after Labor Day. You'll be here for months," she added in a bright tone.

"Mom, I don't want to move home as soon as school gets out in May."

"Of course you do. I mean, where else would you be?"

She hadn't thought that far. "I assumed I'd stay here. At Chloe's."

"You can't."

"Why not?"

"That's too long. It's an imposition. You know that."

"I don't think Chloe will mind. She likes me being here and I haven't been any trouble."

"She isn't going to tell you, but I'm sure she will be more than ready to have her house back by graduation." Lowering her voice, she added, "Try to think of how much you've disrupted her life, Maddie. We can't take advantage of her kindness."

Madison hadn't really thought about her taking advantage of Chloe. But it was true. Chloe was having to buy more food, rearrange her schedule to mesh with Madison's. Maybe even her power bills had risen.

She was kind of embarrassed that she hadn't thought of all those things. Of course, Chloe was really nice. Even if she was annoyed with Maddie, she would never say anything. "I'll talk to Chloe tonight about how long I can live here next summer."

"You'll do no such thing."

"But—"

"Madison, Dad and I have been more than patient in letting you finish out your schooling there, but I've begun to get the feeling that you have been pulling away. You're still our daughter, and you're barely eighteen. Not an adult."

She was barely eighteen, but she wasn't a child. She was an adult, or at least should be able to make some decisions about her life.

But how could she tell her mom that?

"Maybe we could talk about this another time."

"Yes, that's a good idea. Besides, I was not just calling to check in. I wanted to talk about spring break."

"What about it?"

"I thought we could go on a cruise."

"You and me?"

"No, silly. A family cruise. You, me, Dad and Eileen."

"Eileen wants to go?"

"I haven't talked to her about it yet, but she's been working hard. I think she'd be very up for relaxing on a ship. What do you think? Are you up for a week of sun and fun?" Sounding peppy again, she said, "Just think, everything will be like it used to be. You and your sister can share a room and giggle all night. The four of us can explore islands."

"I don't know, Mom." Sure, going on a cruise would be amazing. But rooming with her little sister and having her parents monitor her every move? That sounded the complete opposite.

"Why? Do you already have something planned with your friends?"

She hadn't, but that was as good an excuse as

any. "Kind of. You know how everyone wants to do senior class trips."

"If you don't want to do a cruise, we can do something else."

"Mom, I'm not going to let you give up a cruise just because I'm not sure if I can swing it. That wouldn't be fair to Eileen."

"She won't want to go without you, Maddie. Eileen misses you."

"I miss her, too." A lump formed in her throat as she thought of how much she hadn't checked on Eileen. She'd been a terrible sister.

"I know! Why go on a ship when you could have everyone here?"

"There?"

"Sure. We have a pool now, you know. Everyone could stay here. It will be like a long slumber party."

That would've been fantastic, if she was fourteen. "I'll check and see," she said.

"You don't sound too excited about any of this."

"I am. Like I said, you caught me in the middle of college apps."

"Where is Ben going?"

"Ben?"

"Ben Gissipe. I thought he took you out last summer."

"He did. But just as friends."

"Oh. Now, who are you hoping to go to prom with?"

Cope. But was he the type of guy who would

want to go to his senior prom? She kind of doubted it. "No one. I might go with all the cheerleaders."

"So you aren't dating anyone? I thought you went out the other night."

All her nerve endings felt like they were frayed. Why had she picked up the phone? Thinking of Cope, and how she knew he'd be disappointed if he discovered that she didn't want to tell anyone that he took her out, she knew she couldn't lie. Not about him. Not anymore. "Actually I'm dating someone now."

"Finally! I knew you were keeping something from me. There's the reason you're not giving me straight answers."

Her mother sounded so pleased, Madison felt like hanging up. She hated it when her mother pushed and pushed until she told her what she wanted to know. "I have been giving you straight answers, I just haven't been in a hurry to tell you that I've been seeing Cope."

"Cope? That's his name?"

"Yep."

"Cope who? It doesn't ring a bell."

"Cope Swartz."

"I don't remember you speaking about him before."

"That's because I haven't."

"Well, tell me all about him. Where does he live? What sport does he play? Where's he going to go to college?"

Those three questions were the main reason she hadn't told her mother anything about him. Boy, she'd dug herself in deep with this. "I'm not sure where Cope lives, he doesn't play a sport, and he's not going to go to college."

"I see."

Oh, no she didn't. "Mom, there's nothing to see. He took me out on a first date only recently."

"So you aren't really dating."

"No, we are. I really like him."

"Honey, you could do better. Don't get serious about someone who doesn't have a future."

"Mother, you need to relax."

"Why isn't he college bound?"

"Mom, stop acting so snooty."

"I'm asking you simple questions. You're the one who's acting as if I'm delving into your personal business."

"You kind of are."

"You're my daughter. Of course I'm going to want to know about what you're doing in your free time."

"I'm surprised you haven't been asking Chloe for reports."

"That isn't fair. Even if I have, it's because I miss you and want to make sure you're doing all right."

And...that was the last straw. Even though her head was telling her to close her mouth, don't say a word and end the call, it was like the rest of her was refusing. "Mom, you had a choice about moving. You knew that I'd be going to college in August. You knew that at the very most, you'd only have six months of living here before you could relocate to Arkansas." As more bottled-up emotions poured out of her, her voice rose. "But you didn't want to wait."

She inhaled. "It wasn't that easy, Madison."

"You sure made it seem that way. As soon as Chloe offered to let me stay with her, the house was on the market. When it sold in two days, you were thrilled!"

"That has nothing to—"

She cut her off. "Mom, how about you stop with the secrets and tell me your whole story? The one about how you and Dad couldn't wait to move on and leave me here?" Realizing that her voice had risen, she exhaled. As she swiped away a tear, Chloe appeared in her doorway.

Are you okay? she mouthed.

She shrugged.

Chloe folded her arms across her chest but didn't walk away.

"Madison, I'm sorry, but you've twisted everything that happened around in your head. We had to move. There wasn't a choice. If we hadn't sold the house, then your dad would've had to live in an Airbnb or something for six months. We would've had to pay for both of those. And then would've had to move in May anyway. Plus, there was Eileen's life to consider. You're about to graduate but she'll still have several more years of school."

"I still wished y'all could have stayed."

"Maybe, but it wasn't the right thing to do. After talking to you and Chloe, we decided to list the house. In this market, things could have gone either way. We were celebrating because we not only sold the house in two days, we got over the listing price."

"I get it, but it was still hard to see how happy you were to get rid of our home."

"Honey, I know that's where you grew up, but it was just a house."

She got it. She really did. Dad had to go where he was needed. Eileen needed to get settled. Her parents had really thought they were making her happy by letting her stay while they left.

But it was still hard.

Pulling herself together, she whispered, "But I needed you, too, Mom." Breathing in deep, she continued. "No, I thought I did. Now I've realized that I'm fine. And I'm doing everything you wanted me to do, too. I'm going to school, continuing to cheer, going to church with Chloe and applying to colleges. But I'm growing up a lot, too. I don't need you micromanaging me from four states away."

Chloe walked in farther and sat down on the edge of her bed. There was no judgment on her face. Instead, she just looked worried. "Listen, I've got to go."

"Honey, how about I get you a plane ticket for next weekend?" her mom asked quickly. "You can come out here and see everything. The three of us will spend some time together."

"I'm sorry, but I can't."

"Sure, you can."

She rolled her eyes. This was vintage Mom. She offered Madison a choice, but there really wasn't one. "Mom, I have stuff I have to do here. And... I've got to go. I'll call you back later."

"Madison, don't hang up. We need to talk through this."

"There's nothing to talk about. Everything's already been done. I love you, Mom, but I really need to get off the phone."

"I love you, too. I'll call you tomorrow."

"Okay. Bye."

When she disconnected at last, she fell back against her mound of pillows.

"What happened?" Chloe asked.

"Mom and I got into it."

"I heard that part, but what did she say that made you so upset?"

"Everything." She wiped her face. "I know. I'm terrible, but my mother is living in a dreamworld and it sometimes drives me crazy."

"What dreamworld is that?"

"She started talking about me moving to Arkansas the moment I graduate. And even suggested that

I invite all my friends to Arkansas for spring break because their new house has a pool."

"I see."

Madison chuckled. "Right? None of my friends might want to drink, party and carouse on some beach in Florida, but they really don't want to hang out at my parents' house in Arkansas."

"No, I don't imagine they will."

"Then she asked who I was dating and I made the mistake of telling her about Cope, who is the opposite of my mother's dream boyfriend for me."

"Oh, no."

"Plus, she's so excited about the possibility of me going to college in Arkansas."

"I'm sure she suggested that because that's where they're living now. It would be in-state tuition."

"Yeah. We said other stuff, but then it was like she didn't even hear what I said. She wants to get me a plane ticket so I can fly to see them next week."

"I heard you tell her no."

Chloe's voice was calm. Maybe, tentative? "Yeah. Do you think that's bad?" She hated the thought of disappointing her, too, but she was also pretty tired of trying to make everyone but herself happy.

"It doesn't matter what I think."

"It kind of does. I mean, you took me in and I'm imposing on you."

"You aren't imposing on anything. You're a perfect roommate. You're clean, considerate and are fun to be around."

Meeting her eyes, Madison spied honesty and tenderness shining back at her. She meant it. She wasn't just saying stuff because it was the right thing to do. "Right back at ya," she replied. "But I would like to know what you think."

Crossing her legs, Chloe said, "For what it's worth, Jamison told me a story a couple of weeks ago. It was how Adam's family was always available when he needed a hot meal, or just a quiet place to hang out." She paused, drawing a circle on the comforter with her finger. "That was nice, right? It was obvious that it meant a lot to Jamison. But what's funny is when I said something to Adam about how much he'd done for Jamison…" She waved a hand. "You know, like saying that it was so nice…well, Adam just shrugged. He said that it wasn't a big deal and that he'd liked having his friend there." She stood up. "I kind of think a little bit of that is what's happening with you, me and your parents, Madison."

"I don't understand."

"You needed a place to live here in Medina. I've always liked you and was glad to help. I never look at you being here as a burden."

"But I've seen it as a lifeline."

She nodded. "As far as the move goes, I think your parents were in between a rock and a hard place. Your dad's job depends on him doing what the company asks him to do. When he accepted the promotion he had to accept the transfer. And even though he could've gotten an apartment or your family could've gotten two apartments and your mother divide her time, that would've helped you, but only temporarily. It also would have been really hard on your dad and especially your mom."

"It's all perspective."

"I think so." She stood up. "If you can't visit your parents soon because of school and other commitments, then you can't. Your parents might be disappointed but they'll understand. But if you are staying away just to prove a point with them, then I do think you're being kind of tough on them. More importantly, I think you might eventually regret that choice."

"So you think I should go."

"I think you're currently trying to figure out where you want to spend the next four years of your life. I think you're dating a new guy and you like him and it's exciting. I think you have a lot on your plate. But you don't live in a vacuum. Your mom might have made a choice you didn't agree with, but she still loves you, still enjoys being with you and still cares about your classes, your activities, your college plans and who you're dating. She moved to a different state, but not to a different life."

"You're right." She'd been only looking at the situation from her perspective, and it wasn't even a clear one. It was clouded with doubts and guilt and hurt and worry.

But if she stepped back for a moment, it was easy to see how her actions might be viewed from her parents' perspective. Wow. It was like a light bulb had just illuminated in her head. Making everything that she'd been dealing with clear. "Thanks."

"You're welcome."

"I'm going to call Mom back before I lose my nerve."

"Even if you elect to stay here, I think that's a good idea. She loves you a lot, Madison."

"I love her, too. And, Chloe?"

"Yeah?"

"I love you, too."

"Right back atcha," she teased before walking down the hall.

Feeling better, she picked up her phone and called her mother again.

"Maddie?"

"Hey. I got to thinking. And... I'm sorry. I'd love to see you this weekend."

"You're sure?"

"I'm sure."

"I'll get online and look at tickets and then text you choices."

"Thanks, Mom."

"Of course," she whispered.

Minutes later when they hung up, Madison knew that she'd made the right decision.

CHAPTER SIXTEEN

IT HADN'T TAKEN a lot of urging to accept Mr. and Mrs. Dwyer's invitation to dinner on Thursday night. Not only did he genuinely enjoy Adam's parents' company, Faye was an excellent cook. She could make a casserole like no other. Adam always thought it was hysterical that he liked those casseroles so much.

Jamison had never known how to tell him that while his mom's meals were fine, she'd always tended to make dinner just for the sake of feeding them. Faye's casseroles represented fussiness and effort. Or maybe it was the way she always beamed when she took one out of the oven. Whatever the reason, Mrs. Dwyer's casserole concoctions signified home for him.

After accepting her invitation, he'd thought about the upcoming meal more than once. He'd even found himself smiling when he'd run into the grocery store to pick up a bouquet of flowers for her.

As he'd imagined she might, Faye had smiled brightly at the sight of her favorite white roses. "Jamie, you shouldn't have."

"They're just from the grocery. No big deal."

"They are to me," she said as he leaned down to kiss her cheek and hug her hello.

"I was so pleased when you told me you could come over for dinner," Faye proclaimed as she released Jamison from her hug. "It's been far too long since we've seen you."

"Faye's exactly right, buddy. Don't stay away so long next time."

Jamison clasped Brian's hand. "I won't."

"Mom. Dad. I've told you that the road to our street is open both ways. You need to get in the car and drive down to see us." Adam was still standing in the doorway, right under the gorgeous garland surrounding his parents' front door. He also just happened to be under a beribboned sprig of mistletoe, because his mother had never believed in decorating for anything in half measures.

Yet again, Jamison's first impression of the large brick house all festooned with Christmas cheer was that he'd been wrong. It seemed Adam's mom really could outdo last year's display.

"I know. And we keep meaning to…"

"What your mother is trying to say is that she never knows what to do with Larry, Curly and Moe."

Those names might bring to mind The Three Stooges for the majority of the world, but in the Dwyer household, those names were all about Faye's beloved, barky dachshunds. The three dogs seemed to be best friends, and sometimes even seemed to move in unison. One was blond and had long hair, one was red, and one was black and tan. As if they'd just been waiting to hear their names, they raced toward Jamison and Adam with a barrage of barks, twirls and wagging tails.

Dutifully kneeling down to pet them, Jamison grinned at his best friend. Adam adored his parents but had made no secret that he'd missed the two old labs he'd grown up with. These three noisy little dogs drove him crazy.

Everyone was pretty sure that the feeling was mutual, too. The black-and-tan one—maybe Moe? He stopped in front of Adam and growled.

"Yeah, I'm not a fan of yours, either, buddy," Adam said.

The little dog growled one more time before joining his buddies. Then, the tiny trio moved to stand next to Faye.

"Son, close the door. We don't need to heat the front yard," his dad said.

Meeting Jamison's eye, Adam grinned. His father always, always complained about the electric, gas or water bills.

After closing the door, Adam said, "It's closed. Everything looks real nice, Mom. It's super festive."

"I told Brian you'd like the mistletoe."

As Jamison stifled a laugh, his dad called their names from his spot near the fireplace. "Take off your coats and come sit down in the living room. You boys want a beer?"

"I'm driving, Dad," Adam replied. "Water's good."

"Jamison?"

"Water's fine with me, too."

"Gotcha."

While he and Adam dutifully took off their coats and shoes, dodged dachshunds and walked into the living room, Jamison took a moment to appreciate the gorgeous Christmas tree in the back corner of the room. It was a freshly cut blue spruce and had to be at least nine feet tall. Like always, it sent tart pine scent throughout the room. On the mantel were six stockings. Three for people and three for dachshunds.

He chuckled to himself, already prepared for Adam to grouse on the way home about the dogs being his parents' second set of children.

"Here you are, son," Brian said as he placed a glass on the coffee table in front of Jamison.

"Thanks."

"And here you are, Adam," he said as he placed the second glass down.

"Thanks, Dad."

"I've been looking forward to seeing you ever since Faye reached out," Jamison said. "I can't believe it's been so long."

"It has. I haven't seen you in at least a month. Time flies by, doesn't it?"

"Yes, sir."

"Shame that Chloe couldn't come."

Startled, Jamison gripped the glass he'd just picked up a little bit harder. "I didn't know you'd asked Chloe, too."

Brian smiled at Adam. "I didn't. Faye did. We got tired of asking Adam when he was going to bring her over for supper."

Jamison turned to Adam. "You haven't brought her over here yet?"

"Our schedules have been nuts. Every time I thought about asking, either she or I had a commitment that came up." As if he realized how lame that sounded, Adam added, "I agreed wholeheartedly about her joining us, though."

"Why didn't she?"

Adam exhaled. "Chloe had yet another commitment. Basically, it was that she didn't want to leave that cousin of hers."

Jamison frowned. "What cousin is that?"

He waved a hand. "Yeah. You know. Mindy. Miranda?"

"You mean Madison? She's Chloe's niece. Madison is eighteen and a senior in high school. She's also Chloe's goddaughter." How could Adam still not know this?

"Oh, yeah." Leaning back, Adam crossed his legs. "By the time I finally get it right, the girl will probably have gone to college."

"Faye invited Madison to come over as well, but Chloe said she thought spending an evening here with all of us might be overwhelming," Brian added. "It's a shame, though."

"I told that son of mine that Brian and I would be on our best behavior!" Faye called out. "I think Madison would've had fun. It's been too long since we had a teenager around here."

Jamison thought that Madison would have been just fine, too. The girl was sweet, and Adam's parents were great. He could think of anyone who didn't enjoy their company.

"Maybe they'll be able to make it another time," Jamison murmured.

Brian brightened. "That's what I said. Chloe is welcome here anytime, along with anyone else she happens to want to bring."

Adam didn't look as enthused. "Hopefully we won't have to worry about her bringing any more needy relatives after Christmas break."

"Why do you say that?" Faye asked.

"Well, I know the girl is trying to finish her senior year, but I'm hoping she can start living with some of her friends or something. Chloe needs her life back."

Jamison couldn't help but stare at him in surprise. He'd never gotten the impression that Chloe didn't like Madison at her house. The only problem she'd ever hinted about was that the girl wished her parents had waited to move until she graduated.

"Son, you just want all her attention for yourself," Brian joked.

Looking awkward, Adam swallowed. "That's not it. But I would like it if she was more available."

Jamison tightened his jaw so he wouldn't say anything about Adam's basketball league or young professionals group.

"Dinner's ready. Boys, come to the kitchen and help me bring in the dishes."

"Coming, Mom," Adam said.

"I'll take your glasses, boys."

"Thanks, Brian."

"No prob. I've got to corral the stooges anyway."

At last, after multiple trips back and forth from the kitchen and a flurry of barking, the four of them sat down to the table.

After Brian led them in a brief blessing, Jamison was able to take a good look at the spread before them. To say it was impressive was an understatement. Almost every inch not covered by plates and glasses held a serving bowl or platter. A poppy seed chicken casserole, mashed potatoes, a broccoli casserole, rolls and at least two other sides.

As always, it smelled wonderful and made his mouth water. "This looks amazing, Faye," he said.

"I hope you enjoy it, Jamison." Chuckling, she added, "The two casseroles on the table are in honor of you."

"Love it." He smiled at her. She used to say the very same thing whenever he'd come over years ago. She would probably never agree, but it had never been the food that had warmed his insides as much as her kindness.

He supposed that was why he enjoyed volunteering at Loaves of Love so much. Faye Dwyer had taught him the value of making something for another person. Time and energy spent was just as tangible and appreciated as the finished product.

As they started passing the dishes around, Adam groaned. "Mom, I wish you wouldn't have gone to so much trouble."

"It was no trouble."

"Obviously, it was. You must have spent hours in the kitchen. I suppose you made dessert, too?"

It was all Jamison could do to *not* kick Adam's leg. Anything to get him to be nicer to his mom.

"Of course I made dessert." She looked horrified that he suggested she hadn't.

"See?"

His father shot Adam an annoyed glance. "Son, I know there's a thank-you somewhere in those words, but I sure didn't hear it."

His buddy set down the gravy boat. "Thank you, Mom. It's a wonderful meal."

"You're welcome, son." As they continued to pass dishes, she took a deep breath. "Now, Jamie, tell us all about Bud and Halley."

"They're both fine, but here's some news you're going to like: Bud is in love."

"What? He's so young!"

"I thought the same thing, but he was quick to set

me straight that he wasn't too young to know his heart." Passing the rolls to Brian, he added, "Bud told me that when you know, you know."

"Those are wise words," Brian said as he took the plate. "I knew that boy was brilliant."

"He is brilliant." He grinned. "But honestly, I'm happy for him."

"Well, what's she like? Do you like her?"

"I haven't met her yet. Supposedly next time he comes down. He only came over for a night before going to spend the rest of the weekend with Jenny's family."

Faye's eyes widened. "Oh, my. That's a big deal."

"I thought the same thing."

"I can't believe your kid brother actually thinks he's in love," Adam groused. "I hope she doesn't break his heart."

"I hope so, too, but it sounds very mutual. Honestly, there's no 'thinking' about his feelings. He's totally into her." Smiling at Mrs. Dwyer, he said, "Bud's head over heels for Jenny. There's no doubt about that."

"I'm happy for him," Faye said. Her eyes lit up. "Maybe we'll get a proposal before too long."

"Settle down, honey," Brian said. "One step at a time. The boy has to finish college first."

Jamison nodded. "I thought the same thing. They've got plenty of time before Bud decides to go ring shopping." It was probably going to take him a while to save up for that, too.

"I guess we'll just have to wait on you two," she said with a smile.

Jamison grinned but he noticed that Adam looked thoughtful. When he waited for Adam to deny that possibility, an awful, free-falling feeling of dread lodged in the pit of his stomach.

Was Adam actually thinking about proposing marriage to Chloe? He was a great guy...but hadn't he just admitted that he wasn't even sure how love felt?

Panic set in as he contemplated the possibilities. What if he did propose to her? What if Adam told Chloe that he loved her, but he wasn't even sure?

What if she said yes because she was falling in love with Adam?

What was he going to do if that happened?

He realized that as much as he wanted Adam and Chloe to be happy, he was pretty sure that the two of them weren't meant to be happy together.

He needed to finally admit what he'd been trying all this time to deny. He knew what love felt like.

Because he was in love with Chloe Winner.

But it might be too late to do a thing about it.

CHAPTER SEVENTEEN

When Chloe arrived at Loaves of Love, there were already over twenty volunteers making bread in the kitchen and someone had taped a handwritten note to the outside of the door, stating that no one else was needed for the day.

Since volunteering there had been her plan for the day, Chloe felt a little let down. While she was thrilled that Edna's venture had brought in so many volunteers, she couldn't help but feel a little nostalgic for the way things had been when she first started. They used to be a smaller, close-knit group.

Feeling guilty for wishing for fewer people, Chloe decided instead to one day chat with Edna about the possibility of making a portal so everyone could sign up online. Of course, she was pretty sure Edna would remind her that inconveniencing volunteers wasn't her priority. Empowering people experiencing food insecurity was.

"Now what should I do?" she muttered to herself.

Terri, the volunteer receptionist on duty, looked sympathetic. "I know how you feel. I was really looking forward to helping out in there this morning, too."

Terri's reminder that she wasn't the only one a little disappointed was exactly what she needed. "It's good there are so many people here. That's a blessing."

Terri smiled. "Edna said the same thing. Hey, are you Chloe Winner, by any chance?"

"I am. Why?"

"A guy named Jamison is in the food pantry with Edna, as well as Kayla and Sean Copeland. Edna asked me to let you know they could use your help if you were interested. No bread baking is involved, but she seemed to think you might want to go."

"I'm interested." She would have said yes no matter what, but the fact that Jamison, Kayla and Sean were there was an added bonus. The more she'd been around the Copelands, the more she thought they could be good friends. Pointing toward an open doorway, she said, "They're down the hall, right?"

"Yep. Would you like me to walk you down?"

"There's no need."

"It's easy to find. Just follow the signs," Terri added just as the front door opened and her attention turned to a woman and her child.

"Thanks, Terri," Chloe whispered before heading down the hall.

Sure enough, the way was well marked, but she could have found her way by listening to the laughter. When she entered the large room, Edna was practically doubled over, laughing.

"Chloe!" Sean called out. "Thank goodness you're here. We need to add a voice of reason into this mix."

"Uh-oh," she teased. "That sounds dangerous."

"Oh, it is. Enter at your own risk," Edna declared. "This crew has been cracking jokes nonstop. I'm amazed we've gotten anything done."

"What's going on?"

Jamison answered from the other side of a large stainless island. "Edna threw out some ideas for holiday gift baskets."

"Okay…what's so funny about that?"

"Someone—I won't mention any names—brought up the idea that the volunteers should dress up like elves when the baskets are delivered," Sean said meaningfully.

"Stop. Fine, it was me who had that bright idea," Kayla said. "It's not my fault that I work at an elementary school. Everyone has a great time getting into the holiday spirit there."

"There's holiday spirit and then there's a no-way-on-earth," Edna joked. "I do appreciate your can-do spirit, though."

"Me, too," Chloe said.

"That's because you would probably make a great elf delivery girl," Jamison teased. "You're the right size."

"Oh, no. Do not go there."

"See why I'm glad you showed up? This is what I've been putting up with," Edna joked. "It's not our fault that we're on the petite side, right?"

"Right. My mother told me at least once a month when I was in middle school that I could change a lot of things about myself except my height."

Edna shot her a commiserating smile. "Seriously, would you like to help us? I've gotten some good donations from local businesses. I thought we could use them to buy some mittens and socks and hats... and maybe something like chocolate or candy in addition to food items?"

"I've love to help you. I can go shopping, wrap items, fill baskets, you name it."

"Uh-oh. You've got that accountant look in your eyes." Jamison groaned.

"What does that mean?" Sean asked.

"I kind of like to organize things for fun."

"That's why we need you," Edna said. "Kayla already has my notes and the budget. I'll let the four of you run with it, if that's okay?"

"We've got this, Edna," Kayla said. "Don't worry."

"Thanks," Edna said as she picked up her cell phone which was buzzing again. "I need to take this one. One of you text me later if you have a question or need to go over the budget."

"Will do," Sean said. "We'll keep you informed."

After Edna walked to the hall with the phone to her ear, Chloe said, "I was a little bummed that there wasn't any space in the kitchen, but this project sounds like a lot of fun."

"I think so, too," Kayla said. "I've started a list of action items that need to get done before the official delivery day."

"Which is when?"

"On December 20."

"Okay. Shall we sit down and get organized? I bet we could find a couple of folding chairs in one of the storage closets."

"I think it would be better if we went to one of our houses. Clients are sure to be arriving any moment," Kayla said. "Would you two like to come over to our house right now?"

"Our kids are at my sister's so it won't be too chaotic," Sean added.

"I'm in."

"Me, too," said Jamison. "I really like this project."

"I didn't even think of whether you'll have much time off from your job," Sean said. "With Kayla and me working for the school district, we're on vacation."

"As soon as I know what everyone needs me to do, I'll block off the time at work. I'll either take vacation or talk to my supervisor. He might just give me some time since this is for the community. Hey, Chloe, what about you?"

"I'll make it work." She did have some clients still trying to tie up some end-of-the-year investing and donations, but this was worth a couple of late-night work sessions.

Sean glanced at his phone. "It's almost lunchtime. How about we stop by the deli and grab some sandwiches and meet you two at our house in thirty minutes?"

"Sounds good." After passing on their orders along with some cash to help pay for everything, Chloe followed Jamison out the back door. The parking lot was on the side of the building. With the wind blowing, she was glad she hadn't taken off her coat when she'd been inside. As they walked, she felt the familiar zing that seemed to happen whenever she was around Jamison.

"It's good to see you," she said.

"I was hoping to see you, too. Did you walk or drive here?"

"I drove. You?"

"I walked. Can you take me to Kayla and Sean's in your car, or drop me off at my house to get my truck?"

Going to Jamison's house meant that there was a good chance of seeing Adam. She wasn't quite ready for that. "I'll drive us to the Copelands."

"You'll be good dropping me off later?"

"Of course."

As they walked to her car, he glanced at her. "So, what's new? How's work?"

"It's good. Since it's the end of the year, I've just

been answering a lot of questions about things everyone needs for taxes and such."

"Every time you talk about your job, you smile."

"I like it. It's busy and chaotic, and sometimes feels like I've bitten off more than I can chew. But, that said, I really like having my own business. It's so much better than being another up-and-coming drone at my former employer."

She took a breath. "The big news is that I think that Madison and I have made a lot of progress." Clicking the remote on her car, she unlocked the doors. "Jamison, I encouraged her to see her parents. She's there right now."

"That's a big deal?"

"Yeah. She's been pretending that she hasn't been upset about them leaving. We talked and she stopped holding everything in. I think she feels better."

"She's got a lot on her plate."

She buckled her seat belt. "She sure does. But I guess the same could be said of everyone else."

"Such as the two of us getting ready to work on this new project?"

"Exactly. I'll have a good time going shopping with you and filling baskets."

"As long as no one makes me dress in an elf costume to deliver them, I think it's going to be great."

"I promise, I won't make you do a single thing you don't want to do."

"I'll make the same promise to you," he murmured.

Catching his eye, her breath caught. She was pretty sure he'd been talking about something a whole lot more personal than working on gift baskets.

She sucked in a big breath of cold air as Jamison opened the passenger side door and sat down. She needed to cool off, fast.

And, maybe, finally take some of the same advice that she'd been giving Madison. It was time that she stopped avoiding a hard discussion with Adam. She needed to move forward with her life.

Before it was too late and she lost her chance with Jamison forever.

CHAPTER EIGHTEEN

THE TWO-HOUR MEETING had turned into a three-hour lunch, which had eventually become an opportunity for the guys to watch the Browns play on TV while Chloe helped Kayla work on some napkin rings she'd decided to make for a Christmas party she and Sean were hosting for their families.

"I think it's awesome that your families get along so well."

"I do, too. Sometimes I kind of have to pinch myself when I realize just how lucky I am. Not only did I find the greatest guy at Loaves of Love, but I already knew him in high school."

Chloe knew a little about Kayla and Sean's backstory. Sean was a widower with a six-year-old son when he'd reconnected with Kayla. Back then, she was newly divorced and really struggling. She'd been having such a difficult time that she'd walked into Loaves of Love in order to get food.

Edna had encouraged her to stay and bake some bread, and Kayla had ended up being at the same workstation as Sean. They eventually fell in love. Now they were married, Jackson thought of

Kayla as his mom and they even had a baby named Aubrie.

"I guess you two were meant to be."

Glancing at her husband across the room, Kayla smiled softly. "Sean and Jackson changed my life. It's no exaggeration to say that they taught me to love again."

"I bet they feel the same way about you."

For the first time, Kayla looked slightly vulnerable. "Maybe, but Dannette, Sean's first wife, was great. They were happily married."

"So Sean is very blessed." Personally, Chloe couldn't imagine Sean's first wife being any more suited for him than Kayla. She was sweet, obviously doted on him and always talked about Jackson as if he was her own.

"I suppose he is. Though, I guess we could say that you are, too."

"I do have a lot of blessings, but what are you referring to?"

"Uh, you and Jamison, obviously." Before Chloe could interrupt, she said, "Last month, after we all stood in the reception area of Loaves of Love and talked, I told Sean that you two were the cutest couple." Becoming even more animated, she added, "I love how you two really complement each other. You met at Loaves of Love, didn't you?"

Oh, no. Feeling like she was about to tell a kid that Santa Claus wasn't real, she said, "We did meet there, but Jamison and I aren't a couple."

Kayla looked at her quizzically before she bit her lip in obvious embarrassment. "Sorry. I guess I just assumed…"

"No, we're just friends. Really." When Kayla grinned, like she was sure Chloe was playing a game or something, she added, "I've uh, actually been dating Jamison's best friend, Adam."

"Wait. You're serious."

"Yes. I'm afraid so."

Looking mortified, Kayla slapped both of her hands in front of her eyes. "I'm so sorry. I, well, I'm really embarrassed."

"There's nothing to be embarrassed about." It was on the tip of her tongue to say that mistaking her relationship with Jamison was a common mistake, but what would that say about the two of them? Maybe they'd become too comfortable together.

Could that even be a thing?

"Still…" Kayla darted a glance toward the guys. "I guess I was enjoying both of your company so much I wanted to get together again."

"I'd like that, too." Chloe reached out and squeezed her arm. "I promise, I'm not upset."

"Okay. Good. Maybe I'll set something for the four of us after the New Year. Sean and me, and you and Adam."

"That sounds great." Thinking about the upcoming conversation she really needed to have with

Adam, she forced herself to be completely honest. "I mean, it will if Adam and I are still dating then."

"Oh. So, you and him aren't…"

Chloe didn't blame Kayla for sounding confused. That was no surprise, because Chloe was confused about everything. "I've started to realize that maybe he isn't the right guy for me."

Kayla studied her intently. "You know that I was married before, right?" When Chloe nodded, Kayla's expression turned more somber. "I know we don't know each other very well, so feel free to take or leave my advice. But I would be remiss to not tell you that I learned something pretty valuable while I was married to the wrong guy."

"What was that?"

"You can't make something work that doesn't. Wishing and nagging doesn't help. Neither does prayer. If you don't feel like Adam is the guy for you the moment you get up in the morning all the way through the moment you close your eyes, he's not. And no amount of trying harder is going to change that."

"Thank you for that."

"I hope I didn't upset you too much." She bit her lip, then murmured, "It's just that, well… I had a lot of hard moments that I wouldn't wish on anyone. I'd feel like I'd be doing you a disservice if I didn't share that with you."

"I understand."

Kayla's words had obviously been torn from her

heart. She couldn't fault her for being brave enough to share her experiences.

The only problem was that she had no idea about what to do with the conversation that occurred. No, she did know. She needed to finally break things off with Adam. That was the right thing to do—but boy, what is it going to be painful.

An hour later, Chloe was still thinking about Kayla's words as she was driving Jamison home. Luckily, Jamison had had a lot to say about the football game he'd watched and the plans that they'd made for the gift baskets.

She'd nodded and pretended to be more interested than she was in the Browns' victory or the stories Sean had shared with him about coaching high school football.

She was almost glad that a new batch of snow had started to fall, and so she'd had a good excuse to keep her eyes and attention on the road.

By the time she got to Jamison's house, she couldn't wait to head home and reflect on the day.

"Well, here you are," she said, as she pulled into his driveway.

"You want to come in for a while?"

"Thanks, but it's been a long day. My plan of spending an hour or two at Loaves of Love before running errands and cleaning bathrooms kind of fell by the wayside."

"You're not to going to clean bathrooms tonight, are you?"

"I don't know. Probably not."

Jamison unbuckled his seat belt but didn't move to open his door. "Chloe, is something on your mind?"

"Yeah."

"Want to talk about it?"

"Not yet."

He turned slightly to face her. "Does that mean you'll want to eventually?"

"I'm not sure." When a line formed between his eyebrows, she said, "I'm not trying to be mysterious. I promise."

"Okay. But if you change your mind, you can always let me know. I'll come over."

"I know. But for now, I do want to get home."

"Yeah. The snow is really starting to come down now." He chuckled. "So much for all the forecasters saying that this was going to be a mild winter, huh?" Finally opening the door, he exited. "Be careful driving home."

"I will."

When she was alone again, Chloe realized that she'd been clenching her jaw so tightly she was starting to get a headache.

Something had to be done, soon.

CHAPTER NINETEEN

AFTER KAYLA SHARED that she'd gone ahead and picked up all the socks and mittens at a discount store when she'd spied them on sale, Chloe and Jamison said that they'd bake the fifty loaves of cinnamon bread for the gift baskets. Edna had suggested they do the baking on Sunday evening, since the food pantry was always closed on Sundays.

When Madison had admitted that she didn't have any plans, Chloe asked if she'd come along to help. Madison had agreed in a heartbeat.

Though now, two hours later, Chloe was wondering if the girl was starting to regret her decision. Making, kneading and baking fifty loaves of bread was a hefty commitment—for both her time and muscles.

Added to that was the teenager's need for perfection. She kept doubting herself.

"How does this look, Jamison?" Madison asked as she stared at her lump of bread dough in front of her.

"You're doing fine. Keep kneading it, though. The dough needs to look almost shiny."

"Almost shiny. Got it."

As Madison mumbled to herself, he met Chloe's gaze and winked.

Chloe smiled back, just as they heard the front door click open. A wave of alarm zipped through her before Edna and Wayne walked inside.

"What are you two doing here?" she called out.

"We finished supper early," Wayne said as he helped Edna take off her coat. "And then someone decided that you guys might need some help with those fifty loaves."

"We've got this," Jamison said. "Especially since we brought along Madison here."

"I'm sure you do," Edna said. "But would you mind if we joined in?"

"Edna here realized that she'd been so busy with administrative duties she hasn't been able to work in the kitchen much at all," Wayne explained.

"It's your kitchen," Chloe said. "By the way, Edna and Wayne, this is my niece Madison."

"Good to meet you," said Wayne.

"Hey!" she said before glaring at her ball of dough again.

"You look like you're having a lot of fun," Edna teased as she washed her hands and put on an apron.

"It's okay."

Chloe knew by now that was teenager-speak for she'd rather be doing just about anything other than baking bread. "Hey, Madison? Why don't you see if Cope or one of your girlfriends can come pick you up."

"No. I promised I'd help you."

"And you have. You've been here an hour. You can stay if you want, but now that Edna and Wayne are here, there's no need for you to."

"You really don't mind if I call someone?"

"Nope."

"Okay. I'll, uh, go see what Cope's doing," she said as she walked over to the sink and washed her hands.

Seconds later she was texting on her phone near the back of the kitchen. When she put her phone down, her expression looked remarkably happier.

"Did you get ahold of anyone?" Jamison asked.

"Yeah. Cope is coming to get me. He said he wasn't doing anything much. He's at a friend's house playing video games."

"Looks like your night just got more interesting," Chloe teased.

"Yeah." Walking to her side, Madison whispered, "Thanks for letting me leave."

"It wasn't a problem. You know that. Just be home at midnight."

"I will." As she turned to grab her coat, Madison added, "I couldn't believe that when I told Cope I was at Loaves of Love, he didn't even need me to give him the address. He said he knew where it was." She frowned. "Don't you think that's strange?"

"I don't know. Maybe he's volunteered here before or something?"

"Or saw the sign out front," said Jamison.

"Oh. Right. It is a pretty big sign." She looked down at her phone. "He said he's five minutes away. I'm going to go wait for him."

"See you later, dear," Edna called out.

A couple minutes after that, Madison called out, "He's here!" and then hurried out the front door.

"Ah, young love," Wayne joked as he started measuring flour and yeast into his bowl. "There's nothing like it."

"I couldn't agree more," Edna said. "I used to count the hours until my beau called every night. I bet you did the same thing, Chloe."

"Not really. I was all about college and big dreams when I was a senior in high school. I didn't ever date anyone seriously until the middle of college." She chuckled. "Honestly, I sometimes think Madison could give me dating advice."

"I think you're doing all right," Jamison said before carrying two bread pans to the ovens in the back of the room.

There was something about the way he spoke that made her wonder if it meant more than she realized. She was still stewing on it when Wayne was in the back with Jamison pulling loaves out of the oven.

"Are you still dating that friend of Jamison's?" Edna asked. "What was his name?"

"Adam." After making sure that Jamison was out of earshot, she added, "Yeah, we're still dating."

"How's it going?"

"I think it's about run its course."

"Uh-oh. I'm sorry about that."

"Me, too, but it's pretty obvious that he and I aren't the greatest match."

"When are you going to talk to him about it?"

"Maybe in January?"

"January."

"Yes. I don't want to break up with him at Christmas. I mean, that would be pretty mean, don't you think?"

"Maybe. Or, maybe putting off the inevitable has its own difficulties."

"I suppose. I'm dreading it, though. Adam is a lawyer. It's kind of second nature for him to question something he doesn't agree with."

Edna frowned. "Do you really think he'd do that?"

"I'm not sure." Waving a hand in the air. "I have this fear of getting so irritated with him that I say point blank that he's not 'the one.'"

"Maybe that's what he needs to hear."

"Maybe," Chloe allowed, "but what he asks who is, if not him? I mean, I have no idea."

"Are you sure about that?"

Before Chloe had a chance to answer, Wayne called Edna over to his side. Giving Chloe another opportunity to glance at Jamison yet again.

Leading her to believe that she really did have someone in mind. She had no idea if that made things easier or harder, however.

CHAPTER TWENTY

MADISON'S PARENTS' NEW house in Rogers, Arkansas, was big and fancy. It was brick and stone and had a circular driveway in the front. It had a big lawn of thick, green grass even in December. There were also lots of trees and bushes and flower beds that were lined with the same stone that was on the house.

In the backyard, there was a pool with a cover on it. Her father had grinned when he'd showed her how the retractable cover worked. You could push a button and it would move forward or backward automatically. Next to the pool was a sunken hot tub and a fancy outdoor kitchen.

Inside the house there were two fireplaces, a game room, a formal living room, a big kitchen, a workout space and four bedrooms, each with its own bathroom. Hers was on the second floor in the back. It had its own reading nook and even a little balcony. She could sit on it and look at the pool if she wanted.

In short, it was amazing. Her dad was so proud of what his years of hard work had garnered. Her mother was excited and her younger sister, Eileen, was already acting like she'd lived like a princess all her life.

Thinking about Cope, Madison supposed she had.

They both had.

So it was all amazing, and she knew she should be really excited. Especially since her mom said they could go shopping and she could decorate her new bedroom and bath like she wanted. Her fifteen-year-old self would have been jumping up and down if Mom had told her that she could get all new bedding for her room and even special-order coordinating window treatments.

Now? It felt like too much.

And kind of a waste because Madison had no intention of ever living in that room. Well, not beyond the occasional vacation and trip home.

To her relief, she hadn't had to say much about anything so far. Her flight from Cleveland to Atlanta had been delayed, which made her miss her connection to the airport in Bentonville. Luckily, the airline took care of everything and put her on the next flight, but that was three hours later. By the time she landed, got her bag, got something to eat and a complete tour of the house, it was close to ten o'clock at night.

Eileen had been so eager to tell her about her new school, the friends she'd made, the ballet troupe she was thinking about trying out for and even the new boy she liked, Madison didn't have to say a thing.

Finally, when it was almost midnight, she told everyone that she was exhausted and went to her room. After taking a hot shower, she put on pajamas and finally was able to call Cope. He'd been texting her during the day and had even sounded a little bit anxious that she hadn't been able to call.

"Maddie, you good?" he blurted as soon as he picked up.

She loved that was always his first concern. Every day, no matter what she'd been doing, he always asked about her first. One time, when she'd been upset about one of the girls on the squad not following her directions, he'd listened patiently. Even though it was a given that he couldn't care less about cheerleading drama.

But that was how he treated her. With care. Like she was special. He always wanted to know how she was feeling and if it wasn't good, he wanted to fix it.

It was so different than every other boy she knew. She'd begun to think it was in a guy's genetic makeup to want to constantly talk about himself.

Focusing back on his question, she decided to answer with complete honesty. "I think so."

"What happened? Did your parents say something?" He paused. "Was waiting for the next plane harder than you let on?"

"No, no. Everything was fine. My parents were

nice and Eileen was Eileen." With a laugh, she said, "She told me about her whole life nonstop. She really loves it here." She took a breath. "Anyway, after they came and got me, we went out to eat, then I got a tour of the house and saw my new room."

"What's it like?"

"It has its own bathroom and sitting area. It's in the back of the house, and it even has a little balcony."

"Whoa."

"Right? It's huge."

"It sounds awesome."

"I guess. I think Eileen is jealous. She doesn't have either a sitting area or a balcony. I'm pretty sure she's told Mom that she should be the one to have the bigger room because she's living here full-time and I'm about to go to college."

He chuckled. "I don't blame her. I'd probably say the same thing."

"I would, too. Mom offered to take me shopping tomorrow to choose new bedding and stuff but I'm going to try to get our rooms switched before she does all that."

"Are you sure that's what you want to do?"

"Yeah. I'm not planning to be here all that much."

"You might change your mind."

She knew he was probably joking. Or maybe he was trying to make her remember that their relationship was new. He shouldn't be the reason she wanted to stay near Medina.

But she'd had a lot of time to think while she'd been sitting at the airport. She now knew that she wasn't basing her comments on just Cope. The truth was that she didn't want to just be Rhonda and Jerry's oldest daughter. She wanted to be her own person.

She wanted more independence and that wasn't going to happen if her mother and father were checking to see what time she was going to sleep at night.

"I don't think I'm going to change my mind. And I'm not just saying I want to stay for you."

"No?"

She smiled. "Even if we broke up and you never wanted to see me again, I don't want to move here."

"What if you have to?" He sounded worried.

She didn't know why. "I hope I don't." She'd said the words firmly. Like a firm tone would prevent him from thinking that she wasn't worth the trouble of a long-distance romance.

Though, was it even a romance? He called her all the time. They texted, and he looked at her like she was precious. But they'd never even kissed.

Hating the direction that her head was going, she said, "Tell me about you."

"Nothing new here. I went to morning classes then worked six hours."

"What did you do tonight?"

"Nothing much."

She gripped her phone. Hoping he would say something more, but he didn't. "How's your dad?"

"He's the same. Why?" His voice had turned bitter.

"I don't know. No, that isn't true. I... I just want to get to know you better."

"You are."

"I feel like sometimes all I do is talk about me. That isn't fair."

"Maddie, look. I know you're trying, but believe it or not, I'm trying, too. I don't like to talk about my homelife and I really don't like to talk about my dad with you."

"If not me, then who do you talk about him with?"

"I don't need to talk about him with anyone." He sighed. "Look. It's late. I better go."

"Why?"

"I haven't even started that big project I was assigned in government. It's going to take forever."

It was Christmas break. And after midnight. No way was he going to write a report that wasn't due until January.

That meant he just wanted to get off the phone with her. "Okay. Bye."

"Hey. Don't get upset. I'm just...well, I'm not used to having someone who cares. That's all."

"I understand." And now, maybe she did. She needed to stop expecting that their lives were going to immediately intertwine. Relationships didn't work that way.

She needed to remember that.

"Hey, I'll text you tomorrow, okay? You can tell me about how the big room-switching discussion went."

She felt her shoulders relax at his teasing tone. "It's sure to be a doozy. I'll warn you before I call so you can get mentally prepared."

"I'll be ready. Night, Maddie."

"Night, Cope."

After she hung up, she lay down on her bed and felt herself relax as her body adjusted itself to the mattress she'd had for the last six or seven years. Even though her surroundings were different, she was back in the comfort of her own home. Against the back wall were three unpacked boxes. Her mother hadn't wanted to go through her stuff. She'd be able to pull it out and arrange it how she liked. Feel like she belonged instead of being just a guest in Chloe's home.

She wondered if that would make her feel better about her life. She wasn't sure.

CHAPTER TWENTY-ONE

When Adam had invited her over on Monday evening, Chloe had accepted immediately. She'd been feeling guilty about her increasingly strong feelings for Jamison. Those feelings seemed to be getting stronger every day, and there was nothing she could do about it. It felt as if they were out of her control.

Even though she felt as if she was betraying Adam by even thinking about another man, she couldn't seem to help herself.

It made no sense, especially since neither of them had ever declared any strong feelings for the other person.

Hanging out at his house on a Monday night seemed like the perfect opportunity for her to reconcile her feelings and settle her heart once and for all. She was relieved he'd asked her to do something relaxing and easy.

Usually, "easy" and Adam didn't go hand in hand. Whenever he took her out on dates, it was usually somewhere fancy or notable in Cleveland. She enjoyed getting dressed up as much as anyone, but often the emphasis was on the meal or the crowd or, well, any number of things.

When they didn't dine in that direction, they often shared a quick lunch before heading back to work. Those lunches had served their purpose, but they were ultimately unfulfilling for her heart. Those quick lunches always included their cell phones nestled securely next to their plates. Emails and texts were answered while eating salads and conversing.

Whenever they parted after a brief kiss, Chloe had always felt empty inside, like she'd been looking for sustenance to fill her up but instead had only received rations. She'd felt like they were going through the motions instead of really enjoying their time together.

Instead of carefully styling her hair, she'd pulled it into a ponytail. A pair of worn, loose-fitting Levi's and an old Browns sweatshirt completed her look. When Adam opened his door, she was glad to see he'd also dressed casually.

After a quick hug and kiss, he'd offered her a soda, pointed to a monster bag of chips and a jar of salsa, and announced that was the end of his hosting efforts.

Every bit of Chloe had loved his irreverence. It was what she'd been needing from Adam. She'd wanted his attention and to just be together. Maybe she'd been impatient when she should have realized that Adam did things in a more methodical way.

She made the decision to relax and enjoy their afternoon together and give them one more chance.

"I'm so glad you came over," he said.

"I'm glad you called." She curved her hand around his forearm. "We should do things like this more often, Adam."

"What? Hang out and watch football?"

"Yes. At least the hanging out part."

Leaning over, he kissed her forehead. "Anytime you're up for eating junk food and yelling at the games on TV, come on over. I'm your man."

She kept her smile in place, but some of the warm and gooey feelings that she'd been desperate to enjoy had dissipated. "Tell me about your week," she said quickly. "I want to hear everything."

He blinked. "Oh. Sure. Well, first of all, I made some good progress on the Stewart case." He launched into a long, complicated summary that involved subpoenas and tax laws.

Chloe followed the best she could, then shared her efforts to organize one of her client's portfolios. Adam's glazed look proved that he was as uninterested in accounting work as she was in law. "Church was good yesterday," she said, a little desperately. "Did you go as well?"

"My church has a Saturday night service. I like going before I go out."

She blinked, realizing that he'd gone out on Saturday night before. And…he had no desire to tell her about it.

The conversation continued. But after they talked a little bit more about their families and the weather, there didn't seem to be anything more to say.

"I better turn on the game before we miss the entire first quarter," Adam said.

She'd gotten a soda while he'd picked up the remote, turned on a game and leaned back on the couch. After pouring her Coke into a glass, Chloe sat down next to him.

That was two hours ago.

Yep, for two hours, she'd been sitting on the couch and pretending to watch football. It felt like two days.

Maybe, if Adam had acted like he was really into the game, Chloe could've relaxed a bit. After all, she knew of a friend of her mother's who happily read books next to her husband while he watched sports. It worked for them.

But since Adam seemed to be just as invested in whomever he was texting on his phone as he was in the game, pretending to be enjoying herself wasn't working for her.

She realized then that she couldn't take much more of it. Not of the game that she hadn't wanted to see in the first place, or of the stilted conversation that they were sharing whenever either of them had anything to say.

After the Browns got a field goal and tied up the

game, Adam stood up. "I'm going to get another Coke. Want one?"

"No thanks."

When he walked away, she mentally practiced her speech. She was going to start by telling him what a nice guy he was, continue by adding that she'd enjoyed their time together, and finish by declaring that she was sure there was a better woman for her than him.

All of that was pretty good. She just didn't know how to get started.

"Chloe, what's going on?"

She looked up to find Adam standing in front of her. His expression appeared to be mildly irritated.

"I'm sorry, did I miss something?"

"Beyond that last touchdown return? Yeah."

"Sorry. I've been rehearsing something in my head."

Sitting down, he frowned at her. "Rehearsing?"

It was time. Bracing herself, she looked into his deep brown eyes. "Yeah. See... I need to talk to you about us."

"What about us?"

"I don't think we should see each other anymore." And there went her prepared speech, sailing out the window.

His forehead wrinkled. "Wait a minute. Are you breaking up with me?"

"Kind of." "Breaking up" sounded like it was

ending a real relationship. She wasn't sure if they'd ever reached that point.

"Kind of?" His voice hardened. "What's that supposed to mean?"

"It means that I would like for us to stop seeing each other, but I haven't been considering you and me to be a real couple."

Sitting back down next to her, Adam leaned forward, resting his elbows on his knees. "Chloe. What the heck? We've been seeing each other for months."

"I know." But not every week. Sometimes they were lucky to see each other only twice a month. Two times in thirty days didn't equal a "real" relationship in her mind. "Listen, I don't think the problem is just you. It's me, too. I... I just don't think we're the right fit."

Adam was still staring at her like she was speaking another language. "I call you all the time."

He did call her quite a bit. But Adam's "all the time" and hers were very different. She stared at him. Was it worth it to share her viewpoint? Or would it just prolong the moment?

She had to try to smooth things over. At the very least, share her feelings. She owed him that. "Adam, we don't even text every day. I talk to Jamison twice as much as you."

And just like that, his confusion settled into understanding. His scowl deepened. "So that's it, isn't it?"

"What?"

Standing up, he crossed his arms over his chest. "Come on, honey. Don't play innocent now. I know what the two of you have been doing."

She got to her feet. "You're missing the point. This is about the two of us."

"No, I think it's more like the three of us."

"Jamison and I have not been doing anything, Adam."

"Volunteering together? Grabbing a bite to eat when you are both done?" His voice deepened. "And now the two of you are going over to other people's houses as a couple. What do you call all of that?"

"We haven't been going to anyone's house—" Suddenly, she realized that he was talking about the Copelands. "Adam, that had to do with Loaves of Love. Edna asked Jamison and me to work with Kayla and Sean Copeland on some Christmas gift baskets. We went to their house to plan because we needed someplace to talk." Of course, they all had ended up sharing a meal.

"There's a lot of people volunteering at that place."

"It's called Loaves of Love."

"Whatever. What I'm saying is that it sure was convenient for the two of you to just happen to be put on the same committee."

"There are no committees. This…this just happened."

"I bet."

Hating that he was turning this breakup into her fault, she snapped, "You are making something more of that meeting than it was."

"I know I'm not imagining 'something more' of your relationship with Jamison. Over the last couple of months, it's felt like the two of you have gotten closer. Am I wrong about that?"

What could she say?"

"Adam, I'm not going to deny that Jamison and I have become close. But that doesn't mean I've been doing anything behind your back." She inhaled. "My feelings for you don't have anything to do with my friendship with him. What I'm trying to tell you is that I don't think you and I are a good fit." She knew her voice was starting to quaver, but this discussion was going even worse than she'd imagined. "I am looking for someone to share the rest of my life with. I'm sorry, but I don't think you're that guy. Neither of us is the right person for the other."

He turned toward one of the windows that faced the street. Stared out. "I can't believe this is happening. I live next door to Jamison. We've been friends forever. My whole family thinks of him as part of our family."

He wasn't upset about losing her. He was mourning the loss of a friendship. Hurt and dismay settled deep into her chest. Right where her heart was.

She needed to get out of there. "Adam, this isn't about Jamison."

"Sure it is. He knew how I felt about you. He knew I assumed you and I would get married one day."

Both irritated and hurt, she strode to the pair of coat hooks next to the front door. "If Jamison knew all that, then that's more than I knew."

"Come on."

"No, you stop. You're acting like we were involved in some big, passionate love affair and I just cheated behind your back. You and I both know that this is not what's been happening. When were you going to tell me your plans, Adam?"

"You knew."

She yanked her coat off the hook and pulled it on. "I didn't. You can revise our history as much as you want, but my recollection of our dating was that we occasionally went out. We occasionally talked on the phone. Lots of our conversations were about our workdays."

He frowned. "What's wrong with all of that?"

"Nothing. But it wasn't enough for me."

He exhaled. "What do you want, Chloe?"

"I want it all," she said in a soft voice as she zipped up her coat. "I want nightly phone calls. I want dates. I want time together that aren't dates." Feeling a little stripped bare, she whispered, "I want romance, Adam. I want promises. Feelings.

Laughter. Tears." Doing her best to hold back her tears, she whispered, "I want everything."

Adam's expression flared before he quickly tamped it down. "What you want is a made-for-TV movie. Not reality." His tone was decisive. Each word was clipped. "You've conjured up a list of wants that no man can possibly ever reach."

"I haven't been trying to make us into a rom-com, Adam. What I'm trying to tell you is that I want things that I don't think you can give me."

Looking as hurt as she felt, he exhaled. "If I'm guilty of never telling you my dreams for us, you're guilty of never telling me your dreams. I'm not the only one who messed up, Chloe."

He was right. They might have talked a lot, but they'd never talked about things that mattered. Blinking away a renegade tear, she picked up her purse. "Bye."

Adam didn't turn back her way. "If you were planning to break things off this afternoon, I wish you would've just done it first thing. I've missed the whole third quarter."

That was his parting comment? She pulled open the door. "Don't worry, Adam. There's always another game next week." She just wouldn't be anywhere near him.

It was snowing again. Two of the houses across the street had their Christmas lights on. They twinkled against the flakes and teased her.

Getting into her car, she turned on the engine

and turned the defroster on High. While she waited for the vehicle to warm up and the windshield to clear, she leaned back against the seat and pressed her hands to her cheeks. "Way to go, Chloe," she muttered to herself. "You somehow managed to make a bad situation even worse than you imagined."

When the tears that she'd been trying so hard to hold back finally broke free, she swiped them with the side of her palm.

They were taking her by surprise. She'd liked Adam but she hadn't thought she was going to have a broken heart.

Until she realized that she was crying over the loss of what could have been.

And for how this breakup was going to hurt Jamison.

No doubt Adam was about to stop at Jamison's house later and give him a piece of his mind.

Jamison was going to feel blindsided and betrayed. There was a real chance that he might even be angry. She might have just ruined two friendships this afternoon. All right before Christmas.

She had no idea how to make things better, either. Not anytime soon.

CHAPTER TWENTY-TWO

IT WAS MONDAY, and Christmas was now a a week away. Halley had finished her finals, stayed a few extra days in Lexington to recover and relax, and then had driven to his house the night before.

As usual, she'd texted him, asking if he minded. Even though they both knew he wouldn't. She'd said she wanted to hang out and catch up with him before moving over to their mom's.

Since he still had a lot of vacation days that needed to be taken before the end of the year, he'd cleared a couple more with his boss. This morning, they'd skipped church. Instead, he'd let her sleep in. Then, he'd sipped coffee while she did laundry and listened to Christmas music. Most of his questions were answered with a couple of words.

This wasn't out of the norm. Bud, by nature, was always the chattier of the twins. But Halley also kept looking at him, like there was something on her mind and she was trying to determine how he would react to whatever she was going to say. He was pretty sure that there was something on her mind and it wasn't to spend quality time with her big brother.

Thinking of how Bud had acted about Jenny, Jamison decided that maybe Halley and her brother weren't so different after all.

He was fine with it, though. After she'd finished her laundry, she'd taken a nap, he'd gone for a run, and then they ordered a pair of pizzas from their favorite place. After a little while, they FaceTimed with Bud. Eventually, he and Halley started playing gin rummy. Sure, they could have also hung out and played a couple of video games, but the three of them had always liked playing cards. They talked. They half watched whatever game was on TV. They glanced at their phones. Playing cards was easy.

Although Jamison had considered pressing her a bit to tell him what was on her mind, he decided against it. Halley deserved to have her secrets, and he needed the distraction.

It was a blessing, really. If Halley wasn't there being, well, Halley, he would have been stewing on the fact that Chloe was probably over at Adam's. He knew she'd gone over to his house today to watch the football game but he hadn't spoken to either of them in two days. No doubt they were spending more and more time together and didn't need him there as the third wheel. Which hurt.

Jealousy was a bitter pill and he was having a hard time swallowing it.

"Gin!" Halley called out, bringing him back to

the present. Counting up her cards, she said, "You better be careful, J. If you don't get your head in the game, I'm going to beat you in record time."

"Not going to happen," he teased. "But before you try, go deal with your laundry. The dryer beeped ten minutes ago."

"Fine." She stood up with a huff and walked down the hall.

Deciding it was as good a time as any to heat up some more slices, he got off the couch, too. Then was sidetracked by a pounding at his door.

"Hey," he said to Adam. "This is a surprise." Unable to help himself, he glanced beyond his buddy to see if Chloe had come over, too.

"She's not with me," he bit out. "Is Chloe here?"

"No."

Adam's eyes narrowed as he stared at Halley's sweatshirt. It was powder blue and obviously far smaller than anything Jamison could fit into. Walking inside, he walked across the room and picked it up. "Yeah. It sure looks like she isn't," he said sarcastically.

He was completely confused. "What the heck, Adam?" Jamison said. "Man, you're getting snow all over my floor. Take off your boots."

Ignoring him, he continued to grip the garment. "Wow. She sure didn't waste any time, did she? Where is she now?" He inhaled sharply. "Your bedroom?"

"I have no idea what you're talking about. But

you need to take it down a notch." When Adam didn't move, Jamison added, "And put my sister's sweatshirt down, too."

"You always were a terrible liar. What's she been telling you?" Scanning the room, Adam's voice rose. "Let me guess—Chloe came over here in tears and you decided to console her with...pizza and a game of cards or something?"

Chloe. This was about Chloe. Worry began to thread an uneasy trail through his insides. If she was crying, then Adam had done or said something to her. And it would've been bad, too. She didn't cry for no reason. "Adam, stop ranting and take a breath. What's going on with Chloe?"

Finally tossing the sweatshirt on a chair, Adam folded his arms over his chest. "You tell me. She's obviously came over here to be comforted."

Comforted? "Chloe is not here, man."

"Yeah, right." Raising his voice, he said, "Chloe?"

"Adam, stop. Listen, I don't know what's up with you, but you've got to calm down. You're going to scare my sister."

"I'm fine, J," Halley said as she walked out with an armful of towels and sheets. "Although I gotta say that you sure aren't, Adam. Jamison's going to be really ticked at you for making his floor all wet. Everyone knows he loves this refurbished floor."

Adam's expression went slack before he recovered. "Halley. Hey."

"Yeah. Hey. Good to see you, too." She frowned at Adam as she tossed the towels on the couch.

Jamison wasn't sure if he wanted to laugh at the way his kid sister was putting Adam in his place or glare at him for the aggressive attitude his best friend came in with. Deciding neither was a good idea, he focused on the pile of towels that were now on the couch. "Halley, couldn't you have done that someplace else?"

"No." She shot him a meaningful look. He knew what that meant, too. Adam's behavior was kind of freaking her out—and she didn't like anyone being rude to him. He might be her big brother, but she had the same protective streak.

"One more time, what's going on?" he said with the last of his patience. "Why did you think Chloe was over here?"

Giving Halley one last look, Adam released a ragged breath. "She broke up with me tonight."

"What?"

A line formed between his brows. "You really didn't know that, did you?"

Too stunned to speak, he shook his head.

Looking satisfied with his reaction, Adam swallowed hard. "It was a shock to me. One minute, we're watching the game and the next Chloe tells me that we don't have a future. I couldn't believe it. But maybe you don't feel the same way?"

Halley sat down on the couch and pretended to

fold towels while he gaped at Adam. "What is that supposed to mean?"

"It means that all this time I've been thinking that the two of you are just good buddies but obviously you've been fooling around behind my back."

When Halley inhaled sharply, Jamison realized that the conversation was about to head even further south. It was nothing that his sister needed to hear. "Halley, give us a second, 'kay?"

"Yeah. Sure." She looked from him to Adam and back again. "Do you, ah, want me to take my laundry, too?"

"I don't care, honey."

Adam's jaw twitched as Halley grabbed a couple of towels before finally heading down the hall to her bedroom. When they heard her bedroom door click shut, Adam sat down on the chair next to him. "I promise that I didn't realize your sister was in town. Sorry I grabbed her sweatshirt."

"She's fine." He wasn't all that sure he would get over Adam's accusations anytime soon, though. "Adam, why don't you take off your coat and talk to me."

"No. I'll go. But first, I just want you to tell me the truth. Have you two been playing me for a fool? Have the two of you been seeing each other behind my back?"

His teeth were clenched so hard, it was almost hard to get a word out. "No," he bit out.

"What about the lunch you two got together?

What about the dinner you two had with another couple?"

"What has Chloe been telling you?"

"No, you tell me. I don't want to watch you try to get your stories straight. I want the truth."

He sat down. "Fine. You want to know the truth? I like her. I think she's just about perfect. She and I have a ton in common, and we laugh a lot when we're together." He paused as Adam sat down on the ottoman. "Was I jealous of your relationship with her? Sure I was. She's great. But we didn't do anything behind your back. The lunch and the dinner at the Copelands weren't dates."

"Are you sure?"

"I wouldn't lie to you about that. But, if you want to know everything, I'll tell you more of my dark secrets. A couple of days ago, she and I were walking in the dark, she tripped. I reached for her arm. There was something there. Sparks. When she looked up at me, and I gazed into her blue eyes, I bent down to kiss her cheek, but it wasn't what I wanted to do. What I really wanted was to kiss her on the lips. I wanted to kiss her like she was mine." Looking away, he cleared his throat. "I didn't, but I know Chloe could tell that I was only holding back because of my loyalty to you."

Adam's expression darkened. "I knew it. I knew there was something there, I just didn't want to see it. Way to go, J. You've managed to surprise me and I didn't think that was possible."

Well, that's what he got for being completely honest. "Oh, stop. Nothing happened beyond that. I stepped away and apologized. She did the same. Chloe practically ran back to her house."

"You didn't see the need to tell me about that?"

"Tell you what? That I accidentally kissed Chloe for about a half a second? No."

"You're splitting hairs."

"No, what I'm doing is telling you that I've wanted to do more. A lot more, but I didn't. And neither did Chloe." When Adam still looked like he was about to argue that point, he said, "What happened between you two?"

"I told you. She broke up with me and left."

"Did she make it home okay?"

"I don't know. I was sure she'd call you." He waved a hand. "I was sure she'd be over here now that I was finally out of the way."

"I'm sorry she broke up with you, but I'm not going to take the blame for this. I didn't encourage her to do that, Adam. We made a point of never talking about your relationship."

"Because of your feelings for her?"

"Yeah. And because of my friendship with you. Adam, don't you get it? I value our friendship. It means a lot to me. I not only owe you a lot, but I owe your parents a lot, too. I would never do anything to jeopardize that." Sure, he sounded sappy, but he didn't want Adam to think that Jamison had forgotten all the times he'd helped him out over the years.

Adam studied his face. Then, as if someone had let all the air out of his sails, he leaned back with a sigh. "You don't owe me a thing. Whatever I did to help you in middle school was no more than you helped me later in life. And my parents... J., even when I'm a jerk, my parents are great and they love you like a son. They'd also say that you don't owe them a thing. They love you."

The lump that had formed in his throat made it hard to talk. He nodded.

Adam leaned back. "This is on me, isn't it?"

"Chloe breaking things off?" When Adam nodded, he said, "I don't know if it's on you as much as that it wasn't meant to be. You two were just dating, right?"

"Yeah. It was exclusive, though."

"All right. I get that. But come on. We've both had serious girlfriends over the years. I mean, who can forget Janine?"

His eyes flared. "Janine was a piece of work."

"Yeah, she was," he said with a laugh. Thinking of his first girlfriend, he rolled his eyes. "I still can't believe I was so blind about her true character for so long." They'd been together for seven months.

Unzipping his coat, Adam said, "You mean until she started giving you a hard time about the price of her birthday gift."

"Yeah." Janine had refused to believe that he

didn't have hundreds of dollars to spend on her birthday. "I'm not saying that Chloe is anything like Janine. Only that she's a good example of why every relationship doesn't necessarily end in marriage."

Adam stared at him a long moment, then nodded slowly. "Yeah. Yeah, you're right."

"It's good it happened now instead of after you got even more serious."

"Probably."

"So, how about you take off that coat and those boots and stay awhile. Halley and I weren't doing anything special. Just playing cards."

"Thanks, but I'm going to take off. Tell Halley I'm sorry for barging in here and making her hide out in her room."

"She's fine. But you can tell her yourself. C'mon, stay. We've got plenty of pizza."

"Thanks, but I'm going to head out."

"All right."

Adam paused at the door. "Jamison, we good?"

"Yeah. Other than the fact that I've got to wipe down my floors, we're fine." Neither of them smiled, but a look passed between them before he strode out the door.

Walking to the kitchen, Jamison grabbed a spray bottle of floor cleaner and a couple of paper towels and wiped down the melted snow, salt and grime Adam's boots had left.

As he wiped, he thought about that look they'd

shared. Maybe it was filled with regret? Maybe it was simply acceptance. But whatever it was, Jamison had a feeling that things had changed between them. A line had been crossed. Adam had accused him of going behind his back and Jamison was acutely aware that no matter how much he protested that there was nothing between him and Chloe, there actually was.

"Is it safe to come out yet?" Halley called out.

"Yep. Always the jokester, girl."

"Sorry, I couldn't help but give you a tiny bit of grief. You're in the middle of a love triangle, Jamison."

"I think not. Nobody's mentioned love."

"I'm not talking about you both loving Chloe. I'm talking about you loving Adam while you're falling in love with Chloe."

Just as he rolled his eyes, Jamison realized that she might not be too far from the truth. He did love Adam like a brother. The guy meant as much to him as Bud and Halley did. But was he falling in love with Chloe?

Well, yeah. He'd already admitted that to himself.

Since she seemed to have a better handle on this than he did, he said, "Do you think things are going to get harder before they get better?"

Walking over to the pizza box, she said, "Yep."

"Think there's anything I can do about it?"

"Nope," she said as she clicked on *Home Alone*.

He leaned back on the couch. No longer hungry, he stared at the television. Tried to watch the movie.

But not even Kevin's antics against the idiot burglars or Halley's commentary brightened his spirits.

All he could think about was that he needed to see Chloe soon, but he wasn't sure what to say.

It was the first time he could ever remember that happening.

CHAPTER TWENTY-THREE

BY MONDAY NIGHT, she'd made her decision. After continually hearing about her chances of getting into Yale, Vanderbilt and Dartmouth, Madison had had enough. Enough of the college brochures. Enough of the websites. Enough of analyzing her last four years through her parents' eyes.

More than anything, she'd had enough of feeling like a college's acceptance letter was going to determine the rest of her life. And, if she didn't get a letter to one of her parents' top five choices, then she was a failure and should have pushed herself even harder during eighth grade and high school.

Including that year of junior high had been the kicker, she'd decided. The memories of being a brand-new teenager and caring more about advanced placement entrance exams instead of zits on her face or braces on her teeth were painful. Even back then, she'd yearned for a break from meeting everyone's high expectations.

Madison didn't want to do it anymore.

No, she didn't think she should have to. She was eighteen. She wanted to laugh more, sleep more, and have fun. She wanted to live and enjoy her days instead of working toward an elusive goal. And it was elusive, too. She honestly had no idea what she wanted to do for the rest of her life and was tired of pretending that she wanted to find out as soon as possible.

All Madison did know was that she absolutely did not want to spend another second discussing if she'd volunteered enough or been in enough clubs and groups at school.

Sitting in her parents' new sunroom, with her sister, Eileen, sitting beside her with a soda in her hands, Madison gazed out at the backyard and wished the privacy fence wasn't so high. Why did all these people in this neighborhood not want a single person discovering what was going on in their backyards? What could they possibly be doing?

"Madison, did you hear me?" her father asked.

"I'm sorry, no. What did you say?"

He released a put-upon-sounding sigh. "I asked if there was a chance you could go to that Loaves place a couple of times with Chloe. Do you have time?"

"I bet she could make time, right?" Mom asked.

"I can't do that."

Her mother's expression turned disappointed. "You really don't want to volunteer there?"

It was on the tip of her tongue to mention that she actually had helped out at Loaves of Love before. It was a great place and baking bread for gift baskets had been fun.

But she didn't want to go there again just to make her parents happy. "Why are you two pushing this?"

Dad tapped the tip of his pencil on the notebook he'd started when she'd begun applying to schools. "Because there's a chance one of the colleges might call for an interview. You need to be sure to be actively volunteering somewhere if that happens."

It took Madison a moment to fully understand what her father was getting at. No, that wasn't true. She got it. She just was having a hard time wrapping her head about how laser-focused they'd become on her future.

A year ago, she would have said that she'd talk to Chloe. "Talking" meant nothing. And she would have talked to her, just not about Loaves of Love. She wouldn't have to do anything they suggested, just play the game. It would make them happy and get them off her back. She'd done this dozens of times.

But there was no way she was going to do that to Chloe. Chloe deserved more respect for something she cared so deeply about.

But more importantly, she couldn't do that to the folks at Loaves of Love. No way was she going to volunteer at a food bank for all the wrong reasons. It made her feel icky inside.

"No," she said. When Eileen's eyes bugged out,

Madison turned away from her. She didn't like disappointing her sister, but she was even more tired of disappointing herself.

Her mother tilted her head to one side. "No, what? No, you haven't talked to Chloe?"

"No, I don't want to start volunteering at Loaves of Love just in case somebody at a university calls."

All three of them stared at her. Each looked so shocked, it was almost comical. Almost.

"I think you need to rethink that decision, Madison," Dad said. "I know you don't want to give up your free time, but this is important." He shrugged. "Besides, you probably will only have to go a couple of times. Just enough so if someone calls to check on you they can say that you have been helping out."

"I'm not going to change my mind. Volunteering at a food bank so it will look good for some fancy college recruiter isn't right."

"Maybe it doesn't seem right, but it's the way of the world. They want well-rounded students, dear."

"I *am* well-rounded. I have been doing all kinds of good things. For years. I've made really good grades. I've taken advanced placement classes and earned amazing test scores. I've done everything right." She waved a hand. "And for what? Nothing."

Her father sputtered. "It's not nothing, Madison. We're talking about Yale."

"No, you are."

Studying her face, her mother got to her feet. "I

think we should've waited to talk about this, Jerry. She's obviously tired."

"I'm not tired. I'm fine." Tears were forming in her eyes and threatened to fall but she ignored them. The tears were because she was frustrated. Everyone might as well be on the same page. "What I am is frustrated because you two have not been listening to me!"

"We're listening now," Dad bit out. "Madison, calm down."

"No, Dad. I won't. It's too late for that. I don't think I'd even be able to calm down if I tried. All I can do is tell you the same thing I've been trying to tell you guys for weeks. I don't want to go to an Ivy League school anymore. I want to go to one near Medina. I want to go to college and have fun. I don't want to choose a major the minute I step foot on campus. I don't want to worry about dean's lists. But, most of all, what I really don't want to do is spend the next four years of my life stressing out just so I can get a piece of paper from somewhere I didn't want to go in the first place."

"Where is this coming from?" Her mother narrowed her eyes. "Is it Chloe?"

"Chloe? No!"

"Are you sure? Because it sure seems like you've been talking to her a lot about your future."

"Why shouldn't I? Chloe has a lot of good advice."

"She's not a mother. She doesn't understand what

it's like to think of someone else's needs more than your own."

"That isn't fair. Aunt Chloe isn't selfish at all. And she has nothing to do with my decision about college."

Folding her arms over her chest, her mother groaned. "If it's not Chloe, you must be doing this because of that boy? What's his name again? Kevin?"

"No, Mom. It's Cope."

"Who are you talking about? What is his name?" Dad asked.

"It doesn't matter. You'll probably never meet him anyway." Yes, her voice was snarky, but she didn't care.

Both of her parents gasped while Eileen covered her mouth. Madison was pretty sure her sister was smirking.

"I think you need to move home," Dad said. "Obviously something has happened to you at Chloe's. If she hasn't influenced you, she certainly hasn't stopped you from making bad decisions."

"Nothing's happened! And I'm not moving home because another family is living in it. Just like my family moved away, too."

"Madison, enough with the drama," Dad said. "Take a deep breath and settle down."

"Dear, do you want a glass of water?" Mom asked.

"No. What I want is a break." Getting to her feet,

she turned to Eileen. "Well, dear sister, now you know what not to do with your life. Learn from my mistakes."

"Do not leave this room, young lady. We are not done."

Oh, yes they were. "Sorry, Dad, but you lost the right to order me around like a little kid when you decided that you were too busy to even get on the phone with me once a week. I'm going for a walk. I'll be back in about an hour."

All three of them stared at her with shocked expressions. She didn't blame them. She was shocked at herself, too.

Walking to the front door, she reached for her coat, slipped her feet into her UGGs and walked out the door.

When the chilly breeze brushed against she cheeks, she could feel her tears evaporate.

Angry at herself, she swiped her eyes. Then, as soon as she figured she was out of sight from the house, she picked up her phone and dialed Cope.

He answered on the first ring. "Madison?"

"Hey. Are you busy?"

"I'm still at work."

"Oh. Sorry. I'll—"

"No, wait. You sound upset. Hold on."

"Really, it's okay."

"It's not. Hold on, Maddie."

She could hear him speaking to his manager

about taking her call. Saying that he needed ten minutes because his girlfriend was upset.

He thought of her as his girlfriend. She was stunned. And…kind of excited, too.

"Sorry about that. I got fifteen minutes. Now, what happened?"

What hadn't? "I yelled at my parents." Remembering her parting words, she cringed. "And, kind of at my younger sister, too."

"What about?"

"It all started with my dad saying I needed to volunteer at Loaves of Love in case a recruiter from college called and was worried that I stopped doing good works or something."

"Do they do that?"

"I don't know. It sounds kind of stupid, right? I mean, it's not like I'm going to have to be a super volunteer when I get to college. Anyway, after I told them that I wouldn't do it, things went downhill fast."

"Oh, man. I'm sorry, Maddie."

"Oh, Cope. I can't believe the things I said. I just lost it. My dad got so mad, he said that I needed to move home right away."

"Can they do that?"

"I don't know. Maybe." She brushed a stray tear off her cheek. "I don't think they will, though. It would be stupid for them to pull me out of school this close to graduation. We all know that."

"What did you say when he threatened to move you there?"

"This is where I lost my mind. I think I told them that I didn't have a home anymore."

After a choking cough, she heard him chuckle under his breath. "Sorry. It's just…"

"Dramatic? Crazy? That I acted like the earth was ending and I was the sole survivor?"

"I was thinking more along the lines that you really let them have it." His voice deepened. "I'm really sorry that it went so bad."

"Me, too." Taking a fortifying breath, she added, "The worst part is I can't even think of what I should've done. I just feel like I finally needed to stand on my own two feet." Listening to her words, she groaned. "Do I even make sense?"

"You are. I think you did the right thing."

"Thanks."

More softly, he said, "What are you doing now?"

"I told them that I needed to take a walk and I'd be back in an hour." All she'd wanted to do was call him. To hear his voice but saying that sounded weird. "I'm glad you answered."

"Me, too."

She continued on the sidewalk, barely paying attention to where she was going. She figured she'd get back to her parents' house by retracing her steps. Whenever she was ready. After a few seconds, Madison realized that he wasn't saying anything. Panic set in. Maybe he hadn't wanted her to call and share her drama with him. "Hey, you know what? I should probably let you go."

"Maddie, stop worrying, okay? I have time to talk. Plus, everything's going to be okay."

"You don't know that. They're really upset. I told them that I want to go to college near Medina."

"I thought you were thinking about a bunch of fancy schools."

"I don't think those schools are going to give me my dream."

"What is that?"

"I just want to have a job like my aunt Chloe."

"What is she? An accountant or something?"

"Yeah. I don't know if I want to do that…but I want to have a life. I don't want a big, important job that I feel married to." Like her father.

"Instead, you want to be married and have a family."

Even though they'd just gotten to know each other, it felt like he understood her more than her parents. "Yes." She nodded, wishing she could see his face.

"Maddie, that's sweet."

"Listen, I'm not saying that we have to be the ones who are together… I'm not trying to push you into something."

He chuckled softly. "You just don't get it, do you?"

"Get what?"

"How I feel about you. I more than really like you, Maddie. I love you."

"You sound so sure."

"That's because I am. And listen. I'd love you no matter what, but you're like, this perfect girl."

"Please."

"No. Listen. You're beautiful, Maddie. You're smart. Really smart. You're good with people, and more than that, you care. You're a cheerleader." He laughed. "You are what a lot of people would call the total package. I didn't think I'd ever have a chance with you but I wanted to try. And now that you're being so sweet and talking about how you want to have a future together? Well, it's so good, it's like a dream. There's nothing you can do to push me into a relationship with you. The fact is that I'm already there."

"I wish you were here."

"I wish I was, too. But for what it's worth, I'm glad you're telling your family how you feel."

"Me, too. But I should've done it a better way." Eileen's look, especially, was going to haunt her for a while. She looked both shocked and hurt by the things Maddie had said.

"I don't know if that was possible," Cope said. "You told them a lot of things that they didn't want to hear, right?"

"Yeah. Saying that they didn't want to hear it is an understatement."

"Well, then, go with it. You had to tell them some

time. It had to be done, and you have a lot of strong feelings."

"What do you think is going to happen when I get back?"

"I don't know…other than I'm pretty sure your parents are still going to love you."

"I hope so. I still love them." But did love make everything that they'd said to each other not matter anymore? She doubted it.

"See? Everything's going to be okay."

"You sound so sure."

"I am sure. You've told me a lot about your life. Your parents might have done some things you weren't happy about, but you've had a great life with them."

"You are way too good with words."

"Not really, but I'm glad you think so." He paused. "Sorry, but I really gotta go."

"I understand. Text me later?"

"Count on it. Later, Maddie."

"Later," she teased. Then turned around and headed back to the house.

Cope had been right. She did feel better after telling them her feelings.

Everything might not be perfect, but everything was going to be okay.

Eventually.

CHAPTER TWENTY-FOUR

RHONDA'S TUESDAY MORNING phone call had been a welcome surprise. Though they'd been communicating quite a bit since Madison had moved in, it was usually through texts and an occasional email.

"Hey you," Chloe said when she picked up. "Did you get Madison on the plane all right? I've already checked her flight info and it looks like her flight from Atlanta to Cleveland is still on time."

"She got on the plane just fine," Rhonda said in a monotone. "At least, that what her text said."

Chloe frowned. Her sister did not sound happy. But then, of course she wasn't going to be happy. She missed Madison. "I bet saying goodbye was difficult."

"Not for her. Madison could hardly wait to get out of the car."

"Oh." Feeling dismayed by how bitter her sister sounded, Chloe sank onto the soft cushions of her couch. She'd been looking forward to hearing about their new house and Jerry's new job. And Eileen, of course. She'd been looking forward to hearing about everything, actually.

"Oh? Is that all you have to say?"

"Rhonda, I'm sorry, but you're going to have to back up a few steps. I have no idea what's gotten you into such a snit." She winced. The phrase had come out unintentionally. She used to say her sister got in a snit about five hundred times a day.

As expected, Rhonda inhaled sharply. "I am not in a snit. What I am, is horrified by what you've been saying to her."

"Pardon me?" She stood back up.

"Madison has decided to ruin her whole life. Everything that she's worked for and planned has flown out the window! Now she has grand plans of going to some local school and dating some boy who has no future." After a pause for breath, Rhonda's voice got louder. "Why have you, *of all people*, encouraged this?"

Of all people? What did that even mean? "Hold on there. I didn't do anything!"

"Well, you sure should have," Rhonda said. Then, before Chloe could say another word, she began to rant.

Holding the phone to her ear, Chloe began to pace back and forth in her kitchen. It was either that, or break into her secret stash of Halloween candy that she'd saved in the freezer for special, high-stress situations. Did she have any KitKat bars still in there? She was pretty sure she was going to need five of those in about two minutes.

Though, if Rhonda kept up her rant much longer, she was pretty sure she was going to pull out the big guns and find the Dove bar in the butter bin in the refrigerator. She'd start munching on that while she paced.

When Rhonda finally took a deep, fortifying breath, Chloe spoke. "Maddie's decisions are not my fault."

"They have to be. You're the only difference in her life."

Only? Not by a long shot. "Rhonda. Your daughter moving in with me made a big difference in her life. A giant one. I'm sorry if you don't want to hear it, but your decision to move during Madison's senior year instead of waiting a few months has been very difficult for her. She's had a hard time with it."

"She shouldn't be having a hard time at all. Madison got what she wanted. She wanted to stay in Medina and finish high school there. Instead of yanking her out and making her move, we found a way to let her stay."

Chloe bit her lip so she wouldn't point out that the "found a way" was her. She was the one who agreed to take in a teenager for an entire school year. "What is your point?"

"My point is that my dependable, responsible daughter has changed. She's now acting like everything she's worked so hard for doesn't matter." Her voice rose again. "I think you've encouraged that, Chloe."

"All I've been doing is listening to her. She needs a friend."

"She needs guidance."

Not wanting to bring up the move again, Chloe softened her voice. "Come on, Rhonda. Don't you remember how we felt when we were seniors in high school? She's straddling everything she knows with about a thousand questions about her future. It's a scary time."

"She's also dating that boy."

"Cope?"

"Cope Swartz."

Chloe went to the freezer and dug out the Dove ice cream bar. "Oh, do you know him?"

"No, but I've heard rumors. He's not from a very good family or from a very good side of town."

She ripped open the wrapper. "I don't know what that has to do with anything."

"If you were a parent, you would. You have to be careful about who your kids spend time with, Chloe. Some kids are simply bad influences."

"I don't know about that... He seems to have a lot on the ball."

"Well, what did you think when you met him?"

"Oh." Feeling more uncomfortable, she nibbled on the end of the treat. Tried to find some solace in that first bite of dark chocolate. "I haven't actually met Cope."

"You didn't meet him when he came to the door to pick her up for their dates?"

She popped another square in her mouth. "She's eighteen. An adult. So no. I wasn't home when he picked her up."

"I'm shocked to hear that."

"Shocked?"

"Chloe, you should've been there."

"Even if I didn't like him, what would you have made me do? Step into a relationship that was none of my business?"

"It would have been. You know what? Never mind. I mean, I get it. It's just… I don't know what to do. Jerry and I are at our wit's end. Perhaps I should give his parents a call."

Oh, for Pete's sake. "That's a mistake, and you know it."

"I suppose. I just… I just want her back like she was. Until now, she's never given us a lick of trouble."

"Rhonda, Maddie isn't in trouble now. She's doing fine! The only thing that's happened is that she's changed her mind about where to go to college."

"And the fact that she has a boyfriend who neither you nor I have met." When Chloe remained silent—because what could she say?—deeper hurt entered her sister's tone. "Chloe, when Jerry told her to go to her room, Madison said she was going for a walk instead because she didn't have a room here. She was very snippy."

It was hard not to smile. "Um, you are right. That was snippy."

She sniffed. "I swear, I don't know who she is anymore. It's like she's lost her mind."

"Oh, honey, you're worrying too much. I promise, she's okay. She's great. She's a wonderful girl."

"It all started because we wanted her to volunteer at Loaves of Love, too. Can you believe that? I thought she liked to volunteer."

"I thought she did, too. But maybe she didn't want to make bread?"

"She said that no college recruiter was going to care if she was volunteering right now."

It took a moment to connect the dots. "So you wanted her to volunteer because of college?"

"Yes. She said she'd done enough."

"Maybe she has?"

"I suppose…"

"Just relax. I got in fights with Mom and Dad and you did, too. It's normal."

"Jerry said the same thing. He said that once Madison starts getting her welcome packages and acceptance letters to all the places she's applying, she'll feel different. It is only December."

"Right."

"So, you'll help me convince her to come to Arkansas next semester?"

What? "You really want her to do that?"

"Jerry thinks we need to get her away from this boy and watch her schedule more closely."

"Wow."

"She's going to be mad at us, but it needs to be done. It's for her own good, right?"

"I'm not a guidance counselor, Rhonda, but I don't think it's possible. She's got to finish her classes here so she can graduate on time."

"Maybe so." She sniffed. "Oh, here comes Eileen. She's all upset about her sister. I better go calm her down."

"Yes, you probably should. I'll let you know when I have Maddie."

"Thanks. And…sorry I called you in a snit. I do appreciate everything you've done. Bye."

When she heard the click and then silence, Chloe stared at her cell in aggravation. She felt terrible for Madison.

And, kind of for herself, too. When she'd agreed to let Madison stay with her for her senior year, she hadn't thought too much about what that would involve. All she'd known was that Madison was a responsible girl and had always been enjoyable to be around. She had no idea what she was supposed to do when it came to convincing her to follow her parents' decisions.

Decisions she didn't agree with.

Realizing that her ice cream bar was long gone, she decided to find some support another way. Grabbing her phone again, she called Jamison.

"Chloe. It's good to hear your voice. I heard

about what happened between you and Adam. You okay?"

She realized then that she hadn't even been thinking about Adam. That was telling. Boy, she'd waited too long to break things off. "Yeah. I'm fine." Feeling a little flustered, she added, "I'm sorry I haven't talked to you about Adam. I didn't know what to say." Of course, the truth was that she had so many emotions where he was concerned that she didn't trust herself.

"I didn't call you for the same reason. I mean, I didn't want to swoop in if you needed some time."

"I'd be lying if I said breaking up with him wasn't tough, but it was the right decision." Forcing herself to be completely honest, she added, "I haven't been thinking about him much." Because she'd been thinking about Madison. And Jamison.

"I'm glad you're hanging in there. What's going on?"

And that, right there, was why he was so important to her. Jamison not only listened to what she had to say, but he also took the time to process it. Somehow he managed to do it all with that sexy, swoony rasp in his voice that gave her goose bumps. "Everything."

"Everything?" He whistled low. "You better fill me in."

"Get ready, because it's a lot." As briefly as possible, she described the last conversation with Rhonda.

"Whoa. She was a little out of line."

Relief surged through her. "*Right?* I feel blindsided. I don't know what to do."

"I bet."

She waited. Ready to hear his opinion on the matter. But unfortunately, he didn't seem all that eager to tell her anything. "Jamison, what do you think I should do?"

"About Madison?"

"Well, yes. I mean, that's who is your number one priority, right? Or is it Rhonda and Jerry?"

"It's Madison." There was no question about that.

"See? There you go."

His voice sounded warm. Sweet. And confusing. "No. I don't see anything! What should I do?"

"Chloe, stop worrying so much. The girl knows you love her. Just pick her up from the airport, take her home and listen to what she has to say."

"And then?"

"And then you'll know what to do."

"That's it? Can't you give me some words of wisdom?"

"I'm afraid I'm not doing great with words of wisdom lately. I seem to be making a lot of wrong choices."

She wasn't going to play dumb. Not with that. "How are things with Adam?"

"Pretty cold. Like the Arctic."

"I'm sorry about that."

"Are you sorry that you broke up with him?" he asked.

"Not even a little bit. He wasn't the one."

"You sound so certain about that."

"Believe me, I've had a lot of practice figuring out if a guy is the right one or not. Adam isn't."

"I'm sorry."

"Thanks, but I'll be okay." Especially since there was now someone else in her life who seemed like he might be the person she'd been waiting for all this time.

"You've made me feel better, Jamison. Thanks for listening to me."

"Anytime." His voice lowered. "I promise, call anytime at all. About anything. I'll always answer."

Warmth filled her as everything in her life seemed to ease back to where it should be. "You better be careful. I might take you up on it."

"Sweetheart, I'm counting on it."

After he hung up, she sat motionless for a few sweet moments. Reliving his words. The way his voice sounded.

The way he made her feel.

CHAPTER TWENTY-FIVE

THEY WERE BACK in the friend zone again. Chloe seemed to be at peace with that. He, on the other hand, felt like there was no worse place to be. Especially since Adam was still upset and bitter about the breakup. Now Jamison had an awkward relationship with both his best friend and Chloe.

Walking into Loaves of Love onThursday afternoon, Jamison vowed to put all thoughts of romance—or his lack of one—on the back shelf and concentrate on making bread. Just a couple of days ago, he and Chloe had joined Sean and Kayla on a shopping trip. Everything had gone well. But instead of concentrating on the needs of the people they were serving, all he could seem to do was focus on how different his relationship with Chloe was in comparison to the Copelands' with each other. There was a warmth and easy affection between them that Jamison could only hope for.

After she and Adam broke up, he'd been sure that they'd start seeing each other more. But so far, everything between them felt the same. He was starting to wonder if she'd ever look at him with love in her eyes.

"Morning, Jamison," Edna called out as he stood in the entryway and pulled off his coat and knit hat. "Ready to bake?"

Grabbing the cup of coffee he'd picked up on the way over, he nodded. "I think so."

She tilted her head to the side as she studied him. "What's going on?"

"Nothing too important. Just some personal stuff."

"Personal...family? Are Bud and Halley okay?"

"They're fine. This is all about me, I'm afraid. I've got a relationship that I'm trying to work out."

"Oh?" Her eyes lit up. "I'm great at relationship problems. Want to talk about it?"

Edna looked so confident and excited, he had to chuckle. "Thanks, but no. I'll keep you in mind, though. I mean, if I ever do decide that I need some help."

"Try not to wait too long, dear. Take it from me, if it's love, drawing out problems won't make your heart feel better. Only honest communication does that."

"That's all, huh?"

She shrugged. "Well, that, and a good kiss."

He just about choked on his sip of coffee. "Wow, Edna."

To his surprise, she didn't look the slightest bit embarrassed. "I told you. I'm great at relationship advice. A really good kiss works wonders."

"I'll keep that in mind." He wasn't sure if a really good kiss could make things better between him and Chloe but he was willing to try. "So, uh... anything new going on around here?"

A frown formed between her eyebrows. "Nothing beyond the usual, I suppose." Lowering her voice, she added, "We have quite a few new clients here today. They look dazed and a little lost. Meeting brand-new folks this close to Christmas always makes me sad."

"Me, too." Looking around the space, he gestured to the decorated tree, garland around the doorframe, and the red stockings hung on a laundry line on one of the walls of the large workroom. "This is a good place to be, though. They'll come to realize that."

"I hope so."

Gesturing to the line of stockings, he said, "What's going on?"

"I wanted to do something for all our volunteers. You know, make them feel valued." Edna's eyes lit up. "I'm thinking I might throw a volunteer party."

He made a mental note to be busy whatever night that was. He liked coming over to Loaves of Love to bake bread and to feel like he was helping someone out. Getting together for a party with a bunch of people he didn't know felt awkward.

"You'll come, won't you?"

Edna's hopeful expression made him bite back his real thoughts. "I'll try, but it's a busy time of year. I've already got a lot of work commitments."

"Oh. Yes. Of course. I understand."

He winced at her transparently fake smile. "I'm sure a lot of people will attend. It's nice of you to do this." He was almost relieved when the front door opened and a teenager walked in. He was a handsome kid, tall and well-built. But his guarded look told Jamison everything he needed to know. "I'll head on in," he murmured to Edna as she stood up.

"Cope, it's nice to see you again," Edna called out.

Pausing at the door leading into the workroom, Jamison was tempted to turn around. This was the second time he'd heard that unusual name that month. The only other time had been when Chloe had mentioned that Madison was dating a Cope. He wondered if it could possibly be the same person. Just as quickly, he pushed that thought away. It wasn't his business. People here deserved their privacy.

Walking into the workroom, he went through his usual routine, washing his hands, donning an apron, pulling out a pair of gloves. In the back of the room were Sean and Kayla. He was just about to head toward them when he noticed an older guy named Walter standing by himself. Jamison walked to his table. "Okay if I join you today?"

"I'd be upset if you didn't," Walter said. "How are you doing, Jamison? Long time, no see."

"I'm good. Busy."

Walter's leathery face dissolved into a maze of wrinkles as he grinned. "It is the season after all."

"Indeed." He was just about to walk over to the supply area to grab ingredients when Edna called out to him.

"Jamison?"

"Yes?"

"This is Cope. He's volunteered here before, but it's been a minute. Would you and Walter give him a hand if he has any questions?"

"No problem."

"Thanks. Cope, this is Jamison and Walter. I'd tell you they are old pros but they don't like to be reminded of their advanced years," Edna teased.

"Speak for yourself, lady," Walter quipped. "I'm young at heart and intend to stay that way."

"Good luck, honey," she whispered to Cope. "If you need anything, let me know. And... I'll see you when you're done here."

The teen didn't meet Edna's eyes when he nodded. "Yes, ma'am. Thanks."

Cope finally met his gaze as Edna walked away. "I'm pretty sure I know what to do," he said.

"I'm sure you do," Walter answered, easily taking the lead. "You look like a capable sort."

When Cope's lips twitched, like he was fighting back a real smile, Jamison had to fight back a smile of his own. Edna had been smart to pair the kid with Walter and him. Walter could set the most anxious person at ease. He'd seen it a number of times.

"You got any helpful hints for Cope here, Jamison?"

"Only that the instructions are on this laminated

sheet here. You might want to double-check the measurements if you want your bread to rise."

The boy's shoulders visibly eased. "Will do." He swallowed. "I gotta go wash up and put on an apron."

Walter nodded. "Best go do that, then."

As Cope left them, Walter glanced his way. "Have you seen him in here before?"

"No. You?"

Walter nodded. "Once. About two or three months ago. Poor kiddo looked so awkward a part of me wanted to simply hand him a loaf of bread, give him the twenty bucks in my wallet, and tell him to grab his food and go."

"I'm guessing you didn't?"

"I didn't dare. Edna would have had my hide." Still keeping his eyes on Cope, who was now tying an apron around his waist, Walter said, "It was a good thing I didn't, too. By the time the boy left, he was holding that loaf of bread like it was a trophy. He was pleased with himself."

"I've felt the same way," he said as he started organizing the containers of flour, sugar and salt on the table.

"I forgot how hard these gloves were to get on your hands," Cope said when he returned.

"Yeah. I've teased Edna that she needs to get some gloves in larger sizes," Jamison said. "It's not only women who volunteer around here."

Cope's hazel eyes flickered with appreciation. "What did she say?"

Walter cackled. "I don't know what she told Jamison here, but last time I complained, she told me to get to work."

When Cope chuckled, Jamison was once again thankful that Walter had decided to volunteer today. He was exactly who the boy needed in order to stop feeling so stressed out.

Satisfied that he and Walter had done as much as they could without making Cope uncomfortable, Jamison said, "I guess we'd better get started."

Cope nodded, then mirrored his movements as they each grabbed a stainless steel bowl, the yeast, measuring cups, and got started.

As the minutes passed and Jamison began to stir, then knead the ingredients together, his spirits lifted. Sure, things in his personal life weren't good, but at least he wasn't sitting inside his house staring at a television screen. He'd gotten out, connected with Walter, and maybe even was helping a teenager feel like his day wasn't horrible even though he'd come to a food bank for a helping hand.

By the time he left, he was sure he might even be able to not think about Chloe Winner for almost half a day.

CHAPTER TWENTY-SIX

"Thanks for coming with me," Chloe said as she pulled her vehicle into the Loaves of Love parking lot. "I know this place might feel like a sore subject, but I promise I don't have an ulterior motive."

Madison almost had to bite her lip to stop from laughing at her aunt's earnest expression. Chloe was nothing if not sincere. No way would she try to make Madison do something that had a hidden agenda. That wasn't her. "I didn't think you did."

Chloe flashed a smile. "Good." Pausing before she opened her door, she added, "When Edna called to say that she'd had a big number of first-time clients, some who were too embarrassed to want to bake bread, I knew I wanted to help out a couple of more hours than usual."

"I'm glad to have something to do." Since she was practically on house arrest.

Chloe shot her a sympathetic look. "I'm really sorry about your parents grounding you."

She was, too. "I bet you're also really sorry that you have to be the one who's having to supervise me." Like she was a little kid.

"Well…a little bit." She looked sheepish.

Some of the hurt that Madison had been carrying around like old baggage eased. Seeing that sympathetic expression on her aunt's face was everything! "I knew it. I should have told my mom that she couldn't do this to you. Or me. It's…it's just *wrong*."

"I can't say that I think it makes perfect sense, but I also think that we both know it's smarter to pick our battles. At least you're here."

"That is true." If they'd canceled her plane ticket home, it would've been horrible.

"Your parents are at a loss about what to do with you."

"I know." She'd messed up their perfect plans by being imperfect. Okay, that might not be exactly how it was, but she was really angry right now.

"You know what? Let's stop worrying about you and go bake some bread."

"I'd like that." She shared a knowing glance with Chloe. Her aunt was exactly right. She needed to stop moping around and think about something else for a while.

Stepping out into the parking lot, she shivered. The weather had gotten a lot colder during the day. To make matters worse, it was as cloudy and gray as it northern Ohio could ever be in the winter. "I wish it was spring."

"You and half of the Midwest. But instead, we have Christmas to think about."

"Ho, ho, ho."

"I'm going to call you Grinch if you aren't careful," Chloe teased as she led the way up the sidewalk and then pulled open the large wooden door into the remodeled building.

"Chloe, you did make it." A lady with gray hair and bright eyes called out.

"Of course I did. And I even did one better. I brought Madison again."

"Welcome back, Madison. We appreciate your help."

"Thank you. I'm excited about baking bread again."

"Usually I'd show you around and remind you how to get set up, but you're in good hands with Chloe. Have a good time."

"Thanks."

"Let's put our things away, wash our hands, and get on our aprons and hairnets," Chloe said as she ushered her to one of the sides. "I'm glad you don't mind pulling your hair into a bun."

"I think I wear it this way half the time. It's no big deal." She thought it was funny that Chloe thought she'd care about what her hair looked like. She couldn't care less. For the next couple of minutes, she followed Chloe's directions, washing her hands really well, tying on the apron, arranging the hairnet on top of her messy bun.

"Now, let's take our canisters of flour, salt and tins of yeast to my favorite workstation."

"You have a favorite workspace?"

"I know. It's silly, but I'm a creature of habit."

Madison chuckled as she followed Chloe to her spot, glancing around the room as they walked, trying to guess about how many volunteers were in the space.

And then she just about had a heart attack. Because right there, in the table next to where Chloe was heading was Cope Swartz. She couldn't believe it. "Chloe, Cope's here."

"Really?" She glanced his way. "Oh! He's working with Jamison."

"I can't believe they know each other."

"I didn't know they did," Chloe said. When she looked back at Madison, her aunt's expression seemed a little closed, like she was keeping something important to herself. "Well, isn't that something?"

"Yeah." After putting her flour container down, she said, "I'm going to say hi."

"All right." Chloe wasn't wearing her usual, easygoing expression, though. Instead she looked a little worried.

Madison was tempted to ask her about it, then realized that she already knew the reason behind her awkwardness. Jamison. Of course Chloe was going to be upset to be around him. "I promise, I'll get right to work in a minute."

"I know you will."

There it was again. A thread of worry in her

words. Pushing away her confusion, she walked over to Cope. He, too, didn't look all that excited that they were all at the same place.

"Hi, Madison!" Jamison said. "It's good to see you."

"You, too." Turning to Cope, she smiled big. "Hey, I can't believe you're here. You should have told me you were going to do this."

Cope scanned her face as he straightened. "I, uh, wasn't sure that I would be. What are you doing here?"

She rolled her eyes. "Ah, helping out at the food bank. What else?" Without giving him a chance to speak, she leaned closer to him. "You are full of surprises, Cope," she teased. "What else have you been keeping a secret?"

"Nothing. And this…it's not really a secret."

He wasn't looking at her, though. His focus was on the dough he'd just rolled into a ball.

What was going on with him?

"If you'd told me you were going to be here today, we could've come together."

"Like I said, it wasn't really planned."

"Oh. Yeah, I didn't really plan on doing this, either, but since I have to be stuck like glue to Chloe's side, I figured I might as well come."

"Ah."

"Even though I don't need to earn any more community hours for graduation, I still like making bread. Why are you here?"

"What do you mean?" His voice was hard.

It took her aback, but she pushed away the awkwardness. "You're not here trying to get community service hours, are you?" Suddenly realizing how callous she sounded, Madison added, "Oh. Do you already volunteer here a lot and I didn't know about it?"

"We should talk about it later."

"Oh. Okay." She stood there. Waiting for him to tell her when he was going to call.

"Madison, it's time to get started," Chloe called out.

"Just a minute." Turning back to him, she smiled. "Want to do something afterward? We could go get a coffee or something. I bet Chloe wouldn't tell my parents anything."

To her surprise, Cope looked even more uncomfortable. "Sorry, but I can't."

"Oh. Why? Or, are you with your dad?" She looked around the room. "Is he here, too?"

"I'm here on my own but I'm going to have to leave soon. And I can't talk now. I've got to get this done."

He was shutting her out. Closing her down and she wasn't even sure what she'd done or what had changed. "All right."

"Madison, now," Chloe said.

"Sorry, I guess I've got to go."

"Yeah. Like I said, now's not a good time to talk."

She noticed then that the couple standing at the next table over were glancing his way with sympathetic expressions. Jamison looked like he felt bad for Cope, too. It was obvious even to them that he didn't want to talk to her.

What had she done? It was like he was breaking up with her while she was attempting to rearrange her whole life so she could be with him.

She felt completely crushed.

Swallowing hard, she walked to Chloe. "Sorry."

"Go put on your apron and wash your hands again. It's time to get busy. This isn't your social hour."

Now Chloe was sounding just like her mother. And for what? Because she didn't like how Cope looked? Or because she didn't want Madison to talk to anyone while she was here?

Hurt and frustration settled inside of her. Disappointment and loss, the two emotions that seemed to have taken the most room in her belly stepped aside so she could fight tears and a temper tantrum at the same time.

When she returned to Chloe's side, she smiled at the woman standing across from her. "What should I do first?"

"The instructions for making the dough are right in front of you, honey. Work on dissolving the yeast first."

"Yes, ma'am." She might not be the person Cope wanted to spend time with but she wasn't going to argue. After reading the recipe all the way through, she got to work, silently following each direction step by step.

Beside her, Chloe was doing the same, though her movements were smooth and easy. It was obvious that she'd made this dough many, many times before.

As the minutes passed and some of her awkwardness faded, the tension between her and her aunt slowly dissipated.

Chloe introduced her to Sean and Kayla, who stopped by to say hello. Then she and Wendy, the other lady at their station, started talking about favorite Christmas movies. Wendy mentioned all sorts of old favorites that her grandmother liked. It wasn't until Madison had shared that she was still most partial to *Rudolph* that she realized that Chloe had put them on a common ground. She'd found a topic that was stress-free and with an even playing field. In between movie mentions, Wendy and Chloe took turns with hints and advice about kneading and resting dough.

None of them talked about jobs or school or anything that she usually discussed with adults. After thirty minutes passed, she felt more relaxed than she had in days.

Now she understood why Chloe liked volunteering there so much. Eventually Wendy left. Then Chloe took her two loaves to the back. When she finally placed her dough in the two bread pans, she looked over her shoulder. Just to see if Cope looked any happier to see her.

But he was gone. He'd left without telling her goodbye. She couldn't believe it.

Her spirits sank.

Chloe returned to her side. "All you have to do now is walk your bread pans to the back of the kitchens. There, they'll rise again and then go into the oven. I'll start cleaning up."

"Okay."

"Hey, I'm sorry I snapped at you earlier."

"That wasn't your fault. You were right. Besides, Cope didn't want to talk to me. I don't know why."

Chloe's expression shuttered, like she knew something that Madison didn't.

She wondered what that could be, then pushed that worry away.

After all, her aunt barely knew Cope. What could she possibly know about him that Madison didn't?

CHAPTER TWENTY-SEVEN

It was impossible not to notice that Madison was upset about how Cope had treated her at Loaves of Love. Unfortunately, Chloe didn't know how to help ease her mind. Just as Madison had worn her heart on her sleeve, she'd realized that Cope was guarding his like a Doberman.

Chloe couldn't read minds, but she could usually read people, and everything about his embarrassment and guarded expression screamed that he'd never wanted Madison to discover that he was working at Loaves of Love today. He didn't want her to think less of him because he wasn't making bread to gain community service hours. He was making bread because he'd come there for food. But even though it was obvious to her, Kayla and Sean a couple of workstations over, and likely to Jamison as well, there was no way Chloe would ever tell Madison. Cope's business was his to share.

That didn't make it any easier to watch how heartbroken Madison was by his less-than-welcoming demeanor.

The girl did do her best to pretend it didn't bother

her, however. She followed the directions on her recipe card, talked to everyone around her and generally continued to be the kind of young woman her parents should be proud of.

But as the minutes passed, some of Maddie's smile dimmed. When the teenager had excused herself before scurrying off to the bathroom, Chloe had wiped down both of their stations. She needed something to do besides wonder about what she should say to her.

"Oh, no," she murmured to herself.

Kayla shot her a sympathetic smile.

Even before they'd gotten together for the gift baskets, Chloe had gotten to know Kayla over the last year. She knew that before she was married to Sean, she'd fallen into some financial difficulty and had walked through the doors the first time because she'd been hungry.

Though Kayla hadn't made a big deal about her past, the brave way she'd discussed it had stayed with Chloe. The woman had been embarrassed but desperate. Two things that, when combined, had made her vulnerable.

The way Cope was probably feeling.

When ten minutes passed and Madison still hadn't returned, Chloe picked up her bag and decided to wait for her near the reception table.

"You okay?" Jamison asked when he was on his way out.

"Yeah." As usual, the pull she felt toward him

was front and center. But as much as she wished she could let him know what was going on, she couldn't talk about it.

"I saw Madison run out of the room. Is there anything I can do?"

"I wish there was, but I'm afraid there isn't." Meeting his gaze, she hoped he understood everything she wasn't saying. "Do you mind if I call you later?"

His expression softened. "That's more than fine."

Then, to her surprise, he leaned close and pressed his lips to her brow. "Try not to worry. Everything will be okay."

Unable to help herself, she lifted her arms to hug him. Jamison wrapped his arms around her and held her for a moment. His heat and his scent immediately enveloped her. Easing her worries while sparking the attraction that was always between them. For a brief second, she almost forgot where they were.

After he left, she looked through the windows, hoping to see Madison walking toward her, but after another moment, Chloe turned back around.

Seeing Edna approach was a relief. Hopefully she'd be able to provide some much-needed distraction.

"Thanks again for coming in. Are you all done?"

Chloe nodded. "I'm waiting for Madison and then we'll head out. She's in the restroom."

"Where's your bread?"

"Oh, my gosh. I forgot it."

"I noticed your cute niece working hard in there. Make sure she gets her loaf, too."

"I'll tell Madison, but I'm not sure if we'll need two loaves of bread. I know you were getting low."

"We were, but my callout worked wonders. Not only did we get tons of volunteers, but I received some generous donations. We're stocked up again."

"That's great news."

Edna grinned. "I agree. It's sure going to make a lot of difference in a lot of people's lives." She took a breath. "Anyway, that's why I'm encouraging you both to get your loaves. Madison can always freeze her loaf if she wants. A lot of people do that."

"I'll ask when she comes out." Eyeing the closed bathroom door with worry, she blurted, "Did you happen to see her back there? I thought she was in the restroom...but maybe she's wandering around."

"I did see her, but we didn't speak. I assumed she was either heading to the bathroom or heading out to the parking lot."

"How did she look?"

A line formed between her brows. "What do you mean?"

"I just wondered if she was crying."

Immediately Edna's expression sharpened. "What happened? Did she get hurt or something?"

"Oh, no. Nothing like that." After taking yet another glance at the door, she blurted, "It's none of my business, but I'm afraid that the boy she's been seeing was also making a loaf of bread. She didn't understand why he wasn't thrilled to talk to her."

"Ah." Sympathy filled her expression. "I did happen to notice a certain handsome teenager leave here with a crushed look. I wondered what had happened."

Well, that told her everything she needed to know. She didn't want to share Cope's secret but she also wanted to find a way to encourage Madison to not be too upset with him. "Any suggestions on how to handle this?"

"I'm sorry, no."

"I was afraid of that."

Edna sighed. "Chloe, I don't know if this will help, but perhaps you might want to consider whose pain might get greater if you say too much."

She had a good point. Madison might be feeling ignored or even a little heartbroken, but if Chloe told her the real reason he'd given her the cold shoulder, then his trust in Loaves of Love would be compromised. He might not return, and if he didn't, then that would have a great many damaging consequences for him. And, perhaps, whomever he lived with.

"Here she is," Edna said. "Good luck and…try not to worry too much. If there's one thing I learned from raising my kids, it's that you can't make every hard decision or situation easier. Sometimes it's out of your hands." She paused. "Which is probably a good thing."

"You're right. Thanks for that." Turning to Madison, whose eyes were slightly red, Chloe smiled brightly.

"Here I am. Sorry it took me so long."

Though it was on the tip of her tongue to ask Madison if she was okay, she didn't dare. It was obvious the girl wasn't. "Edna and I were just chatting and she reminded me that we didn't get our loaves of bread."

"Oh. I didn't come here for a loaf. I'm okay."

"I said that, too, but she reminded me that we could freeze one at the very least. Let's go in and get one loaf."

"All right."

When they walked in, Madison was staring at the ground, like she was afraid to spy someone else she might know. It was the complete opposite of the cheerleader's usual confident, sunny expression.

"The finished loaves are over here," she said in a soft voice. When they reached a stainless steel cart filled with about three dozen loaves of bread, each one neatly encased in a plastic bag and secured with a twist tie, she said, "Go ahead and pick one, Maddie."

"They all look the same."

"I guess they do."

Madison reached out, obviously intending to grab one, but paused and stared at the collection. Then she carefully reached for one. "This one."

"Great. Thanks, Wayne," Chloe said to Edna's

husband, who happened to be the volunteer in charge of watching the oven timers and removing the finished loaves from the oven, and then eventually taking them out of the pans. Yet another volunteer washed and dried the bread pans and then placed them with all the other cooking supplies.

By the time they got to the car, Madison seemed calmer, but she was looking at her phone a lot. Though that wasn't a rarity, Chloe knew that she was hoping to hear from Cope.

It was time to say something. Not to divulge Cope's secret, but to help Madison remember that she wasn't alone. "I'm sorry you're upset," she said as she backed out of her parking space.

"I guess that's pretty obvious, huh?"

"A little bit." Okay, it had been more than obvious to probably everyone in that kitchen, but Madison didn't need to know that.

"I don't know what was up with Cope. Didn't you think he was being weird?"

"You know I don't know him."

"But come on. You know men. I mean, you're best friends with Jamison and you dated Adam for months."

She couldn't ignore the way Madison had said "Adam." He was definitely on the outs in her book. "Maddie, Adam isn't a bad person, he just wasn't the right one for me."

"I guess not. You sure liked him, though."

"I did. But that's why we were dating. It takes

time for a relationship to mature. Sometimes you discover that they aren't the right person for you… and sometimes you realize that they are." Like Jamison.

"That's how I felt about Cope." Looking even more torn up, Madison added, "I thought he was perfect for me. But maybe he isn't. Maybe I just wanted him to like me."

"I think you are blowing things out of proportion. People can have bad days, Maddie."

"I get that, but this was different. No, he was different. I'm certain." Folding her arms over her chest, Madison studied her face. "Aunt Chloe, did you really not think he was hiding something?"

She did. She was pretty sure poor Cope wanted to hide his situation so much that he'd rather Madison think he was a jerk than in the kitchen because he was hungry.

But sharing that wasn't going to do either of them any good.

"I don't think it matters what I think," she said. "You need to call him."

Her blue eyes widened. "And say what?"

"Tell him what you just told me." She waved a hand. "But, you know, in a nicer way."

Madison literally leaned backward, like she really needed to get away from those words. "I can't do that. He would hate me."

"He's not going to hate you, honey."

"He's not going to be happy if I push him to explain himself."

"All right. Then don't do that, either. Don't push Cope into talking about something he doesn't want to talk about. Just chalk it up to him having a bad day and move on."

"I can't." She lowered her voice. "It sounds stupid, but I think whatever he didn't want to talk about was important." She pressed her hand to the middle of her chest. "It's like I can feel it in my heart."

"Then it sounds like you made up your mind."

"But what if he gets mad?" As Chloe pulled into the garage, Madison's voice cracked. "I don't know what to do and I can't ask my mom. Why won't you help me?"

Chloe was starting to realize that Rhonda might be controlling, but she was also tougher than she'd ever imagined. This parenting thing wasn't easy. It was about a whole lot more than being a good friend. She exhaled. "Let's move inside to talk."

"No." Looking increasingly frustrated, Madison shook her head. "If we wait, you're going to put me off. Just tell me what you think."

She closed her eyes, prayed for the right words to pop into her head, and then said, "Okay, I think you should think about this. There might be things going on with Cope that you have no idea about. You might think his attitude had everything to do with you, but maybe it had more to do with some other things going in his life. Something that he's embarrassed about or doesn't feel comfortable sharing."

"Like what?"

"Maddie, I don't know. But I do know that pretty much every person you meet is either dealing with something hard, or has dealt with something in the past. But they hide it."

"Maybe."

"Maybe? Madison, darling, look at you. Everyone who only knows you slightly only sees a pretty blonde girl with a great figure and a fun personality. They see a cheerleader and think you must be popular. Other people might have classes with you and see that you make good grades and imagine that you never have to study. Others might know that you're doing volunteer jobs because you are trying to get into fancy, exclusive and expensive colleges."

Her blue eyes clouded. "That's not fair."

"You're right. It's not. Because they don't know the whole story. They have no idea that your parents moved, that you aren't very happy about it and that you are still struggling with what to do about your future."

"I guess that's true," she whispered.

"What I'm trying to tell you is that you aren't the only person putting on a good face." Chloe swallowed hard, hoping and praying she hadn't just said too much.

"Do you think Cope is hiding something he doesn't want me to know?"

"All I'm saying is that maybe you shouldn't be too hard on him until you know why he acted that way."

Little by little, some of the tension faded from her expression. "Thanks."

"Of course. I hope I helped."

"You did." She smiled as a hint of humor lit her eyes. "Can I return the favor?"

"About what?"

"About reminding you that not everybody you're hanging out with should just be a friend."

"I have no idea what you're talking about."

"I just don't think that Adam is the only guy you know who thinks you're pretty awesome."

"Someone else thinks I'm pretty awesome?" She teased.

"Yep."

Chloe grinned. "And who might that be?"

"You know."

"Are you talking about Jamison?"

Madison smiled as she got out of the car. "You said his name. Not me."

"Wait! Don't just leave me sitting here."

"Sorry, but I can't do that. I've got a lot to do before I visit Cope."

"You're going to go to his house?" She couldn't help that her voice sounded as hesitant as she felt. It was times like this when she realized that she was in way over her head. Part of her wanted to celebrate that Madison believed in Cope enough to risk his anger. The other part of her felt that she should be saying something wise and wonderful to Madison. Tell her how patience was a good thing and that she shouldn't push another person to share something that they weren't comfortable discussing.

She'd never imagined that she'd have to deal with such emotional, tough life lessons when she'd agreed to let Madison live with her for a year.

Oblivious to everything that had been going on in her head, Madison nodded. "Yep. I listened to everything you said and realized that if I want to know the real Cope, then I need to go see him at his house." She held out her hand. "Oops. I can borrow your car, right?"

"Of course." Chloe handed over her car keys.

"Thanks."

"Please, be careful." And she wasn't just talking about driving. She was talking about her words and Cope's feelings.

"I will." Madison smiled before walking out the door.

Watching her leave, Chloe felt a burst of emotion well inside of her. She was proud of the girl. She was going after something she wanted. It might not be the wisest course of action, but her heart was in the right place.

That said, Chloe was worried about Madison,

too. Everything about her, from her tone of voice to the way she was striding toward the door, was full of confidence and hope.

Five minutes later, as she stood at the window to watch Madison drive down the street, Chloe leaned her head back with a sigh. What had she done?

Just as importantly, she wondered when she was ever going to get brave enough to go after what her heart wanted. She was pretty sure that was Jamison.

The only problem: she had no idea how to go about telling him her feelings.

Huh. Maybe she should have been the one driving to a boy's house. Since she'd given Maddie her vehicle, that wasn't possible. It looked like now the only thing she was going to be able to do was sit around and wait.

Walking toward the kitchen, she decided to put on the kettle, make some hot tea, turn on her Christmas tree lights and watch old holiday movies until Maddie returned.

It was probably going to be a while.

CHAPTER TWENTY-EIGHT

JUST AS SHE parked the car on the street in front of Cope's house, Madison fought off a wave of dizziness. Honestly, she was pretty sure she was about to throw up.

Unfortunately, it wasn't the first time this had happened. Back when she was in sixth grade, she'd had a difficult pair of teachers. They'd been demanding and loud. She'd been half-afraid of them. And, because of that, she'd started having trouble sleeping, then eventually had begun to experience true anxiety. Eventually, her parents had not only had to have multiple meetings with the teachers and administrators, but Madison had to see a therapist.

"You are about to get a panic attack," she said to the empty car. "Stop visualizing the worst of what could happen and start concentrating on the best. Think about what you have control over."

Breathing deeply, Madison imagined Cope smiling at her. Pulling her into his arms when she asked about the real reason he'd been at Loaves of Love.

As wonderful as that vision was, she had to laugh. No way was Cope going to be happy to see her. But even if he was going to get mad at her, there was no way she was going to stay away. She really liked him.

She loved him so much that she wanted to be his girlfriend. She wanted to go to college near him. She needed him in her life. And that was why she knew that she had to get out of the car and knock on his door.

"You can do this," she said.

Feeling a little bit better, Madison stepped out of Chloe's car, then reached in the back and got out the box of cookies from the Blue Door Café. She'd stopped by to get a coffee, then on impulse bought a dozen Christmas cookies, too. It felt too weird to come over empty-handed.

Now she was feeling like the weird one. She was eighteen years old, not some church lady paying a social call. But, just like her visit, Madison couldn't seem to get herself to backtrack.

For about the hundredth time, Madison wished she could have asked her mom for advice. Her mother would've told her what to bring—or what not to bring. She could've even told Madison how to bake some cookies herself. Chloe might be able to make bread, but she wasn't very handy in the kitchen.

Oh, well. There was a pretty good chance that Cope wouldn't even see them, anyway. He'd answered her text when she'd asked what he was doing, but nothing about his reply had seemed very warm or nice.

When a pair of boys rode by on their bicycles, staring at her as they passed, Madison knew that she needed to start walking. Grabbing her purse, she clicked the lock on Chloe's car, crossed the street and went up the front walkway. Then, before she lost her nerve, she rang the doorbell.

The door was pulled open after barely a second. Madison braced herself.

But Cope wasn't facing her. Instead, it was a tall, thin man with a haggard expression.

He stared at the bakery box for a good fifteen seconds before lifting his head. "Yeah?"

Her palms started to sweat. "Mr. Swartz?"

"That's me. What do you want?"

This was getting worse and worse. "I'm sorry. Are you Cope's dad?" When he continued to glare at her, she took a step backward. Looked to the right and left. "Or, um, do I have the wrong house?"

"What do you want with Cope?" His eyes narrowed. "Are you from some do-gooder organization or something? Is that why you're bringing me food?"

Every word had been drenched with disdain. "No. My name is Madison." Hoping her name might ring a bell, she attempted to smile.

He didn't.

Realizing that her worst-case scenario vision

hadn't been near bad enough, she said, "I'm a... I'm a friend of Cope's."

His eyes narrowed.

Feeling more awkward with every second, she added, "Is he home?"

"Yeah. Yeah. Come on in."

Before she had time to close the door behind her, Mr. Swartz was yelling down into the basement. "Copeland, get up here!"

"Why?"

"Because someone's here to see you."

"Who?"

"It's a girl. Madison."

When Mr. Swartz turned back to face her, he still wasn't smiling. But he didn't look as angry. But maybe that was her imagination?

When she didn't hear any footsteps on the stairs, she began to wonder how she could continually make straight As in school but be a total idiot where Cope was concerned.

This man was acting like she was an imposition, and she probably was.

He also didn't look like any father she'd ever met. He looked ragged and exhausted. He smelled of cigarettes, too.

As the silence stretched, she began to realize that everything in the house looked tired. Not dirty, or like it needed a good washing. No, it was more like even the faded curtains on the windows were desperate for a breath of fresh air. Seeing the filled ashtray, she figured that had something to do with it.

After a couple of seconds, she heard footsteps on the stairs. Nerves got ahold of her as the enormity of what she'd done settled in.

Suddenly, the worst thing wasn't going to be that this wasn't Cope's house, it was that it was, and he was going to hate her for being there.

And then, there he was. He was still wearing the same thing he'd worn at Loaves of Love. A pair of faded jeans and an untucked long-sleeved T-shirt. His hair looked like he'd just ran his hand through the strands in an attempt to comb it.

It didn't work.

"Madison, what are you doing here?"

Neither Cope's voice nor his expression said that he was glad to see her. He looked pissed.

She should've been prepared for that.

"The girl brought you cookies, son."

"Yeah." He didn't look all that pleased about it, either.

Feeling even more awkward, she thrust the bakery box toward him. "I was at the Blue Door getting a coffee and thought you might like some cookies."

Which was probably the stupidest thing to say. Ever.

Cope didn't reach for them. Instead, his head tilted slightly to one side, like he was trying to figure her out. "How did you get here?"

"I borrowed Chloe's car."

"How come you brought me food?"

Avoiding Mr. Swartz's gaze, she shrugged. "I don't know. I, um, didn't want to come over without bringing anything."

"Why?"

Feeling more stupid, she shrugged again. Why had she not thought this through?

"Copeland, give that poor girl a break and invite her in," his father barked. "She's been standing on that same spot for five minutes looking like she was about to get kicked out for soliciting."

A pained expression crossed his face. "Dad, don't say stuff like that."

"I'm only speaking the truth."

"She doesn't look like she's soliciting."

"Well, she doesn't look like she's coming over to see her friend. Worse, you aren't treating her like one."

"Dad, don't start telling me how to treat a friend."

As she listened to the two of them, the complete awkwardness of the whole situation hit her hard and she started giggling.

Cope looked her way. "Are you...laughing?"

"I'm sorry." She attempted to cover her mouth with her palm, but to be honest, it was only a half-hearted effort.

He stepped closer. "What's so funny?"

His voice had lowered. It was sweet, too. Like he was desperate to make sure she wasn't getting ready to run out of there. "You and your dad bickering. Sorry. I'm not making fun of you. It was… well, it surprised me."

Finally, finally humor entered his gaze, too. "That makes two of us." Reaching for the box, he said, "Thanks for bringing us cookies."

"I hope they're okay."

For the first time since she'd shown up on his doorstep, warmth filled his eyes. "Me, too. Want to get out of here?"

"Okay. I mean, yes, if you want to. Or we can stay here."

"I don't want to stay here." After handing the box to his dad, he reached for his coat, which was hanging on a hook by the door. "I'll be back later, Dad."

"Yeah, all right."

"Bye, Mr. Swartz," Madison said. Sure, it was awkward, but she needed to say something.

"Bye, missy. Don't let my boy boss you around too much."

Smiling, she said, "I won't."

Cope reached out his hand. "Come on."

Sliding hers in his, she followed him out the door. Even though the weather was really cold, it felt soothing compared to the stale air in Cope's house.

Immediately, she felt awful for thinking such a thing. That was his home. Pasting a smile on her face, she said, "Where would you like to go?"

"I don't know. I only said that to get you out of there." Looking pained, he added, "But now that you dropped off that food, if you want to leave on your own, you can."

A lump formed in her throat. "You mean without you?" When he nodded, she shook her head. "Cope, I wanted to see you. When I saw you at Loaves of Love, I realized that you've been doing all the work. You are always the first to call. Or text. Or suggest we do something."

"So you decided to just show up at my house?"

"I didn't think you'd mind. Why do you mind? Did you not ever want me to come see you?"

He looked away. "Madison, let's not pretend my living room is anywhere that you want to be."

"It wasn't so bad. Your dad was nice."

"He's a lot of things. Nice ain't one of them."

"It's so cold, let's not just drive around." Remembering the money her dad had sent to her account, she added, "Let's go out for pizza. My treat."

"You don't need to buy me food. Or bring me any."

She knew he was still thinking about her seeing him at Loaves of Love. Even though she had a bunch of questions about that, there was no way she was going to say a word about that. "If you don't want to get pizza, we can go somewhere else. Your choice. I'm starving, though."

"All right. Pizza's fine."

Feeling like she could finally breathe again, she said, "Maybe after, we can drive around and look at all the Christmas lights."

"You want to do that?"

"Well, yeah." Liking that idea, she said, "We could even park downtown. They're supposed to have some food trucks there. They'll have people making hot chocolate and hot cider."

He smirked. "You're such a girl."

"I know. Does that bother you?"

"That the prettiest girl in the high school came over to my house and wants to hang out with me? Not one bit."

A warm feeling slid inside her. Wanting him to get on even ground, she pulled out her car keys. "Want to drive?"

"You don't mind?"

"Of course not."

As they got in, Cope adjusted the driver's seat, then spent a couple of minutes messing with the mirrors, too. Then he pulled onto the street and headed south. Toward Tony's Pizza Parlor.

It started to sleet, but since he didn't seem to care, she fussed with the radio until she found a station playing Christmas music.

Cope groaned. "Oh, man, you're going to make me listen to this stuff, too?"

"Yep. I'm going to put you into the Christmas spirit if it kills me, Cope." When he looked like he was going to scowl, Madison took a chance and placed a hand on his leg. "Relax, Cope. Everything's going to be okay."

When he looked at her, three things happened all

at once. The brakes on Chloe's car locked up, the light they were approaching turned red...and the truck to the right of them pulled out without looking in either direction.

Breathing in deep, Cope tried to pump the brakes as he hit the horn.

She screamed as the vehicles collided.

Seconds passed before she was fully aware that Cope was hurt, she was bleeding and sirens had surrounded them. Her last thought was that she hadn't imagined this worst-case scenario, either.

CHAPTER TWENTY-NINE

SHORTLY AFTER GETTING home from Loaves of Love, Jamison's brother, had called. They were back in town and had stopped by their mom's house so Bud could introduce Jenny to her.

Jamison had been floored. Not only because Bud was in Medina, but his brother hadn't asked him to be at their mother's house for the big introduction.

It was then that he'd realized that his brother was showing him that he might be younger, but he sure wasn't Jamison's "little brother" any longer. He was a grown man and didn't need his older brother smoothing things out for him any longer.

Jamison wasn't sure if he felt sad or dismayed by this realization. Maybe a little bit of both?

Luckily, there wasn't much time to dwell on that because after Bud had filled him in, he asked when Jamison could meet him and Jenny at the Oak and Barrel.

An hour later, the three of them were seated in a booth in the cozy, upscale restaurant on the edge of the town's square.

As Jamison had expected, Bud's fiancée was

adorable. Jenny had curly dark brown hair, freckles on her nose, and had studied education and dance in college. She wanted to be a ballet teacher one day, which Jamison could totally see. The young woman had an ethereal look about her that suggested she was both a talented and graceful ballerina.

But what mattered most to Jamison was that she had an infectious smile and it was always focused on Bud.

His younger brother looked so proud sitting next to Jenny. She now had a diamond ring on her hand, which was firmly clasped in his own.

As the two of them sat across from him at Oak and Barrel, he tried to figure out why Bud had not only changed his mind about introducing Jenny to their mother before Christmas and then had called to ask Jamison to meet them for dinner.

Bud had never been known to easily change his mind or to do things on the spur of the moment. He knew Bud well enough to know that something was on his mind, and that it probably had something to do with the ring. His younger brother had never been all that shy about telling Jamison what he wanted or needed. This hesitancy was new.

After the three of them had eaten cups of beef barley soup, been served their meals, and were almost through, Jamison began to get worried. Bud had already mentioned that he and Jenny had plans to see her family after dinner. Time was running out.

When Jamison spied Jenny raising her eyebrows

at Bud and even give him a little nudge, Jamison couldn't take it anymore. The suspense was killing him.

"Bud, what's going on?"

His brother swallowed. "What do you mean?"

"I mean that even though I like meeting you for dinner and I'm real glad that I got a chance to get to know Jenny better, I'm pretty sure that you've got something on your mind. Am I right?"

Bud looked down at his half-empty plate. "Yeah."

After taking a sip of water, Jamison leaned back. Waited.

"Bud, just say it," Jenny whispered.

"Okay, fine." He took a deep breath and blurted, "Jenny's pregnant, we're going to get married on Christmas Eve, and I want you to be my best man."

Pregnant. Wedding. Best man. Christmas Eve.

That was a lot. He wasn't sure what he thought Bud might share, but it wasn't that. "Wow," he said under his breath.

Bud scowled. "Wow? Wow? That's what you've got to say?"

"No. Of course not," he added quickly. "But, it's…it's a lot to take in, Bud."

"Take it in fast, J."

His brother's panicked expression finally shook some sense back into his head. Pulling himself together, he smiled at Jenny. "You're right." Standing up, he walked to the other side of the table. "Congratulations!" After Jenny and Bud climbed out of the booth, he hugged them both. "I'm so happy for you, honey," he said to Jenny. "I'm sure you're going to be a wonderful mother. And, Bud, it goes without saying that I think you're going to be a great dad. I'd be honored to be your best man."

"Yeah?" Bud almost squeaked.

"Yeah." Pulling him into another hug, he added quietly, "Dad would be really proud of you, Bud. I am, too."

Jenny's smile brightened as she curved a hand around Bud's arm. "See. I told you everything was going to be okay."

His brother's voice lowered as he leaned closer to his girl. "Yeah, I should've listened to you."

The moment was sweet. Jamison would've maybe even have felt like ordering a cake or something to celebrate…if a hundred questions hadn't been blaring in his head. "I now get why you went to see Mom."

"That was the reason," Bud said as they slid back into their side of the booth.

Turning to Jenny, he said gently, "And I'm guessing that you already told your parents, too?"

"We did," Jenny said. For the first time, her smile looked strained. "It, um, was a shock. A little yelling was involved. And tears."

"Oh, no."

"It was to be expected. But Bud told them that they needed to settle down so we wouldn't upset the baby." A dimple formed in her cheek. "That worked like a charm."

"What happened with Mom? Did she yell?"

Bud's expression was somber. "No. She didn't say much at all. Well, not much except that she was disappointed in me."

"I'm sorry." He supposed he shouldn't have hoped for anything different, but he was crushed for Bud.

"Me, too. But it's how she felt. And, I don't know. Maybe she's right to feel that way."

"Dad's been gone a long time. I know you don't remember him all that well. But he would be pleased that you found a woman like Jenny. I know that."

Bud didn't look too sure about that. "We didn't plan on this, of course…but we're excited."

"Me, too. What did Halley say?"

"She squealed and started calling herself 'Aunt Halley.'"

"I'm glad."

"My brother and sister were excited, too," Jenny said. "I mean, once they got over the shock of it."

"I bet everyone is going to have the same reaction. Anyone who sees the two of you together knows that you two are meant to be."

"I knew from the first moment I saw Bud that he was the man for me," Jenny said.

When it looked like Bud was about to start kissing his fiancée and getting syrupy, Jamison blurted,

"So, tell me about the wedding. It's on Christmas Eve?"

Jenny nodded happily. "It's going to be at our church. At four o'clock, but my pastor said he'd be happy to perform the ceremony...as long as I wouldn't mind the sanctuary being decorated for Christmas." Her smile turned blinding. "If we had planned for this for a year, I would still have wanted a Christmas wedding. Those would've been my colors anyway."

"Red and green?"

"No. Green and gold. With poinsettias, of course."

"Ah."

Bud leaned back in his chair. "It's useless to talk about wedding color schemes with Jamison, Jenny. If it doesn't have to do with a park or nature trail, he's clueless."

"I'm afraid that's true. If Chloe was here, she'd tell you the same thing."

"See, I told you that there was something between them," Jenny whispered to Bud.

Hearing the confidence in her tone took him off guard. "We're just friends," he said.

"Yeah, that's what you keep saying," Bud said.

As the waiter brought out slices of pie, Jamison made sure to keep the conversation on happy things. He didn't want to pepper them with questions. Though he sometimes felt like he had a hand in raising Bud, he wasn't his parent. Then, of course, he figured that they'd already been through a question-and-answer session with her parents, too.

Bud relaxed again.

By the time Jamison had asked for the bill and they'd tentatively mentioned a few dates for everyone to get together before the wedding, it was time for Bud and Jenny to go.

When Jenny excused herself to run to the ladies' room, Bud said, "Are you sure you don't want me to help you pay for dinner?"

"Of course not. I've got this."

"Thanks for being so cool about everything."

"You're welcome, but I'm really happy for you. And don't worry about Mom. I'll talk to her."

"It's okay. I don't know why I expected anything else."

"She loves you and she's proud of you."

"I know Mom loves me, but she's pretty upset," he said with a frown.

"She'll get over it. Especially when she starts thinking about how happy Dad would be." Reaching out, he gripped Bud's arm. "And I promise, he really would be excited and happy for you."

"Thanks," Bud said.

When Jenny returned, Jamison hugged them both and sent them on their way.

Then he couldn't believe it. Just as they were leaving, Chloe walked in. And of course, she stopped to chat with Bud and Jenny and pointed Jamison out.

He stood up again as she approached. And wondered what in the world he was going to do about her.

He had a feeling that everyone was exactly right when it came to his feelings for Chloe. They'd long since morphed into something far stronger than mere friendship.

After Bud and Jenny walked out the door, Jamison strode toward Chloe. "What's going on?"

"Nothing. I decided to splurge and pick up something from here to eat at home."

"Where's Madison? Waiting on you?"

"No, she went to see Cope."

"Oh."

"Yeah. I'm afraid she's going to push him to talk about being at Loaves of Love. If that happens, things aren't going to go well."

Jamison was afraid of the same thing. "That's a tough one. She might be tempted to never bring it up, but then it would be the elephant in the room."

Chloe's expression softened. "Exactly. I tried to give her a little bit of advice, but in the end, I felt like I had to keep my mouth shut."

"I would've done the same thing." After all, he'd kind of just done that with Bud.

Reaching out, she pressed her hand on his shoulder. "Thanks for saying that."

It seemed only natural to move her hand down a few inches until it was pressed over his heart. "Of course." Suddenly, all he could feel was the warmth of her hand over his heart. Her expression conveyed the same thing. Right there near the entrance to the restaurant. "Hey, what do you think about bringing your dinner over to my house?" he asked.

"That would be great." Looking sheepish, she added, "Madison needed my car to see Cope so I walked here. I really wasn't looking forward to walking back to my empty house."

Just as he was about to give her grief about walking such a long way in the cold at night, her phone rang.

She fished it out of her coat pocket. When she saw the screen, she frowned. "Hello?" she said hesitantly. "Yes. Yes, this is she. What? What? Oh my gosh." Tears filled her eyes. "Yes, I'll be right there. Thank you."

"Chloe, what happened?"

"That was University Hospital. Madison was involved in a car accident. She and Cope were hurt."

Pulling on his coat, he took her hand. "Let's go."

"You could just drop me off..."

If was obvious she was in shock. "Chloe, if you think I'd be anywhere else in the world but by your side, we're going to have to have a serious talk real soon."

She blinked. "You mean that."

"Absolutely. Where you go, I go. Now, come on," he said as he wrapped his arm around her shoulders and led her out the door. "We need to get on our way."

Chloe didn't say a word. All she did was lean into him.

That was enough. It told Jamison everything he needed to know.

CHAPTER THIRTY

SHE'D DONE SO many things that were wrong, she could barely count them all. Sitting next to Cope as he drifted in and out of consciousness, Madison carefully held his hand and tried to stop crying. Which was something pretty pathetic in itself. Her boyfriend was in the emergency room and she'd wrecked Chloe's car. But what was she doing? Crying as she heaped guilt on her shoulders. Like that was going to do a single thing to help Cope.

"How's he doing?" Cope's dad asked as he entered the room after stepping outside to use his cell phone. He'd arrived soon after the ambulance had brought them in. He'd talked to the doctors and nurses while she'd gotten seven stitches in her eyebrow. Later, he'd sat with her again while she was waiting to get one of her wrists x-rayed.

Somewhere along the way he'd told her to stop calling him Mr. Swartz. So, she was now calling him Lee.

Quickly swiping the tears with the side of her hand, she said, "I don't know. The nurse who came in said that he was doing better."

Lee walked to Cope's other side, his expression wary as he looked for signs of improvement. "What do you think, Maddie? Does it seem like he has a little more color in his cheeks?"

She shrugged as she sat down in the other chair. "I don't know." The truth was that she was afraid to have an opinion. She thought Cope seemed to have more color in his face, but maybe that was just the way the lights in the room were illuminated? No way did she want to give his father false hope.

He stared at her intently before exhaling. "Yeah, I don't know, either." Reaching out to Cope, Lee ran a hand along the blanket they'd put over his chest.

He looked so sad, her tears began to fall again. "Lee, I'm so sorry."

He shook his head. "You don't have a thing to apologize for. You weren't driving. Cope was." He shifted again. "It wasn't his fault, either, anyway. The cop I talked to said a truck pulled out too fast without looking. That, along with the sleet, and maybe your aunt's brakes? All that played a part. It was an accident."

"If I hadn't stopped by, he never would have left."

"Maybe not. I can't say that him staying home with me all afternoon would've been better for him. For some reason, Cope likes being with you a lot more than me."

She smiled at him. "I didn't know he talked about me."

"He didn't. Not too much, anyway." He swallowed. "But the truth is we don't talk about much of anything these days."

Watching Cope's chest rise and fall, she whispered, "I know what that's like."

"Oh, yeah?"

"Yeah. I haven't been getting along with my parents lately. We've been butting heads a lot."

"I reckon that's normal. I bet they're worried sick about you."

"They were, but they also said that I shouldn't have left Chloe's in this weather." Or let someone else drive her car.

Lee folded his arms across his chest. "I don't know your parents, but when Kate was alive and I was doing better, she and I sometimes wished we could make Cope a little boy again. It's not always easy to watch your kids grow up…especially when you know you're disappointing them."

His honesty, though not all that easy to hear, helped ease some of the tension inside her. "I told my parents that I resented them moving before I graduated."

"This is just me, but I figure you have a right to an opinion."

"Even if it's wrong?"

He chuckled. "Yep. Though I have to tell you, spouting your opinion isn't much easier when you're right."

"I guess not."

"Are they on their way out here?"

"I don't know. I told them I was fine, but I guess they'll decide what to do after they talk to Chloe."

"She's who you're living with?"

"Yeah. She's my aunt. She's my mother's younger sister."

"It'll be okay."

Returning her attention back to Cope, she sighed. "I hope so. I wish he'd open his eyes."

"Me, too."

Something about Lee's honesty got to her. She liked how he didn't try to say all kinds of stuff to make her feel better or tell her a bunch of stories because he couldn't take the silence. As the clock on the wall continued to tick and the machine hooked up to Cope continued to quietly beep, they sat together, both staring at him.

It was comforting to know that Lee was doing the same thing she was. Silently hoping and praying that Cope would open his eyes and be okay.

"Madison?"

She turned to see Chloe and Jamison at the door. Even though she didn't want to leave Cope's side, Madison knew that the nurse wasn't going to allow four visitors in the room.

"Hey," she said as she met them in the hall.

Chloe's eyes widened as she seemed to take in every drop of blood and speck of dirt on Madison's clothes. "Oh, honey. I'm so sorry we didn't get here earlier. How are you?"

She shrugged.

"How are you feeling, honey? I know the airbag deployed. Are you bruised and sore? Did a doctor check you out?"

"I've got some bruises from the seat belt and the airbag, but I'm okay." Belatedly she remembered her taped wrist and arm. "I might have broken something in my arm. The doctor's looking at the X-rays."

Chloe pointed to her forehead. "Looks like you got a cut, too."

"Yeah, but I got stitches. I'll be fine."

Her aunt looked even more worried. "Oh, honey. I'd hug you but I don't want to hurt you."

"I know. I... I'm not really up for a hug right now, anyway." All she wanted to do was go back and sit with Cope.

Jamison glanced into the room. "How's Cope?"

"He's asleep. Or unconscious." She blinked. "Can it be the same thing?"

Worry lines formed on Chloe's brow. "What did the doctor say?"

"Lee told me that they said that Cope had a bad cut on his head, which made him be asleep right now. I think he has some other things wrong, too. But no one wants to manhandle him too much until he regains consciousness."

"I'm glad you get to sit with him," Jamison said.

"Me, too."

Lowering her voice, Chloe asked, "How's Cope's dad?"

"His name is Lee. He's nice. I like him."

"May I go in and meet him?"

"Sure."

"I won't be a second, honey."

Madison watched her aunt walk to Lee's side before turning to Jamison. "Thank you for coming."

"No need to thank me. I'll tell you the same thing I told Chloe. There's nowhere else I'd rather be."

"We wrecked her car."

He rested a palm on the back of her neck. "She couldn't care less, Maddie. All Chloe has been thinking about is you and Cope."

For some reason, that made her want to start crying again. "She's been really good to me."

Jamison shrugged. "She loves you," he said simply.

"I love her, too."

"See, it's going to be okay."

Turning back to stare into Cope's room, she nodded.

"Here comes Chloe. Why don't you give her a hug and then you can go back in."

When Chloe walked to the doorway, Madison stepped into her arms. Immediately, Chloe carefully wrapped her arms around her. "You're right. Lee seems very nice. I'm glad." She smiled slightly. "Okay. Jamison and I are going to head back to the waiting room. We'll check back in about an hour."

"You don't have to stay."

"Yeah, honey. We do. We're not leaving without

you. And, I have a feeling that that guy in there is going to want to see your pretty smile whenever he decides to open his eyes."

"Thanks," she whispered.

When she walked back in, Lee was on his feet. "Cope? Cope, can you hear me?"

Madison hurried over. After looking at Lee's face real quick, she stared down at Cope. And saw the best sight in the whole world.

He was staring back at her. "Cope, you woke up!"

"We were getting worried about you, son," Lee murmured.

"Yeah." His voice was hoarse. "Maddie, are you okay?"

"I… I'm just fine."

"Sure?" It seemed like it was taking every bit of strength he had to scan her face.

Even though tears were sliding down her cheeks, she ignored them. Instead, she sat back down in her chair and reached for his hand. "I'm sure. I promise, me and your dad have been getting to know each other while we watched you sleep."

"You and my dad?"

Cope sounded so incredulous, Madison couldn't help but giggle.

To her surprise, Lee chuckled, too. "Looks like all kinds of miracles have been happening in this here hospital room, son. Wonders never cease."

"Yeah." Cope almost smiled.

As a pair of nurses hurried in and motioned for Madison and Lee to move out of their way, she realized that everything was going to be okay. It didn't matter where her parents lived or where she was going to college or that Cope and his dad were struggling. All that mattered right now was that everyone who mattered to her was okay.

That was enough. More than enough.

CHAPTER THIRTY-ONE

AFTER TWO HOURS of sitting with Chloe in the University Hospital waiting room, Jamison was ready to take her and Madison home. Chloe looked exhausted and Madison was wearing a dazed expression. Even though the teenager kept saying that she was fine and that Cope was the one to worry about, both Jamison and Chloe knew that she had to feel achy and sore from the accident.

At least they no longer had to worry about her having a broken arm or wrist. The X-rays showed that the bones were in good shape. The slight swelling was from a sprain. Pretty much every doctor and nurse had said the same thing that he'd been thinking—that Madison's injuries could have been far worse.

After touching base with the nurses and Lee one more time, Chloe had finally convinced Madison to leave Cope's room. Jamison was impressed. For a while there, the girl had been acting like she intended to sleep in the waiting room until she could see Cope again in the morning.

The minute he saw them head his way, he walked to their sides. "Ready?"

"We are." Chloe's voice sounded artificially bright. "Let's get out of here."

"My truck's out this way, Mad."

Maddie's jacket had been ruined in the accident so she had a hospital blanket wrapped around her. He'd offered to go back to Chloe's house to get something else, but Madison had repeatedly said she was fine and not to worry.

After they got in his truck, he blasted the heat and headed to Chloe's house. "Are you two hungry? I can go pick up something."

"Thanks, but actually... Edna called and said that she and Kayla got together and made us a meal," Chloe said. "She said it's already on the front porch in containers. All we'll have to do is heat it up when we get home."

"That's amazing."

"You're welcome to stay. I think it's a lasagna."

It sounded great but he didn't want to impose. "I'll catch you another time."

"Please stay, Jamison," Madison said. "I'm going to take a shower, eat a peanut butter sandwich and then collapse. You can keep Chloe company."

"You don't feel like eating lasagna?"

She shrugged. "Not really."

"Are you worried about Cope?" He'd heard that the doctor was only keeping him overnight as a precaution.

"Not really. I think it's all just catching up with me."

"That's understandable."

Twenty minutes later, Madison was in the shower, the lasagna was in the oven, and he and Chloe were sitting in front of the fire. Her Christmas tree's twinkling lights cast a pretty glow in the room and the pine-scented candle smelled a whole lot better than the hospital waiting room.

Wrapping his arm around her, he kissed her jaw. "Better?"

"Yes. Finally." She snuggled closer to him as she stretched her legs out in front of her. "I think I finally calmed my sister down."

"Is she still going to fly out?" At first, Rhonda had acted like she was going to get on the first flight available.

"She is, but I convinced her to wait at least a week. There's nothing Rhonda or Jerry can do. Plus, I honestly think that Rhonda swooping in and attempting to fuss over Maddie is going to backfire on her. Not only does Madison want to be by Cope's side as much as possible, she's still unhappy about them trying to ground her from four states away."

"I can't really blame her for that."

Smiling up at him, she said, "Me, neither."

As the minutes passed, Jamison debated the pros and cons about having their own "big" conversation. Maybe he should wait? But then, again, he felt like they'd waited long enough. "Hey, Chloe?"

She turned her head. "Yes?"

"I meant what I said before we left the restaurant. There was nowhere else I would have rather been than by your side today."

"I knew you meant it." Biting her bottom lip, she said, "Have I thanked you enough for everything?"

"Yeah, but that's not what I was getting at."

Chloe's pretty eyes widened but she thankfully didn't look shocked. "I know. You're talking about us."

"Yeah." He took a deep breath. "If there was a playbook for relationships, I'd pull it out and figure out what to do next, or how to say what I'm feeling, but there isn't."

"I don't want the 'right' words. I'd rather you just tell me."

"Okay." He dropped his arm from around her shoulders and shifted. Reached for both of her hands and linked their fingers. "For the last couple of months I've been trying to give you a little bit of space. I didn't want to hurt you and I didn't want to hurt Adam. But it wasn't easy…because I had fallen in love with you."

"And now?" Her breathing had quickened.

"And now, there's no 'falling' involved. It's official. I love you."

Chloe inhaled sharply. "You love me."

He picked up one of her hands, pressed his lips to her fingers. "I do. I'm completely, wholeheartedly, can't-go-back, don't-want-to-even-try in love with you." There. That sounded awkward as all get-out, but he didn't care. It was the truth.

Her eyes lit up and she grinned.

She was killing him. "Chloe, say something."

"I'm trying! It's just that I can't think of anything to say that's nearly as poetic."

He laughed. "Are you really critiquing me right now?"

"No." She giggled. "I loved it. I think it's the best speech ever."

"So you love the speech?"

"No, Jamison Smith. I love you."

Thank God. He reached for her face, pressed his hands against her cheeks, caressed her soft, flushed skin. And then finally, at long last, kissed her.

Chloe leaned into him. Wrapped her arms around his neck, and sighed as they kissed again. As he tried to show her how much he cared for her without words.

Holding her in his arms felt wonderful. Like she belonged there. And the way she was responding? Chloe was showing him that she felt the same way.

He could hardly believe it and didn't want it to end.

"Oops!"

Breaking apart, Jamison took a breath. "What was that?"

Chloe smiled. "That was Madison."

Turning, he saw the teenager standing just outside the living room. It was obvious she'd been on her way to the kitchen. "Sorry, Madison."

"Oh, don't mind me. I was just getting a glass of water. I can get that, and then sneak right back to my room. Carry on!"

Carry on? "Did she just say what I think she did?" he whispered.

"I think so," Chloe said around a giggle. "I guess I don't have to worry about her being upset about us finally getting together."

"I guess not." Unable to help himself, he reached out for the end of one of her curls and curved it around his finger. "So, what do you want to do now?"

"I want to do exactly what my very smart niece suggested." Reaching for him, she added, "Carry on, Jamison."

He was more than happy to comply.

EPILOGUE

THE CHURCH LOOKED gorgeous and smelled like Christmas. Jamison had never thought he was the type of person to care about such things, but even he could admit that Jenny, her family and the entire church staff had outdone themselves.

Bud and Jenny's wedding didn't look thrown together in the slightest. Along with all the greenery, white poinsettias graced the altar and pretty bouquets made of white roses, carnations and baby's breath tied with white satin ribbon were at the end of each pew. Finally, an arrangement of white candles illuminated the space. Chloe had gasped when she saw the sanctuary and whispered that the photographs were going to be incredible.

All Jamison cared about was that his brother and his bride were happy.

"You hanging in there?" Adam asked. "You good?"

"I'm better than good. Today's a great day."

"Yeah."

Jamison had a lot to be thankful for this Christmas Eve. Not only was Bud completely in love and getting married, but the tension between him and Adam had dissipated. They'd finally talked, and though it hadn't been easy, their honesty had cleared the air. Adam had shared that he felt betrayed by Jamison and Jamison had straight up told him that not only could he not help how he felt… but Chloe had a right to her feelings, too.

Time, and a new gal named Sherry, had seemed to do the trick. Adam was once again dating someone he was excited about, and everyone who'd met Sherry seemed to think the two of them were a good fit.

Usually Jamison would have given his buddy a ton of grief about getting serious about someone so soon. But, since Adam's new love interest meant he was no longer thinking about Chloe, he decided to call it a win.

"Adam?" the wedding planner called out. "We need you!"

"I gotta go."

"I know."

Adam, because he'd been like another big brother to Bud, was one of the couple's groomsmen. He was going to be escorting Halley down the aisle.

"Hey, Adam?"

"Yeah?"

"Look after Halley, would you?" Bud's twin had been teary-eyed all day.

Adam's expression softened. "Of course, J. Don't worry."

Finally relaxing, he folded his hands behind his back. Found Chloe sitting with his mom on the third pew. Jenny had asked if everyone coming to the wedding would wear something red, green or ivory.

Jamison had thought that was weird, until he realized that all of the women seemed pretty excited about it.

So, while he was wearing a black tuxedo with a red bow tie, Chloe was wearing a gorgeous red gown. She'd somehow managed to pull up most of her hair in some kind of twist. Jamison thought she always looked pretty, but tonight she seemed to glow.

Beside her, his mom was in an emerald green dress and was smiling, too. Two rows back, Madison was sitting with her completely recovered boyfriend, Cope. Cope had on a pair of black pants and a white shirt. Beside him, Madison was wearing a red lace dress.

"I can't wait for this to be over with," Bud said as he walked to his side.

"Why? What's wrong?" He'd thought everything had been going well.

"Nothing. It's just been a long day."

"You're just anxious to see Jenny."

"Well, yeah." Bud pulled on the collar of his shirt. "This tux is so uncomfortable."

"You look great. Stand still."

"Fine." He stuffed his hands in his pockets. "You got the rings, right?"

"I got them. Relax."

"Just wait until you're the one getting married. You're going to feel just as on edge when you're waiting to see Chloe walk down the aisle."

He grinned. "I bet you're right." He and Chloe needed a little more time dating before he got down on one knee, but Jamison was planning to propose before Valentine's Day. The truth was that he'd already felt like he'd waited an eternity for her. He couldn't wait until she was wearing his ring.

As music started to play, all thoughts of decorations and the future vanished as the pastor joined them and then the procession began. He could practically feel Bud's heart begin to pound as one of Jenny's sisters walked down the aisle with her escort. Then, just thirty seconds later, there was Halley and Adam. Halley was wearing a long, shimmery ivory dress. She also had tears of joy in her eyes as she exchanged a look with Bud.

And then, after two more bridesmaids came down the aisle, the music changed and Jenny appeared on her father's arm.

She was beaming and only had eyes for Bud.

Jamison got choked up as a thousand memories of his little brother filled his head. Bud chasing after him, hugging their black Lab, playing baseball. Skating for the hockey team. Constantly asking Jamison questions about school and girls and life.

"Who is giving Jenny away?" the pastor asked.

"Her mother and I," Jenny's father replied.

Jamison swallowed as Bud reached for Jenny's hand like he couldn't bear to not touch her.

It was sweet. It was love.

Jamison stood to the side, listened to the pastor's words. Held his breath as his brother said his vows. Fished in his pocket for the rings.

Clapped with everyone else when the pastor pronounced them man and wife.

Then, just seconds before Bud sailed down the aisle with Jenny, his brother looked back at him.

"Thanks," he whispered. "For everything."

"You're welcome," he whispered back, but he wasn't sure if Bud noticed. He and Jenny were kissing again and the whole congregation was on its feet. Clapping and cheering and teasing the newlyweds. Just how it should be.

Later, as everyone was posing for pictures before heading to Jenny's parents' house for the reception, Jamison finally was able to hold Chloe close.

"You looked good up there," she said after a lengthy kiss.

"Funny, I was thinking that you looked awfully good in the third row."

She smiled. "And here I didn't think you noticed."

"I noticed." He winked. "I could barely take my eyes off of you."

Chloe laughed, obviously thinking that he was

saying something over-the-top just to make her smile.

Jamison knew he'd spoken the truth, though. And...suddenly realized that he didn't want to wait to propose until the middle of February. "You know what? You look so pretty, it would be a shame for you not to wear that dress again."

"I agree, but there aren't a lot of places to wear a long, red, satin gown."

Making a decision, he said, "Maybe you could wear it again on New Year's Eve. People get dressed up then."

Her smile wavered as confusion filled her eyes. "I agree that that's a good time...but I thought we were going to hang out at my house instead of going out."

"We can still do that."

"So you want me to wear a fancy red dress while we sit on your couch for New Year's Eve?"

"Why not? I'll get some champagne."

She giggled. "Jamison Smith, you sound like you're up to something."

"I am." He looked at her intently. "Unless you think it's too soon to wear that dress?"

Slowly her smile faded as she seemed to understand that he wasn't talking only about her dress. After a few seconds, she seemed to gather herself. "No." She swallowed. "I mean, no, I don't think it's too soon at all."

Reaching for her hand, he kissed her knuckles. "I'm glad you feel the same way."

"Hey, J!" Halley called out. "Stop kissing Chloe and come over here. Bud wants a picture of the three of us together."

"Sorry, Chloe. I gotta go."

"I know. Go get that picture. I'm fine. I'll be waiting right here until you get back. I promise."

Her words rang in his head as he crossed the room to stand with Halley and Bud. As he stood next to his brother and sister, they laughed and joked. It was a perfect moment.

Glancing around the room, he spied their mother laughing with Jenny's parents. Noticed that Adam was holding Sherry's hand. Cope was helping Madison pull on her coat in the back of the room. So many of Bud's and Jenny's family and friends were still in attendance, lingering to watch the happy couple pose for pictures.

It was a good moment. No, it was a good day.

Jamison supposed it should be. After all, it was almost Christmas...and next year was sure to be even better. He was blessed.

SITTING IN THE far left back pew, Edna held Wayne's hand as she fought back a fresh wave of tears.

"You cry more at weddings than anyone I ever met," Wayne teased as he handed her a handkerchief.

"Oh, stop. I can't help it. I'm so happy for them."

Looking at the attractive couple posing for pictures, Wayne's expression softened. "Me, too. I know they're young, but I think Bud and Jenny are going to be just fine."

"Hmm?" She blinked as she realized that Wayne was talking about the bride and groom. "Oh, I agree. Bud and Jenny are going to have a long, happy life together. I am sure of it." Lowering her voice, she said, "I was actually thinking about Jamison and Chloe. I'm so happy they solved all their problems and are finally together. They were being so stubborn, I was starting to worry that might never happen."

As they watched Jamison join Bud and his sister Halley for a group shot, Wayne chuckled. "You're lucky that your meddling worked out."

"I wasn't meddling. All I did was give them a helping hand. Just like I did with Sean and Kayla."

"I hope your matchmaking days are done, though. There's no way you're going to be successful a third time."

Thinking of a certain dental receptionist named Kinsey, Edna smiled. "We'll see."

After carefully folding up Wayne's handkerchief, Edna slipped it into her pocketbook. "We better head over to the reception. I heard their cake is white chocolate with peppermint icing."

Taking her hand, Wayne guided her down the aisle toward the front door of the church. "Hey, look at that! It's snowing outside. Looks like we'll have a white Christmas after all."

Edna smiled in contentment. A wedding, good cake, and fresh snow all on Christmas Eve? It was no wonder everyone said it was the most magical time of the year.

* * * * *

Be sure to look for Shelley Shepard Gray's next book in her A Matchmaker Knows Best series, available in April 2026 wherever Harlequin Heartwarming titles are sold!

Get up to 4 Free Books!

We'll send you 2 free books from each series you try PLUS a free Mystery Gift.

FREE Value Over **$25**

Both the **Harlequin® Special Edition** and **Harlequin® Heartwarming™** series feature compelling novels filled with stories of love and strength where the bonds of friendship, family and community unite.

YES! Please send me 2 FREE novels from the Harlequin Special Edition or Harlequin Heartwarming series and my FREE Gift (gift is worth about $10 retail). After receiving them, if I don't wish to receive any more books, I can return the shipping statement marked "cancel." If I don't cancel, I will receive 6 brand-new Harlequin Special Edition books every month and be billed just $6.39 each in the U.S. or $7.19 each in Canada, or 4 brand-new Harlequin Heartwarming Larger-Print books every month and be billed just $7.19 each in the U.S. or $7.99 each in Canada, a savings of 20% off the cover price. It's quite a bargain! Shipping and handling is just 50¢ per book in the U.S. and $1.25 per book in Canada.* I understand that accepting the 2 free books and gift places me under no obligation to buy anything. I can always return a shipment and cancel at any time by calling the number below. The free books and gift are mine to keep no matter what I decide.

Choose one:
- ☐ **Harlequin Special Edition** (235/335 BPA G36Y)
- ☐ **Harlequin Heartwarming Larger-Print** (161/361 BPA G36Y)
- ☐ **Or Try Both!** (235/335 & 161/361 BPA G36Z)

Name (please print)

Address   Apt. #

City   State/Province   Zip/Postal Code

Email: Please check this box ☐ if you would like to receive newsletters and promotional emails from Harlequin Enterprises ULC and its affiliates. You can unsubscribe anytime.

Mail to the Harlequin Reader Service:
IN U.S.A.: P.O. Box 1341, Buffalo, NY 14240-8531
IN CANADA: P.O. Box 603, Fort Erie, Ontario L2A 5X3

Want to explore our other series or interested in ebooks? Visit www.ReaderService.com or call 1-800-873-8635.

---

*Terms and prices subject to change without notice. Prices do not include sales taxes, which will be charged (if applicable) based on your state or country of residence. Canadian residents will be charged applicable taxes. Offer not valid in Quebec. This offer is limited to one order per household. Books received may not be as shown. Not valid for current subscribers to the Harlequin Special Edition or Harlequin Heartwarming series. All orders subject to approval. Credit or debit balances in a customer's account(s) may be offset by any other outstanding balance owed by or to the customer. Please allow 4 to 6 weeks for delivery. Offer available while quantities last.

Your Privacy—Your information is being collected by Harlequin Enterprises ULC, operating as Harlequin Reader Service. For a complete summary of the information we collect, how we use this information and to whom it is disclosed, please visit our privacy notice located at https://corporate.harlequin.com/privacy-notice. Notice to California Residents – Under California law, you have specific rights to control and access your data. For more information on these rights and how to exercise them, visit https://corporate.harlequin.com/california-privacy. For additional information for residents of other U.S. states that provide their residents with certain rights with respect to personal data, visit https://corporate.harlequin.com/other-state-residents-privacy-rights/.